Of Gods and Boys

Harry F. Rey

Winnipeg, Canada

Editors: Craig Gibb & Francisco Feliciano

Published May 2024 by Deep Hearts YA, an imprint of Deep Desires Press and Story Perfect Inc.

Deep Hearts YA
PO Box 51053 Tyndall Park
Winnipeg, Manitoba R2X 3B0
Canada

Visit deepheartsya.com for more great reads.

Of Gods and Boys

Chapter 1
Achilles the Great

Ain't nothing worse in the world than waiting outside juvie to get picked up by your mom. Two years of hard work, poking the eyes of the wrong crowd, covering the asses of the right ones, all gone to shit as I stand on the other side of the impassable fence, kicking broken twigs away from my duffel bag.

Countless times I put on a fearless face inside that cursed place to confront the smooth cheeked psychos, the type that stands in an animal pen in court like a teenage Hannibal Lecter. You gotta mark your territory inside, and you gotta fight to keep it, and let every boy in that great big cage know damn well Achilles the Great is not a guy to be messed with. But you have to be smart about it. Acting like a gangster will get you thrown in solitary quicker than a denied appeal. There's times when the best thing to do is sense the drop-shift in atmospheric pressure going on around you, and make sure as shit to get back in your cell before things kick off. That place needs a twenty-four-seven tornado siren with the amount of times the pressure changed without warning. 'Cause when things do kick off, the Beasts will be out hunting, sniffing the air for the scent of blood, banging their night sticks on the bars and yelling:

"Who stabbed the psycho? His lawyer's coming down from Dallas and they'll sue the shit outta you."

We all knew the Beasts likely slashed the new guy themselves 'cause they got bored of jerking off into the oatmeal. Evolution might be blind to prejudice, but survival ain't. In juvie, it's not the strongest that survive, it's the smartest. And I was dumb as shit to let the Beasts know my mom was coming to pick me up when I could've taken the two dollars fifty the State had to offer for the bus home. Armed with that information, another moment inside and Achilles the Great would've been shredded, not just my carefully-won reputation.

Spending those long years in juvie, fifteen, sixteen, seventeen, is like never moving on from tenth grade. Except there's new faces every few months, not each year. But by the time I was four months in, most kids who'd been there when I came were already moved on. Sure, some returned, but not for a while. By the time I was a year in, I was the longest one inside. That's how I got my reputation: Achilles the Great. I ain't a god, despite what the kids in there think. Just because I never once treated another kid unfairly, just because I made sure the weak ones had protection and the strong ones didn't abuse their power, doesn't make me worthy of some kinda poetic justice. I'm just a guy named after a hero. Nothing more, and so much less.

Mom gave me that name as a final "fuck you" to my Greek Orthodox Dad. They were practically divorced in the delivery room, and she wrote out the birth certificate herself, saving me from a life of being called *Constantine Konstantinos.*

Darwinian evolution is the last thing I remember from school. And only because the teacher kicked up such a fuss about teaching it; throwing Bibles at us till we heard the principal, Mrs. McKenna, clattering down the hallway, her flat shoes hard against the linoleum floor and her dreadlocks casting a shadow through the door's window. She booted the door open and spun a fiery tirade like a Baptist preacher and we were a class of Grade A sinners.

I don't know what shocked the teacher more, being fired on the spot, or that twenty-five fifteen-year-old's in Southeast Texas couldn't figure out what a Bible had to do with Darwin. "Welcome to the future, bitch!" Adam yelled at her as she packed up her messy desk and cursed the whole damn lot of us to burn in hell. But I didn't have much time to laugh. Before the bell rang for the next period, the cops arrived, executing a warrant on me I hadn't a clue about. The whole school came to our classroom to watch me being dragged away in handcuffs. Carla slipped three copies of *The Origin of Species* into my bag, and two of the Bible, as the cops slammed my face into the desk and kneed me hard in the balls for good measure.

What juvie made of me arriving that evening with a black eye, busted lip, and five copies of books—both of which were at one time or another banned by the Board of Education—was anyone's guess. But my painted face, and the persistent rumor I was in for a grizzly, violent murder, got my reputation off to a stellar start.

All that fades into hot air the minute Mom pulls up in her rickety station wagon. The boys watching from inside juvie holler from the library window as she leaves the country station blaring out the open window. But Mom being Mom, she's out the car and wrapping her big arms around my neck like a starving gull. And because she parked in the middle of the street, half a dozen angry horns now herald my freedom and draw all the eyes from the barred windows onto the scene in the street. The animals left in the Darwinian cage hoot and catcall as Achilles the Unknown, then Achilles the Feared, and finally, Achilles the Great, wipes lipstick from his cheek.

"Jesus, Mom, you're embarrassing me."

"Don't use that word," she slaps me round the ear and throws my duffel bag, without the books this time, into the back of the car. Oh yeah, Mom *hates* Christianity. With a passion. But the inmates could yell all they like, because I'm done. The Beasts can click their tongues and place bets on when I'll be back in. *See you soon*, the words they left me with coated in a sly grin. But, hell, I'm free. As free as a seventeen-year-old out on parole can be.

"Wave goodbye to your friends," Mom says without a trace of irony—Greek Moms don't do irony—as the crescendo of horns honking behind us reaches boiling point. I glance out the window as she goes through the motions of turning on her blinker and looking in the rear-view mirror at the caravan of angry trucks. Across the high wire fence, the barred windows are banging. Mom or not, the boys inside are sending me off. Some friends, some enemies. But stay in there long enough and you'll learn the shifting alliances between kids mean jack shit. There's a real-life enemy, and it ain't us. And honestly, I'm sad Achilles the Great won't be there any more to protect the ones that need it most. 'Cause to be perfectly fucking honest, not even a lifetime of being raised on a steady diet of Greek gods and heroes and myths and tragedies will prepare you for life inside the cavern of the Beasts.

"So, did you make any friends?" Mom asks as we drive down the highway, doing fifty-five in the fast lane.

"What? No, Mom, you saw me literally last week."

"What about that nice boy Julio you were always telling me about?"

"He wasn't nice, Mom. They put him in solitary because he tried to set me on fire. Don't you listen?"

"Well, your father's coming round for dinner. I thought you two should bond. He hasn't seen you in all this time."

"Whose fault is that?" He hadn't bothered to visit once. I knew why. She knew why. The defense attorney for the entire Konstantinos clan, Julia Astraeus, knew why. But no one was allowed to say why. Even though we were all thinking it, all through the trial, and all through the last two fucking years.

"You know why he couldn't visit, Aki."

"Even the entire social studies class came to visit, remember all those inaccuracies they found in the evidence? How the police just never bothered to DNA test the glove. No fingerprints whatsoever. Jesus, Mom, one of those kids is now doing pre-law at Columbia because of it. But Dad can't take one day—"

"Don't say that word!" A truck honks by, forcing Mom out of the fast lane where she clearly doesn't belong.

"What word? Fuck, sorry, okay…"

Mom clicks her tongue as we pull off the highway, still far from home. But I can feel a rant coming so I don't risk another slap round the head by asking her where the hell we're going.

"Religious freedom, they say. And listen to what they teach you. I mean look at that."

We turned into a mini mall with a fifty-foot-high mechanical Jesus under a cross made out of assault rifles. *Billy Christ's Guns n' Ammo welcomes you to Target.*

"What are we doing in here?"

"I need some coals for tonight."

"It's fifty degrees. Why are you barbecuing?"

She doesn't answer because she pulls the station wagon into the handicapped spot right out front. Like she'd ever let them take that sticker away.

"I thought you might want some new clothes and body washes and such…so, here." She pulls a gift card still wrapped in plastic from her bra.

"Five hundred dollars, are you crazy? Thank you…" I lean across the stick shift and throw my arms around her. She squeezes back.

"It's from your Uncle Zotos and me. He's also coming tonight." She lets go and starts to fumble under the seat for her purse. "He wants you back wrestling."

"Mom, I don't know about that. Like, I haven't done it since school…I mean I don't even think I remember how."

"Well"—her arms flap as she groans under the seat—"Zotos wants you back at his gym five days a week."

I grin. "We'll see about that." The only thing I want to

do for the foreseeable future is sleep till two in the afternoon. Boys were always talking about the first thing they'd do when they got out. Go straight to Sizzler's or hook up with the girlfriend they swore was waiting for them. I didn't care about any of that. Not going to the beach, not going fishing, not walking in the woods or going to Disneyland. Nope. When the Beasts woke us up at six in the morning, seven on a Sunday, the only thing keeping me sane was knowing that as soon as I get home…not Mom, not a tornado, not Zeus himself would get me out of bed before I feel like it.

"No, we won't see, Achilles. Look at you." She lunges at my waist, grabbing all the flab and skin she can find. "You're the only boy in the world who comes out of jail fatter than when he went in."

"Jes…gee whiz, Mom. Lay off a bit. Sorry I don't look like I did when I was fifteen, but I was trying."

She raises a suspicious eyebrow. I don't know what magic she uses, and I probably never will know, but I've never been able to lie to her. Ever.

"You swapped your gym time for the library. You swapped your outdoor exercise classes for the library. You dropped out of mindfulness for anger management on day one and went straight to the library."

"How…how do you know this?" My face twists in shock and horror at this revelation of how much time I'd spent in the library. But it was the place you were least likely to get stabbed. "What, did they send you a letter every week or something telling you what I did and ate?"

"No! It's on the app." Mom rummages in her bag, then

takes out the same lime green cell phone and purse combination she's had for years. She flips the purse section around the back with all her store cards and Costco membership in the see-through card holder where a normal person would have their driver's license. Tapping only three times like it's on her home screen, she thrusts the phone in my face. The smudgy screen protector with Candy Crush dots burned into the retina made it hard to see, but there it is. The Texas Juvenile Justice System app.

Congratulations! Your son, Achilles Konstantinos (FYD24601), has been released on probation.

Probation end date: Undetermined.

"Undetermined?" I yell, throwing the hefty purse-phone back at her. I roll down the window desperate to suck in some air. My head spins. The car whirls like the whole world is being tossed by a giant. The rumble of vomit burns a hole in the back of my throat like whenever I saw a newbie eat a porridge pot at breakfast.

"They said three years on parole. Three. And then I'd be done. Why doesn't it say three years parole, Mom? Why?"

She buttons the purse-phone back together and drops it in her bag along with her car key chain that's got more keys on it than a chief warden. "We got a better deal."

"We? Who's we? And why didn't Julia say anything to me?"

"Oh, she's useless at parole hearings. Uncle Zotos convinced the judge to let him help with supervision. He said getting you back into wrestling was the best thing for you."

"So I have to go do wrestling five times a week or they send me back to juvie?"

"You like wrestling."

"Mom. You can't be serious. What about the end date? What, do I gotta become state champ or something before they'll let me fucking finish with it?"

"Enough, Aki. Zotos just wants you there every day to keep an eye on you for the judge. Part of the deal is if you can qualify for a competition, that means training properly, passing a drug test—"

"I don't take drugs."

"Passing a drug test," she says again, louder. "Then that'll count toward your supervision."

"Count toward? Part of the deal? What the fuck's the rest? Defeat Argus in single combat?"

"Well," Mom said, a bit more nervously. "Mrs. McKenna—"

"What the hell does she want from me? I've not been her student in two years!"

"She's got a catch-up class at night she wants you to come to. And it was Mrs. McKenna who swayed the judge round to the other half of the deal."

"Which is?"

"If you get your GED, as well as qualifying for a wrestling competition, they'll end parole."

The world falls into an enormous silent bubble. Like I'm being dragged to the Underworld, asshole first. This isn't freedom. This isn't even close. The doors of the car suddenly seem way, way tighter than the walls of my cell.

Two years counting down the days had all been one big lie. I'm not free. In fact, I've never been farther from it.

"Mom, you can't be serious. Two years in prison and now I have to go every day to Zotos's gym and train with sweaty meatheads for a dumb-ass wrestling competition, then go every night to school…school, Mom, at night, or I'm breaking parole?"

"Uncle Zotos and Mrs. McKenna are your supervision team. They'll keep the judge informed about how much you're applying yourself."

I throw my head back on the headrest, forgetting how hard it is.

Fucking Texas. What kind of state *elects* their judges? Most don't even need a law degree. I know mine certainly didn't. My case was the first the trial judge had presided over since getting elected, and every five minutes the prosecutor had to approach the bench to explain some legal term he didn't understand. Like "innocent before proven guilty", for one.

"Listen, Aki, it's a good deal. Get your GED and qualify for one competition and that's it. All this can be over in three months. Now, isn't that better than three years?"

"Okay, but I'm all fat, as you pointed out, Mom. And GED? How am I meant to catch up on two years of work in three months?"

"Mrs. McKenna is coming for dinner tonight, so you can ask her yourself. Now, come on," she opens up the car door into a chilly breeze, "if we're going on a shopping spree, we're gonna need some donuts first."

This is exactly how she sets me up for failure. Calls me

flabby but makes athletic competition part of my parole conditions. Then buying donuts and likely cooking up an entire farmyard animal for dinner.

I step out as well, slamming the car door shut even though the old station wagon can hardly take it. The rolling purple skies smell like a storm brewing in the Gulf. But I like the air. I like the wind coming over the suburban flatlands. It reminds me of peering out the cell window with Marcus, staring up at that great big purple sky.

"That's not purple," he'd say. *"That sky is mauve."*

Maybe all this could be done in three months, and I could wipe the slate clean before I turn eighteen. Or maybe I'd be right back where I woke up this morning, fighting Beasts without any magic swords or bows or armor. I sniff the air of supposed freedom. It smells like fried dough and powdered sugar.

Chapter 2
Achilles the Lover

"Hey, who's this little guy?" I ask as Mom boots open the screen door to the backyard, flapping her arms to try and waft out the smell of cooking from the kitchen.

The goat isn't so little though. He trots up to me, bleating as goats do. I lean down and scratch behind his ears as Mom dumps all our shopping bags on the couch and heads back into her domain. The goat chews at the end of my T-shirt and nuzzles into my crotch.

"At least the grass looks good," I call out. But Mom already has her music blasting, singing along to the exact same Greek songs I remember from my last night in this house two years but an age ago.

I sit down on the patio as the goat sniffs around, young and unafraid.

"Here, boy," I say, offering him a tuft of grass.

He bleats and happily starts to chew out of my hand.

"I think I'll call you Marcus," I tell the goat, even though the goat doesn't care. Maybe because this is the first real-life creature, except Mom, I've seen in these few hours I've been in alleged freedom. I assume the spirit of Marcus is inside this goat, waiting for me on the outside like he promised.

Marcus was the only real friend I made in juvie, and he's the only guy I truly miss from there. From anywhere, actually. We only had about six months together, but our friendship was fast from day one. Neither one of us was the typical juvie type in southern Texas; that is, not Hispanic. Marcus gravitated to me from the start. I'd already built a decent reputation as the son of the scion of the Gulf Greek mafia, and Marcus was a six-foot three Black guy from the wrong side of Houston. Together, we were unstoppable. Even the Beasts tended to let us alone.

But Marcus committed the worst sin of all in juvie. One so great and terrible there's no turning back from, no hope of redemption or making amends. He turned eighteen. On the morning of his birthday, I watched with silent tears as the Beasts dragged him out of our cell. The spit-hood and chokehold gave the Beasts all the free punches to the entrapped Marcus they'd never been able to take before. Since the staff at the adult correctional facility were waiting downstairs to take him away, what did it matter if the Beasts gave him a few kicks to his blindfolded head while screaming racist slurs in his ear. What was he gonna do, file a report?

Marcus had six weeks left on his sentence when they transferred him to adult jail. But after a week, I heard he got another year slapped on for walking funny or sitting down before they told him to or some cooked up bullshit like that. Of course they'd do that. Those private prison companies will do everything they can to keep you inside, up to and including breaking your legs on the day you're meant to get out, just so they can plant a knife or meth in your cell while you're getting plastered up.

And especially a juvie transfer who probably came with a way higher price per head to claim back from the State, for all that *psychological support* they'd be giving him. At least the juvies are mainly run by the State. They can only get away with so much. But to the adult prisons, Marcus was a golden calf ready to be sacrificed to their CEO gods. I knew they'd never let him go. And he knew the same thing.

I don't judge Marcus for what he did. I can't, because, truthfully, if I'd been in his position, I probably would've done the same thing. What was the alternative? Endless years of torture? And what's worse, even when he did manage to make it out, what kind of life was there waiting? When the only work you're likely to get is paying off debts to those who'd "protected" you on the inside, till those "debts" found you back on the inside? There was no breaking that cycle. Ain't no rolling that rock up the hill.

I remember a story from *The Odyssey* Mom used to read to me before bed. This guy Sisyphus was the first king of Corinth until Zeus condemned him to push a massive boulder up a steep mountain for all eternity. Every time he was about to send it toppling over the crest, the sheer weight of the rock turned it back and the boulder rolled all the way back down, thumping on the ground far below. And once more, Sisyphus had to trudge back down the mountain and push it all the way up, knowing perfectly well it was cursed to fall back down. Every time, until the end of time.

I remembered that scene so well, when Odysseus

witnesses Sisyphus's torture in Hades. I asked Mom: *"What did Sisyphus do that was so bad?"*

Mom had an answer, of course she did. She had many things to say about the evil of Sisyphus. The king had been wicked and cruel, twice cheating death. The king played a trick on Thanatos, the personification of Death, chaining him up in Hades so no human would ever die again. Naturally, that caused utter chaos to the natural order of the world. Death is part of life, and as hard as it is, if no one ever died, the world could not go on.

That's why Zeus condemned Sisyphus to his eternal punishment. Fair enough, thought five-year-old me when Mom first told me the story. But what about Marcus? Had he stolen his way into Hades' domain and captured Thanatos? Had Marcus guilt-tripped Hades' wife Persephone into releasing him from the Underworld, promising to quickly return, only to thumb his nose at the gods and live far into old age since even Death himself was now deathly afraid to track down Sisyphus at risk of being chained up again?

Hardly. Not even close. Not even nothing. Marcus hadn't even committed a crime, only been caught walking down the wrong street in the wrong neighborhood on the wrong night. Nope, I won't judge Marcus for cutting short his waiting life of torture by hanging from the ceiling pipes in his adult cell. I can only pray Hades will treat him fairly, and Persephone will give Marcus even a sliver of kindness he'd never got in his earthly life.

"Are you hungry, Marcus?" I ask the goat. He's bleating and trotting around the lawn, probably sick of staring at the same square fence day in, day out. I know the feeling. "Let's see if Mom has something nice for you."

But as soon as I'm inside, the front doorbell rings.

"Door!" Mom yells. How she can hear a doorbell ding over the clattering pots and blare of the music from burned CDs, I've no idea. I catch sight of her happy in the kitchen, perusing a steaming cauldron of dolmades and chain smoking as she always does when competing in the contact sport known as Greek cooking. I say chain smoking but it's not really. I just don't know what to call it when there's three extra-long cigarettes burning all at once at different stations of the kitchen. One in an ashtray on the counter by the marinating octopus tentacles, another on the kitchen table next to the pot of yogurt and unpeeled cucumbers, and yet another between her fingers as she squeezes a whole lemon, by hand, into the gigantic pot of stuffed vine leaves.

I open the front door with nothing in my mind.

"Carla!" I stare at her in shock. Seventeen-year-old Carla looks every part the woman fifteen-year-old Carla always wanted to be. It's the first time I've seen her in two long years. Her mom never let her visit, so we talked on the phone a lot. Enough to maintain one level above a friendship. She tosses aside perfectly ironed black hair, which flows from her Longhorns baseball cap, and plasters on that pageant-sized smile that has enchanted me since eighth grade.

"Aki!" She dives inside and wraps her arms around me like a squid clinging to the side of a shipwreck. I grab the petite frame I remember so well, lift her up and swing her round my body like the wrestler I used to be as we both shriek and laugh and soak up each other's skin. "Your mom wouldn't tell me when you were getting out. I had to go down to the courthouse to find out!"

I smile. Some things never change. But it's a wonder of the world to look at her here, standing in the hall, in the flesh. I beam at her effortless style; from the denim shorts I know she cut herself and the strappy white top showing off sunset-colored skin far more tanned and tender than two years ago, just below the dangling hoops in her ears that I know are pure gold.

"Who is it?" Mom screams from the kitchen.

"It's Carla."

A pot clatters.

"Hola, Mrs. Konstantinos."

"Does *she* want to stay for dinner?" Mom shouts. Carla nods enthusiastically, but I reckon it ain't for the food.

"She does, Mom."

"Does she eat octopus yet?" I throw Carla an inquisitive curl of my eyebrow. She shakes her head. Wise decision.

"Still no."

Mom returns to expressing her feelings about Carla loudly in the kitchen, no doubt striking up another cigarette while launching into a personal dialogue with Nemesis herself.

"Is she cursing me in Greek?"

"Best not ask."

"Oh, what's all this?" Carla asks as she spies the mountain of Target bags swamped across the couch.

"We went shopping on the way home, I got some new clothes."

"Oh yeah? Well, maybe after you can give me a fashion show." After...? Carla leans over the couch, squeezing her arms close together. I remember that look all too well. Even after two years barely remembering girls existed, I would never forget the way Carla looked at me.

"I haven't even been into my room yet," I say as we gather up the plastic bags, "so I don't know what to warn you about, but I'm sure there's something messed up inside."

But she just smiles, and I do too. With Carla here, now I really feel free. Putting a face, and a body, back on the other half of our Sunday night phone calls. She'd kept me updated on the social ecosystem at school; what happened at the school baseball and football games I'd missed, how Charlie had led the wrestling team to a complete disaster at state finals, and always the latest on who everyone was dating in the tangled web of suburban Houston... Well, almost everyone. We never talked about who Carla was dating. I never asked, and she never said. Although once I did; one year, two months and three days since I'd seen her. I heard her mouth stretch wide in a grin down the phone as she said: *"Tell me who you're dating and I'll tell you who I am."*

"No one," I responded with the same stupid smile.

"Me neither."

But I'd never expected a girl like her to remain attached to a guy like me. I wasn't the youngest wrestling captain the county had ever had any more, and it's hard to maintain a ranking of being fourth best in the State from behind bars. Mrs. McKenna always used to call me the top jock in the school. She used to say: *"You have to set an example for these kids. They'll follow you.*" I guess that task had fallen to someone else. But I'd never much cared, either before or after. Carla could date who she wanted because honestly, just having her as a friend had been a million times better than a girlfriend too young to grow bored and resentful of her man locked up.

We take the bags down the hall, and I suck in a deep breath as I open the door and flick on the light. It's not an overgrown jungle like I feared. Just a normal bedroom of a guy who was once a fifteen-year-old kid; Drake posters on the wall and, above my desk, a corkboard full of ticket stubs from gigs at the Toyota Center. The ribbons and wrestling trophies are neatly arranged around the small statue of Thamyris, the fabled singer to the gods who Mom said had watched over me since birth.

"I'll put the bags on the bed," Carla says, struggling to find a pathway through the stacks of glossy Greek magazines covering the floor like pillars of a fallen temple.

"Oh yeah, she said she was using my room for storage."

Carla hops on the bed, picking up a random Greek celebrity magazine from the pile and flicking through it. Her shiny, stuck-on nails are new. She tucks her hair under the Longhorns cap once again as she chews gum and looks at the pictures. I never knew her to be a baseball fan before.

I carefully step over the stacks of imported magazines mom has delivered by the crate, snatching a few of the Target bags and dumping them on the desk to root around for the gift I'd gotten Carla.

"I got you something," I say, pulling out the small wooden box with a heart-shaped lock. "Here's the key." I chuck her a small silver charm to add to the bracelet I'm glad she still wears. She takes it with a deep smile.

"What are you putting inside?"

I root around in my duffel bag for the gift to go inside the box, and finally find it. A pocket-sized notebook, every page, every margin, filled with words scrawled in blue ink.

"I wanted to send you letters," I admit, starting to feel a bit embarrassed at the sort of gift the fifteen-year-old Carla might've liked, but the seventeen-year-old version had probably grown out of judging by the gold earrings and man's cap. "It was eight dollars a stamp…and, well, I reckon your mom wouldn't be too keen for her mailman to see all those envelopes stamped with the juvenile justice department." Carla watches me fumble over the words with the kind-hearted smile that always made my chest thump. And her hair. I can't get over how shiny it looks. How much it fits her face more than the scraggy curls she used to wear it in.

I look down at the cheap wooden box containing a battered, yellowing notepad, and feel waves of shame sent straight from Poseidon.

"Every time I thought about you, or heard a new word in Spanish during a gang fight, I wrote it down in this notebook…because…well, because you always told me to tell you what I was thinking and, you know, no one else ever did that. And since I couldn't write you or text you and every call out of that place is recorded, I wrote them all down here. All my feelings. Those quiet things I wish I could've whispered in your ear. Two years' worth." I have to cough to find my voice again.

"I kept it hidden in the library 'cause they don't let us have pens in our cells, much less anything else. But when I heard something I wanted to write down, especially the Spanish stuff I thought was beautiful, sometimes I'd stay awake all night, repeating the words over and over again so I wouldn't forget them if I fell asleep... Anyway," I say, putting the notepad inside and snapping the box shut, "this is for you."

"Aki..." She takes the box, seeming to be genuinely touched. At least for a moment. Her eyes widen and prickle with tears as she goes through the motions of unlocking it and holding the notebook delicately in her hand, as delicately as she held my feelings. My heart drums mercilessly, wondering what she might think, what she might say. But she's speechless. How could Carla, of all people, be without words?

She sniffs away something like a tear, puts the notebook back inside without opening it and locks it with the key which she slides into her pocket. Like that's the only safe place for her feelings like how the box is the only safe place for mine. I'm glad it's locked away. I can breathe again.

"But what about this fashion show, huh?" Carla asks, delicately wiping the corners of her eyes to save her mascara. I didn't know if I was allowed to ask what was wrong. Was she sad because of the time we'd lost? Or the time we had? Or because there was someone else—many someone elses probably—and I was just that guy she once dated who went to juvie she wanted to see one last time. She leans back against the wall as I root through the clothes, trying not to cut myself on our shattered love.

"I thought this shirt was nice," I say, pulling out a lightweight, short sleeved burgundy button-down.

"That's cute. And thank God it's not stripes. Every boy in school thinks he can pull off the vertical stripe fad and I'm like, honey, no. You need to be tall and thin and white, not short, stubby and Mexican."

"Or Greek."

"Papi, you're the buffest boy in school. You don't need stripes. That is a cute shirt…and I'm sure it looks very sexy on you."

"It looked fine. Only six bucks."

"That's good!"

"Yeah…" I hold it tight, thinking about how many other boys have given her a fashion show.

"So come on, let's see it on. Fuck, I missed that body, Aki." She stretches out on my single bed and kicks off her sneakers, just like she used to.

"Okay… but Carla I'm not the same as before. It was two years ago, and I didn't really have a chance to work out in juvie."

"Papi, I don't care about that. I've just missed you. I need my big Greek god to come and hold me in his arms.

"Fine," I say, dropping the shirt. "But I'm turning off the light."

"Deal."

"I'm sorry Carla. I don't know what happened."

"It's fine, don't worry about it," she says, balling up a wet wipe and tossing it into the trash can beside my desk. Not that there was much of anything to wipe away.

"I guess I'm just stressed," I say, lying back on the pillow and covering myself up with the blanket, hands squeezing my pounding head. Carla wriggles her clothes back into place and lies down beside me. "And I was anxious about seeing you and all these parole conditions they're making me do…"

"Aki, relax," she says, propping herself up on my pillow and playing with the hair on my chest. "I can't imagine what you're going through right now. Of course it'll take time to adjust. And when your mom is out there blasting nineties Greek techno music like we're in fucking Aya Napa."

"That's actually in Cyprus, but yeah, she likes the nostalgia, I guess. I dunno."

She lays across me, and I run my fingers along the groove of her soft, smooth back. Exactly the same as before, but completely different. It feels like everything is wrong. I'm in the wrong place touching the wrong person. It's so strange to think but I actually miss the certainty of the cell. The routine. Being woken at dawn and locked away by eight in the evening. The same food on certain days like they were holy feasts. Hot dogs on Monday, pizza on Friday. Once they brought in a new caterer who switched up the menu, putting pizza on Friday and scrapping hot dogs altogether in favor of something called meatless Monday.

The riot went on for two straight days. The Beasts only got us back under control by throwing a barbecue the next Monday and promising it would never happen again in a rare act of solidarity. After all, they eat the same food we do. So much for the vegan option in the Texas juvenile penitentiary system.

My head is too busy with thoughts, and Carla senses it. But she doesn't try to prod. She used to bawl me out so bad for never telling her what I felt or thought. *"But Carla,"* I'd say, *"I don't tell anyone how I feel. Or what I think. Or what I care about."*

Now all my thoughts are locked away in that wooden box. I liked that they sit there, accessible in the abstract but out of sight. I don't have to *think* about my thoughts if I know they are written down, waiting to be looked at if and when the time should come. I hope it doesn't.

"How are you dealing with all this?" the state psychiatrist, whichever one it was that month, would ask. They didn't stick around for long. They only came to us to get college credit then move on up to the big house. So, what were we meant to say about something we could do nothing about to a person we'd never see again? I never liked any of the psychiatrists anyway, except one. His name was Reynard; a big, broad-shouldered Midwesterner addicted to Texas barbecue. He used to sit in the chair, a long coat draped across his shoulders like he was some kind of dame from a black and white movie, legs crossed, like, ball-crushingly crossed, and reacted to all the crazy shit I said with phrases I'd never heard before like: *"What in the Black Jesus?"* or *"Shania save us."* He also called me honey. He said he probably shouldn't, but *"when in Rome."*

I think I only ever told the real bad stuff to him. He stayed for six weeks at most, but he felt easy to talk to.

About whatever I wanted. The Beasts used to joke that he just came by to molest me. They could see we had a connection, that I was telling him stuff, and they didn't like that one bit. They made the county social worker come along to sit in one of our sessions; of course to report back any complaints I might have about the Beasts. I've never seen anything like what Reynard did to her. We were already sitting down in the small office outside the library, and she knocked once and tried to come in, all humble like, clutching a little notepad and tape recorder. A small woman, but her presence loomed large.

But Reynard's was larger. *"Get your cottage cheese ass in that two-bit H&M knock-off three-dollar sale-bin pant suit away from my patient before I call up every hairdresser in town and let each one of them raw dog me in the ass so they'll keep on letting you get that jumble-sale tuft-weed perm that looks like the pubic hair of a mangy old tomcat."* She left. And the Beasts left us alone. They knew he had powers they couldn't even begin to comprehend. Reynard wasn't planning to work in a correctional facility, thank God. He told me he was going to work with queer youth. And in our last session, he told me to get in touch with him through the University of Houston if I ever wanted to talk.

"You all right?" Carla says.

"Yeah…sorry, babe, just my mind is like…ugh. Too much."

"Want some weed?"

"What? No, Carla, you know what they'll do if they catch me with that?"

"It's fine, my mom's got a prescription."

"I don't want any, Carla, no. And don't bring it into this house again either."

"I didn't, Aki. Fuck, I'm just trying to help." She stretches across my chest and picks up the Greek magazine she'd been looking at earlier from the floor. She spreads the cold, glossy pages over my bare stomach and flicks absent-mindedly through the clashing colors of celebrity shots.

"Who's this?" she asks, looking at a double spread of a dark-haired young woman in a low-cut top, her arms folded and standing against the backdrop of white-painted homes on a typical Athens road. Carla twists the magazine around so I can read the Greek headline.

"She's the new leader of the Hellenic Communist Party. It says…" I quickly scan the first parts of the article. "She says despite being thirty-six, she's ready to become prime minister." I glance at some of the quotes pulled out and side barred in the page and snicker out loud.

"What's so funny?"

"Some old male news anchor asked her if she thought it was cruel to expect people to vote for a childless woman who's nearly forty."

"Seriously?"

"Yeah, then she called him a son of a whore on TV and…" I flip over the page and catch the conclusion of the story. "Then he got fired and she jumped ten points in the polls."

"I love her boobs," Carla says, flipping back to the woman's picture. "Those are *exactly* what I want. See how they're not too much at the top? I don't want them to look like a couple of water balloons."

"You're getting a boob job?"

"Yeah," she says excitedly, "I told you, remember? For graduation."

"Wow…okay. But it's like, serious surgery, no?"

"And?" Carla chucks the magazine back on the floor and kisses me between the hair on my stomach. "If I'm going to move to Miami—"

"Since when are you moving there?"

"I told you, Papi, there's a dance crew I wanna get into."

"Oh."

"Don't be sad," she hugs my belly, far more squidgy than the last time she splattered it with kisses. "As soon as you can travel out of state you can come visit." She looks up at me, this girl I used to know so well, now as strange as a foreign ghost. "What're you gonna do?"

Now all the stress comes flooding back.

"I have to do the stupid wrestling again. They made it part of my fucking parole conditions; can you believe it? Who does that?"

"Why not? You were good at it."

"Yeah, but no one does Greco-Roman wrestling after like tenth grade. And they're making me do my GED. Fuck, I wish I could go back inside."

"Aki, stop, first of all you gotta get your GED no matter what, so it's good they're making you do that. And I'll help you study. I got straight A's in English and I can tutor you in Spanish."

"Yeah but is your mom gonna let me come over to your house?"

"Oh yeah. Ha…that might be a problem. She'll probably want to call your parole officer first."

"Fine, it's Mrs. McKenna anyway."

"Holy shit."

"Yup. Told you I'd rather be back inside."

Carla snuggles up beside me, wrapping my arm around her shoulders and smelling my scent like she'll soon never see me again. As if that is all the faith she has in me surviving Mrs. McKenna: parole dementor.

"Poor Achilles." She smooths away my messed-up hair and brushes her soft lips against my cheek. "Life's hard."

I shrug. I know it could be harder, although I'm not sure how. That's the beauty of growing up Hellenic. Because whether things are going wrong or right, there's absolutely nothing you can do to change the fates; only keep sacrificing to the gods and hope one of them might take pity on you if their games get a bit too cruel. None of this personal salvation nonsense or heaven through faith and good works endlessly taught by those "inspirational speakers" in juvie. Nope, in the ancient Hellenic religion, we humans are just the playthings of the divine beings on Mount Olympus. Like, life is a great big soap opera and the gods are a bunch of drunken writers with union contracts.

"Hey, I've got something that'll cheer you up." Carla slides her phone out from under the pillow and taps it open with a fingerprint.

"Holy fuck, they've got fingerprints now?"

"Yeah…but that's not what I wanted to show you."

"Fine, but, Carla, what if someone steals your fingerprint?"

"Aki, are you being serious? How's someone going to steal my goddamn fingerprint? Cut off my thumb so they can get into my phone?"

"Well…maybe. But I don't mean like that. Your data. Carla, the biggest piece of evidence that I didn't do what they said I did was that they didn't have a matching fingerprint. Or any fingerprints."

"Is it rude if I say it didn't help?"

"That's not what I'm saying. I just spent two years locked up with guys who are now fucked for the rest of their lives because some government computer has got their fingerprints. And you're just giving it away to your phone?"

"If it gets hacked, I'll use a different finger. Happy?"

"Happy? No. I just hope for your sake no one's going to steal your data, 3D-print a copy of your thumb and leave your prints all over a murder scene."

"Can I show you this thing now?" Carla holds the phone up and makes a face in the camera, and a couple of virtual bunny ears pop up.

"What the fuck?"

"You try."

I stick out my tongue and all these flowers and eggs start rolling out on the screen.

"It's an Easter bunny filter," she says, but I was too busy playing with my face on the camera, amazed like a child at Christmas we'd never had. "Let's do a TikTok."

"I don't know what that is."

"This! Just stick out your tongue again and I'll record it."

"Carla, no, it looks like I'm naked! And I've not shaved

and my hair's a mess. People will think we've been doing stuff."

"Well…we almost were."

"And what will your mom say?"

"Relax, Aki. My *mom* is not on TikTok. Only kids at school will see, come on." Her nails tap away on the screen. *Look who's home!* she types, then sends to…to TikTok, I guess. I'm suddenly afraid to ask who'll actually see it.

"Will you hold me?" she asks.

"Of course, babe." Carla flips around to face the wall and I thread one arm under her, the other clutching her stomach as I breathe in the warm scent of her neck. I stare over her shoulder like a watchman as she taps rapidly through short videos of people I used to know from school. "Is that Marcel?"

"Yeah, he's tall now, right?" Suddenly replies start to flood in, her phone buzzing every few seconds with people responding. "Look! Everyone's so excited you're back! They all miss you."

"I missed you, though, not them," I say, batting away her phone.

"Aki…" she giggles, "careful this is new. I accidentally smashed the last one."

"You don't need a boob job," I say, nuzzling her skin.

"We're hanging at the strip mall tomorrow night, you know, across from the Domino's? You'll come hang out with us?"

"Well if tomorrow's Friday then I guess I'll be at Uncle Zotos' gym. Same as Saturday, same as Sunday, Monday—"

"Good so it's right there. Nothing big, we just sit around the parking lot for a while. Cops don't care; they prefer we're all in the same place. Look," she thrusts the phone back over her shoulder. "Everyone's asking for you. Bojo has a truck now."

"Has he," I say, unable to stifle a yawn. But with Carla's warm body next to mine, and the smells and sounds of mom's cooking wafting in from the kitchen, I let the exhaustion of two years creep up on me. Sure, the moment I close my eyes I'm transported back to the cell and those sweltering summer nights when the Beasts turned off the air for fun and the howls of newbies crept through the walls like cubs calling out for their dead mammas. But all I have to do is think of Marcus snoring away in the bunk below, and then I feel safe again.

"There's no Beasts out there, Aki," I hear him say in that long Texas drawl. *"You're safe now, son. Just sleep."*

Finally, I can breathe.

Chapter 3
Achilles the Hungry

I wake up to the strangest sensation. Peace and quiet. The room thumps with silence. The walls of my childhood bedroom don't vibrate from the trucks rumbling on the street outside all through the night, or the creaking fifties plumbing, or the vain cries of a scared newbie as the Beasts prowled, waiting to pounce at the slightest scent of blood.

The silence is the scariest thing of all. Carla is gone, so I have nothing to cling to but the sweat-drenched sheets as my heart drills down to a less frantic place. I'm safe, I try to tell myself. But it doesn't work. I find my boxers among the scattered magazines on the floor, slip them on and, yawning, head out of my room to take a piss.

"Aki, you're up!" Mom shrieks. Her and Carla are setting the table as a soft breeze comes in from the screen door. Uncle Zotos and Mrs. McKenna are sitting next to each other on the couch sharing a bottle of ouzo, and both turn to wave with a wide smile. All of this I see with half-shut eyes while scratching my ass. Hardly the best impression to make on my parole board.

"I'm gonna take a shower," I announce to the uninvited guests.

"You're right, Saphie," Zotos says to my Mom. "He has gotten flabby."

"I'll bring your new shirt," Carla says quickly, clearly keen to get out from under my mother's grasp.

"I'll do it Carla," Mom shoots back. The room skips a quick heartbeat, waiting to see if these two big cats can stick around the same cage for a night. Carla seems ready to relent, she's no big cat, and I'm about to hotfoot it to the bathroom when something clatters on the patio outside.

"*Gamo!*" a harsh male voice swears in thick Greek.

"Is that Dad?"

I can hear the sizzle of meat on the barbecue. I wonder if Marcus the goat is out there, butting his head into Dad's legs as he tries to do his manly duty while shooting ouzo through each nostril.

"Go get yourself ready, Aki," Mom says, rushing out to the garden like it might catch on fire. "We don't need to see your bits and pieces flapping around."

Happily, I leave them to it. No one asked for a welcome party. I certainly didn't. And if I had, it wouldn't have included my former principal, my dad, and his sworn nemesis Uncle Zotos. But the hot steam of the shower in the Pepto-pink bathroom soon left me not caring they were here. Growing up, I think I'd spent longer in this room in the house than any other. The long hours I'd do push-ups and sit-ups on the tiled floor so as not to stain the carpet in my bedroom with sweat, then stand up and stare at the bathroom mirror, wondering if I'd got bulky enough for Zotos's liking.

Maybe Zotos prepared me for the Beasts. The master

of Greco-Roman wrestling in greater Houston stole every young Greek boy he could get his hands on like he was the pied Piper of Southern Texas. Like the Spartans of old, mothers would sacrifice their sons on the altar of Zotos, and, in return, he would give them back toned, muscled young men, brimming with muted anger and more raw power in their upper body than sense in their brains. In short, the ultimate young Greek man who in one picture would show up his cousins back home drafted into the army. When Zotos chose you, it was an honor.

I wash my body over and over again with the soft floral scents of my mother's perfumed potions. The Axe shower gel is still wrapped in the Target bag in my room. I don't want to look down at my body. It's a far cry from the marble statue of a naked Ares that Zotos compares us to every weigh-in at the gym. Each ounce of body fat is another hundred push-ups. But I've spent so long inside I started to think I looked normal. Not fat, but not barrel-chested with an eight-pack either. Just a normal body with hair and a bit of cushion around the waist. But normal was never good enough for Zotos.

"Hey, Aki."

I wipe away the steam and see Carla holding my new clothes and a clean towel. She watches me rinse off the last round of soap. I decide five times is enough. I already smell like a meadow.

"Thanks," I say, shutting off the water, stepping out of the glass doors and taking my towel from her. She sits on the closed toilet, watching me dry off. Probably counting each extra bit of fat on my body too that never used to be there.

"Do you think I'm fat?"

"Don't be ridiculous!"

But I don't believe her. I throw the towel over my shoulder and wipe the steam from the mirror. I investigate my thighs, way thicker than before.

"It's muscle here," I say, knocking my legs like a wooden door. "Tell Zotos to come in and see."

"Hey, you want to relax? I came in to speed things up because your Mom and Dad are out there screaming at each other."

"Oh yeah, they do that when they're together."

Carla hands me my boxer shorts. I see her staring with a sadness I don't like as I put them on. Another thing I used to give her which I now can't. Another thing to weigh me down and make me feel like shit. Fuck, I wish I could go back to juvie.

I come out of the bathroom and everyone is sitting patiently at the table which is filled with every serving bowl and silver platter in the house. The typical result of about a week's worth of Mom's cooking. Dad is quietly drinking, his chest angry and red, so he must've been told off already.

"Look at my handsome boy!" Mom knocks Carla out the way to wrap me in a kiss. "You smell like patchouli!"

"That's a lovely shirt," Mrs. McKenna says. But it barely fits. My arms are about to split it open and I need to have three buttons open in order to breathe. All I need is a thick silver chain with a crucifix buried in my chest hair, a clinical lack of morality, and a borderline drinking problem and I'd be Dad.

"Well, Saphie, I must say," Mrs. McKenna says, "this all looks so lovely."

Funny, I've never seen Mom blush like that.

"There's plenty for us all," Mom declares, lifting up the scalding pot of dolmades with one bare hand and spooning the sticky vine leaf cigars onto our plates with her other hand.

"What's on the barbecue?" I ask, but Mom purposely ignores me.

"Now I hope you're ready to work hard, young man," Mrs. McKenna says, cutting up the food on her plate with a knife and fork while the rest of us dig in with our hands. Although Carla beside me only swirls salad around her plate to give the appearance of eating.

"I guess," I say with a full mouth. There's nothing like Mom's dolmades. Cooked on the gas for a day or more, the lemony rice and meat stuffed inside burns my tongue while the caramelized vine leaves stick to my teeth. I love it. I would eat only this, but Mom always insisted it was only a starter. "Carla's going to tutor me in Spanish and English."

"Oh is she now?" Mrs. McKenna raises a suspicious eye. "I hope Carla isn't going to neglect her own college application?"

Carla ignores her, or doesn't hear because she's staring at the octopus tentacles Mom just put on her plate. I wait till Mom's moved on to serving Zotos and scoop the tentacles up.

"Miss Gonzales?"

"Eh…no. I mean…" Carla watches in horror as my Dad chews down tentacles like a sea monster.

"I can't say I'm filled with confidence."

"The boy doesn't need college," Dad says.

"The boy needs his GED," Zotos throws back. There's a reason these two men don't sit beside each other. "And to be at the gym at eight am tomorrow," he adds, glaring at me.

"Then you'll come straight to school," Mrs. McKenna says, the two of them appearing to enjoy this complete control over my life. "As much as Miss Gonzales' pedagogical skills fill me with confidence, I've set you up to be tutored by the brightest student in the school."

"Oh so he agreed to it?" asks my Mom.

"He will. He wants to go to CalTech but needs a bit of social consciousness on his application." Zotos gives an approving nod.

"Who you talkin' about?" Carla asks, to Mrs. McKenna's barely-contained horror.

"The person to whom I am referring," she says with over-the-top correct pronunciation, "is Jesús Alvarez."

Carla snorts with laughter.

"The chimp?"

"I beg your pardon?"

Even dad looks on with trepidation. The hooked eyebrow of Mrs. McKenna would frighten a Gorgon. Especially since comparing anyone to a primate in front of your Black principal isn't the smartest idea. Carla's face drops as she picks up on her faux pas.

"I mean he's like a geek," she says to me. "Like math

club, debate club, Dungeons and Dragons club." I figure the last one is a joke. I can't believe the makeup of our school would've changed that much in two years.

"That geek will have a master's degree and a job in Silicon Valley by the time you're on your second abortion and third stint in rehab." Mrs. McKenna snaps back. I can't say any of us feel strongly enough to disagree.

We all return uncomfortably to our plates.

"Christos," Mom says, taking another glass of ouzo out of Dad's hand. "Let's go bring in the meat."

Mom and Dad head outside while Zotos picks up the only other thing he ever talks about. Taxes.

"… and that's why you should be buying a share in a group rental, " he says through a mouth which is never not full. Mrs. McKenna looks like she's lost the will to live. "The tax deductions alone cover the investment. And with landlord rental property insurance, it's the closest you'll get to a low risk, high yield long term investment."

"Well," Mrs. McKenna says, understandably draining the ouzo bottle into her glass. "I do appreciate the very thorough explanation. But I'm a public school principal, I don't have that kind of time."

"Nonsense. Your accountant will do it for you."

"I don't have an accountant."

"You don't have an accountant?"

What is it with accountants who can never believe that someone else doesn't want to use their services? Zotos takes it as a personal affront.

"You'll come to me. First thing tomorrow and we'll set you up. I bet I can save you five, maybe even ten percent like that." He snaps his fingers, satisfied to tell off another accountant-less individual.

"I thought you ran the gym?"

"Oh that all started as a tax break. I run the accountancy firm next door."

"I do appreciate the advice, but I certainly can't afford an accountant. I always felt they were a waste of money for ordinary people like me."

"Waste of money?" Zotos practically chokes on the last of his ouzo. "Nonsense. I'll have my best people on your case and you'll be *making* money in a year! Saphie and mine's father started that firm fifty years ago and I do the taxes for every Greek in the State of Texas. Even for some of the Turks."

"Again, it's very kind of you to offer but—"

"You won't pay a cent. Pro-bono for life."

"That's very generous but—"

"Please. After everything you've done for Aki. I insist. I'll even have my best guys come to you."

"What's going on here?" Mom asks, coming back inside followed closely by Dad carrying a large silver platter.

"Just putting tax dollars back in the pockets of our hard-working public school teachers. Saphie, that smells incredible."

It does smell incredible. The edges of the cubes of meat are perfectly charred as it practically falls off the bone. Mom quickly clears a place in the middle of the table, stacking empty salad bowls as Dad leans across Carla and I to slam the heavy mountain of meat smack in the center of the table. The sight and smell take me right back to childhood.

"Wonderful!" Mrs. McKenna says while Mom gives her the first serving. Suddenly I feel sick. Blood rushes to my head and I feel my heart thumping in my temple. "What kind of meat is this?"

"Goat."

"Mom…did you…did you cook Marcus?"

"Who the hell is Marcus?" Dad asks while chewing on a loose bit of fat, and dropping a rib each onto mine and Carla's plate.

"Aki, darling, you love goat."

"Mom…" I scrape my chair back from the table, well aware I'm making a scene. It was my fault for naming the goat, I knew that much. And for naming it Marcus. But still, eating the creature who just hours ago had brought a smile to my face, the first smile since Marcus… "Mom, you should've told me you were going to sacrifice the goat."

She sucks a breath in through her teeth, knowing I've said the magic words that will set my dad off.

"Sacrifice?" he yells, emptying his mouth of the half-chewed goat right onto Carla's plate. The poor girl is trapped between my fuming father and embittered mother. Just like my entire life. I think both of us are seconds from being sick. "Sapphira," he bellows, "did you sacrifice an animal to heathen idols in the backyard of this house?"

"Where am I meant to do it? In the park with the damn health inspector and the morality police watching?"

"Devil worship!" Dad yells and storms off into the kitchen where I see him pull another ouzo bottle from the cupboard, snapping it open and gargling straight into the sink.

"Mmm!" Mrs. McKenna says loudly and obviously backing up my mom. "It's delicious. Tell me, Saphie, do you do some special ceremony as well?"

Zotos happily tucks in as well as Mom casually removes Carla's spit-upon plate and fills another bowl with salad and meat for her.

"Oh, just a few words to Zeus to look out for Aki. And to Apollo, of course, for knowledge. And Athena for wisdom. Thamyris…" She tears a piece of meat from the bone with her teeth, happily watching at least some of her guests enjoy the food. "That's Achilles' personal protector—"

"It's an affront to Christ!" Dad yells from the kitchen. But he's ignored. I always thought their marriage was like one big trick orchestrated by a bored god.

"Did you both grow up traditional Greek?" Mrs. McKenna asks.

"Oh yes," Zotos says. "That's why our great-grandparents came to America. So they could freely practice their religion."

"It's not allowed in Greece?"

"That's the reaction you get," Mom says, pointing at Dad with a bone, still washing his mouth out in the sink in between muttering psalms and kissing his crucifix.

"It was the Ottomans who enforced tolerance," Zotos explains. "That's the only way their multi-ethnic empire held together for so long. But when Greeks started to fight for their independence in the nineteenth century, there was little room left in the Greek nation for anyone who wasn't Orthodox."

"Hillbillies," shouts Dad from the kitchen. "Rednecks from the mountains who believe in superstitious bullshit."

"Oh, be quiet, Christos," Mom shouts. "You're from Galveston."

"Paul the Apostle brought Christianity to Greece, is that right?" asks Mrs. Mckenna.

"Yes, but the ordinary folk didn't pay him much attention. Only when the Christian Eastern Roman Empire carried on from Constantinople after the fall of the West did the upper classes take note. Many ordinary folk continued the Hellenic faith right up to the wars of independence in the nineteenth century, especially in the north and Illyria as only southern Greece was liberated in the eighteen-twenties. But this greater Megali idea, the unification of all Greek peoples in one nation-state, left no room for people like us."

"But you're Greeks? Greeker than the Greeks!"

"But we're not good *Christian* Greeks," Zotos continued, helping himself to the meat on my plate. "It's like how the founding fathers of America view the Black man. A burden upon their clean, homogenous state. Greeks like us had our homes and farms stripped by a newly liberated and vengeful Church strolling around the countryside like a plantation owner, and they did everything in their power to make life unbearable. The DNA of the modern Greek nation is as sectarian as the DNA of the American republic is racist. But it has its positive side."

"Does it?" she says with surprise.

"Well, of course, it does. It's why I, a wrestling coach and accountant, can find common cause with a beautiful goddess masquerading as a high school principal." Zotos clasped her hand and kissed it dutifully and Mrs. McKenna rolled her eyes, but offered a slight smile. Both Carla and I swapped horrified stares. "I hope there's not a Mr. McKenna I'll have to battle. Because you know I have all of Mount Olympus on my side."

"No, no. No Mr. McKenna anymore."

Thankfully, Dad sweeps in from the kitchen and breaks the nascent, awkward flirting between my two parole officers.

"Carla, I'll take you home. Your family are good Catholics; they'd be horrified at this Satanism." Dad yelled the word as if it was supposed to have an impact. Mom only giggled and waved away his furious face, then tops off her and Mrs. McKenna's glasses from an open bottle happily sitting on the table that Dad had obviously been too blinded with rage to notice.

"Achilles, come with me," Dad barks.

"Christos, no! The boy hasn't eaten a thing."

"He's eaten enough! Now come with me and we'll take your girlfriend home."

That was the most awkward comment of the night. Carla and I exchanged another nervous glance. But at least we were both on the same page. Neither of us agreed we were boyfriend and girlfriend. But we didn't need to go into detail with Dad.

Chapter 4
Jesus the Provider

We drop Carla off—she seemed glad to get away from these crazy Greeks—but Dad doesn't take me home.

"My boy!" he yells, slapping the steering wheel with giddy excitement. "You're out! My God, I remember my first night of freedom. I only did six months inside the first time, but fuck, son, there wasn't a straight-walking whore left in east Texas after I was through." He slaps me on the thigh and digs his nails into the flesh. I start to worry he's going to lunge for the other bits of me just to check I'm the same red-blooded son he'd betrayed two years ago.

"Thanks for that image, Dad."

We roar down the highway toward the glittering flatlands of Houston sinking in the distance. Driving into it from the higher lands outside the city always feels like descending into a circle of the Underworld, the city sticky and the air close even on an early spring night. The blinking lights of the skyscrapers rising from the swampy concrete indistinguishable from the oil rigs pumping out in the gulf. It makes the city seem far bigger and more terrifying than it really is. An open sewer at the end of America.

"Aki... Two years away, that's a man's job. We're all proud of your sacrifice. You know that."

"I didn't have a choice."

"Neither did our lord and savior Jesus Christ, son. But he gave himself up. And you did too. You were brave."

"Yeah, well, I don't think you can compare either of us to Jesus. Not when you made me take the rap for you."

The next thing I know, a screwdriver is pressing into my throat. He moved so quickly I didn't notice him reaching for the glove compartment, and now he holds the screwdriver tightly, applying enough pressure to almost break the skin. But his eyes stay firmly on the road. A bump, a pothole, a swerve or a crash would send the rusty metal straight through my skin. I swallow hard, but it makes it sorer. The belt locks me into the seat, and once again the idea of freedom feels like a Homeric literary device.

"I made you do nothing, got it?"

"All right, Dad. Fuck."

That answers the question of if Dad is going to ever take responsibility for what he made me do. The answer is the screwdriver now lying in his lap. I breathe out, but it's not a relief.

"Here we are," he says, turning off the highway into what looks like the entrance to Hell. A dimly-lit building that would double for an abandoned warehouse on an Ecuadorian soap opera, the only thing we ever watched in juvie, stuck out of feral land like a single tooth in a hillbilly's mouth. "The happiest place on earth."

I look in terror as Dad slams the car door shut in the nearly-empty parking lot, reaching under his trousers to scratch his balls then sniff his fingers. What I wouldn't give for a pack of Beasts patrolling my cell and keeping the world out.

He leaves the car parked across three spaces. It doesn't look like anyone's coming off the highway for this place. With a heavy sigh I get out of the car and our feet click on the concrete as I follow him to the double doors keeping the world safe from whatever demons lay inside.

"Charlie!" Dad greets a big bald Black man sitting at a table just inside the entrance. He's wearing a purple suit jacket over a black turtleneck, as well as a full-on brass knuckle duster across his hand, as if he uses it so often there's no point in taking it off.

"Christos, my man." Mr. Knuckle-duster gets up, all six-foot-four of him, and gives my Dad a friendly slap on the back. "Hey, is this your boy?"

"Sure is. Ain't he handsome?" Dad grabs my cheek. "Say, is Charlene working tonight?"

"Dad," I hiss. "I don't want to go to a strip club."

For some reason, they both chuckle like I've been left out of the joke.

"Go take a seat," Charlie says. "I'll have her sent down when she's ready."

"Good man, tell her my boy's just done two years inside, so she'll need to go gentle."

We walk through a bead curtain into a smoky bar room scattered with lonely tables and lonelier men.

"Dad, I don't want a lap dance, please." But I answer my own question. There's no stage inside. No pole for a woman to dance around. And certainly no one giving lap dances. It's just a bar with a dozen tables, a few occupied by middle-aged men drinking alone. An older woman in a frilly blue dress waltzes over from the ill-equipped bar and greets Dad with a broad smile.

"Christos," she says, leaning down to kiss him on either cheek. "This is your boy?"

"The very one."

"Well he is a looker, ain't he? Charlene will make short work of him."

"That's the hope. Couple a' whiskeys, Dolly."

"Right away."

She swishes away, all smoke and perfume, and Dad pulls a cigar out from his shirt pocket. There's a matchbook on the table, and he snaps one off and lights himself up. I roll the matchbook between my fingers. *Bootlegger Bordello*, it says.

"Dad…"

"She's a dame, that Dolly."

"Dad. Is this a brothel?"

"Brothel?" He blows a ring of smoke out his mouth. "Son, this is where boys like you become men. Ah, thanks, Dolly," he says as she brings over the glasses then retreats back to the bar.

"But I don't want to be with a prostitute," I hiss.

"Oh, come on. Don't tell me that Carla ain't as frigid as an old maid. Two years inside, boy, you must be hungrier than a marooned sailor."

"No, Dad, I'm fine. Please, I don't want to do this."

"Drink your whiskey."

I drink it down in one anxious gulp. It burns the back of my throat and I swallow away a cough. The dark-lit bar is sadder than a life-sentence. A woman floats in from another bead-curtain entrance across the other side of the bar. She wears only a threadbare dressing gown. Like the kind you get in an ER.

"Phil?" she calls out as if he's waiting for his dry cleaning. One of the men sitting alone at the next table closes his book, takes off his glasses, drains his glass and gets up. Like all this is normal. He's even wearing a wedding ring. And he leaves his coat on the back of the chair.

"Hiya, darlin'" the woman says, kissing him on the cheek as he follows her through the beaded curtain.

"Dad, please, can we go?"

"I just wanted to do something nice for my boy."

"Mom took me to Target."

"Well that's your mother's way of showing affection. I happen to know how to look after my boy." He taps his cigar into the ashtray, then puts it back in his mouth and takes three quick puffs. I notice three gold teeth in the back of his mouth I've never seen before. Not only that, I don't recognize the man sitting across from me. Maybe he was always there, this cigar-smoking, whiskey-drinking whore-monger. But I never saw it. I guess that's the part of Dad I was always shielded from. Till…till I wasn't. Till the night he turned up at our back door, covered in blood and breathing so hard Mom was terrified he was going to have a heart attack. Mom patched him up and they talked long into the night, that's all I knew.

I don't doubt Mom knew the full story. And I never doubted she had no other choice. Given Dad's record, a simple parking ticket would probably have sent him away for the rest of his life.

"Christos!" A shrill voice lacquered in barbecue sauce and menthol cigarettes swims up to our table. Charlene, I assume. She smiles softly at us both, sizing me up like I'm about to be fitted for a suit. I don't know what I expected, but it wasn't her. Voluptuous red hair bounces around her shoulders and curves. She's beautiful, there's no doubt about it, but I have the overwhelming urge to hide under the table. "So, this is the fella?"

Charlene leans over, chest squeezed between her arms in a move Carla had tried earlier to far less effect. But I only see Charlene's eyes. Great green goblets of emerald drawing me in like a gorgon. Yet she singularly fails to turn me to stone.

"Eh, change of plan, darlin'," Dad says. "My boy's beat. First night of freedom and all. Sorry to bring you all the way down."

Charlene giggles and dismisses his apology. Her body loses interest in me, but her eyes stay drilled into mine.

"Never mind. He does look tired." There's something otherworldly about those eyes. They don't release me. Even as Charlene swirls her hair around Dad and he places his free hand firmly on her backside, her gaze doesn't release me. It's like she's weighing up my soul. I try to speak, but only dust and air comes out.

"You know I don't do refunds, Christos."

I want to say what she's doing is wildly inappropriate. Taking my father's hand still damp from the condensation on the whiskey glass and drawing his fingers all the way down her chest. But I can't say it.

If there comes a point in every boy's life when he stops seeing his Dad as some kinda superhero, and instead a flawed and broken man, then for me it was when I was old enough to have the agency to slam my bedroom door whenever he came to visit. But tonight was beyond even that. It was a rejection of Christos the man. Not just Christos the father. After two years inside, I'd seen my fair share of bad kids. Boys who weren't just in there because of the corrupt police, the state's racism, or the tricks and tribulations of manipulative agents. Some of them just had a screw loose. But I'd choose a night in a locked cell with the power off with one of them over watching my dad being directed to feel Charlene up while she stares at me.

"I'll, uh, be right back, son." Dad drains his glass and gets up from the table, wearing a sly grin.

"Give me the car keys," I snap. "I'm not sitting here. I've got no ID."

I turn my eyes away as he fumbles in his pocket and flings the keys at me. I catch them in both hands as Charlene leads him through the beaded curtain, waddling like a rodeo champion. I drain my glass, too, hoping the whiskey will be pure enough to kill whatever germs I've breathed in from this place.

"That was a good thing you did for your father," Dolly says, sweeping back to the table, dropping her own cigarette butt into the finished glass, which sizzles out and leaves a dank stench of damp tobacco that at least covers up the odor of pure bleach. That's how we washed everything in juvie as well; undiluted bleach dumped over anything the Beasts thought was dirty. Boys included.

"I didn't have much of a choice."

"He doesn't deserve it." I've nothing to say back. I just play with the car keys, waiting for her to waltz away so I can get the hell out of here. "Do yourself a favor, kid. Don't ever come back here."

"You can walk from here, son, right?"

We wait alone at the traffic lights. Out the window I gaze at the strip mall. Zotos's gym next to his accountancy store. The lights finally turn out as we approach eleven. The whole strip mall is closed, save for Domino's. Dad doesn't want to take a right. It'll add another ten minutes to his journey. Better I walk for twenty.

"Yeah," I say, unbuckling my belt as the lights turn green.

"See ya, son. Nice to have you back."

I get out of the car without responding, slamming the door. But Dad's off like a shot, roaring through the empty streets and leaving me high and dry once again. The whiskey-tinged exhaustion has me ready to lay down on the street till dawn. I feel stuck in one of those dreams when your legs won't work, and you can't run from the thing that's chasing you.

But then I catch a whiff of dough and cheese. Real cheese. Not the curds the state fed us. Domino's calls me like a siren. Electric lights of red and blue twinkling just across the street. There's a couple stools inside the empty take-out restaurant. Eating alone is the thing I want most in the world right now. I'm fucking starving.

"Hi," I say to the slight young Hispanic boy behind the counter. His red hat is pulled low, blue shirt buttoned up to the collar. It feels like I'm the only one who's been in here all night. The boy puts down his book, stretches and yawns, and looks me up and down.

"What can I get ya?"

"What's the most pizza I can get for twenty bucks?"

He bursts out laughing. It's funny how it doesn't annoy me. His smooth face and dark brown features light up like an electric chair as he laughs.

"What are you, homeless?"

"No," I say, although it doesn't offend me. I easily could be. Half the boys inside were. "I've just got twenty bucks though and I'm starving." I fish the bill from my pocket and slap it on the counter as if to prove I can pay for whatever it is this will buy me.

"What do you fancy?" he asks as I settle into the stool by the counter. I try to understand the dazzling array of options on the menu. Stuffed crusts and burger rings and pizza bases dressed up like chili dogs.

"I...really just want a cheese pizza."

"Okay," he says, still smiling. He hops back on his stool which I can see is meant to belong on this side of the counter. "Well, we can do you a stuffed crust with..." He's staring at me, grinning. I wonder if something fell on my face at that disgusting whore house. "Oh my God, you're Achilles Konstantinos!"

"Yeah..."

"I saw you on Carla's TikTok earlier. Welcome home!"

"Oh, uh, thanks. I guess? Who are you?" I realize he's wearing a name tag. It says Brad. I would not have pegged him for a Brad.

"I'm also at Jefferson High," Brad says.

"Oh, okay. I don't think I remember you, I'm sorry."

"Of course you don't. You were the biggest jock in the school." He's practically blushing. "I wouldn't expect you to know the likes of me. Sweet lord did you really only get out today?"

"Yeah," I say, now it's my turn to blush.

"Poor baby, you must be starving."

"Nah…well, a bit."

"Carla didn't make you a welcome home meal?"

I shake my head.

"Yeah, well I was in home economics with Carla. She burned spaghetti." I crack a smile, never having had the image of Carla cooking in my mind before. "Like, on fire." Brad grins back. "Mr. Michaels had to get the fire extinguisher." I shrieked with a laugh.

"Brad…stop."

"It was only like two weeks ago. You didn't notice her eyebrows were a bit wonky?"

"Can't say I did. But, no, she didn't cook for me. Not today."

"All right," Brad says, climbing up on the stool with his knees and putting half of his thin frame across the counter, pointing out the menu items. He's so close to me I can see all the way down his shirt, smooth brown skin smelling of subtle perfume, not like goopy cheese or marinara sauce like his uniform. "So let's do you a stuffed crust cheese lovers. Mozzarella, gouda, gorgonzola?"

"Sure."

"Goat cheese?"

"No, no goat cheese."

"No probs." He jumps off the stool, heads to the fridge and pulls out a bottle of Pepsi Max.

"I, uh, don't think I've got enough…" I say, trying to add up the numbers in my head.

"Oh, be quiet. Put your sewer money away. Let me treat you, for heaven's sake."

"Are you sure? You really don't need—"

"Please," Brad says, sauntering into the spotless kitchen. "I'd *love* to get fired from this shit hole. I could collect unemployment."

"You don't need the job?" I ask, reaching across the counter to grab the Pepsi and two plastic cups from the stack.

"I'll be going to college after the summer. Get the hell out of this hick town. You want pepperoni as well?"

"No, thanks." I gulp down the cold soda. It shoots through my veins like I imagine meth or heroin would. Suddenly I feel almost normal, not like a zombie dragging around my heavy head. "God, that's the first soda I've had in two years."

"No way!" Brad shrieks, slamming the pizza into the metal machine and dancing back to the counter. "Don't you make toilet wine inside or something?"

"Not quite. Orange squash is all we got."

Brad stares at me, like he's come face-to-face with

someone famous. But then spins around and leaps across to a standing freezer full of ice cream tubs. He pulls the door open and swings back on it, revealing a world of flavors I don't recognize.

"Let's have a starter!"

"I…I've no idea what these are. What's a *Netflix and Chill'd?*"

"Oh my God it's so good!" Brad says, pulling a pint out and tearing off the lid. "It's peanut butter ice cream with sweet and salty pretzel pieces and fudge brownies!"

"Fuck me," I say with a grin, grabbing the plastic spoon Brad passes me. "I'll have to do double time in the gym to get rid of this."

"That one over there, with all those hot wrestlers?"

"Eh, yeah. It's my uncle's gym. I don't know about hot, though." But I don't really care, not with the first taste of real, decadent ice cream warming me up from the inside.

"Sometimes I go look through the window on my break," Brad says, digging a massive piece of chocolate brownie from the tub. "And watch those boys duke it out with each other. It's incredibly erotic."

"Uh huh…good to know," I say, laughing nervously. What was I meant to say? "I can't say I feel the same. When you're on the mat, all you can see is a great hulking Greek boy ready to floor you."

"Why the hell would anyone want to do that? I mean, I personally can see the attraction of being flung around by half a dozen wrestlers…they don't do six on one, do they?"

I shake my head as I ingest the meaning of the joke,

then the image forms and cracks into a smile made wider by the sting of the ice cream on my teeth.

"They're making me do it," I tell him, digging deeper into the tub for the salty pretzel piece. "It's part of my parole."

"Seriously? This fucking state."

"That's what I said!"

But our eyes don't meet across the half-eaten tub for long because the timer on the pizza oven buzzes.

"Dinner time!" Brad swishes back into the kitchen, plastic spoon still in his mouth, slides the sizzling pizza into a box and slices it up. "Here you go. Fingers crossed it's as good as you hoped." But I don't get up. I don't want to leave.

"Can I stay and eat here? I don't think I can finish the whole thing by myself after so much ice cream."

Brad smiles under the low cap and black hair hidden underneath. He takes the spoon out his mouth and drags the stool on his side of the counter closer to me.

"It's huge," Brad says with a sly smirk, "but I'm an expert in…eating pizza."

I thought all I wanted was silence; to eat alone after two years of every single meal being eaten on the edge of a volcano permanently on the verge of exploding, and ruining the sub-standard food in the process. But this is so much better. Brad waits till I take a slice, and watches open-mouthed as I burn the roof of my mouth on the bubbling cheese.

"Argh," I say, shooting down Pepsi.

"Oh sorry, it's probably still really hot."

"No, I love it." And I mean it. "I can't remember the

last time I ate hot food." I take another bite and it burns again, but the pain is worth it. This is what freedom tastes like. Being able to eat a piping hot pizza at five to eleven on a mid-week night, free to walk home whenever I want. Or not. Brad nibbles on one piece only as I wolf down one after another; each cheesy bite better than the last.

"What's it like inside?" he asks, playing with the end of his crust he doesn't want to eat.

"Long," I say, truthfully. "The days are long. Classes, and not just regular school ones, but stuff like anger management, ethics, and stuff."

"Really?"

"Yeah. It used to be far worse a few years ago I heard. Or even in some other places now. Kids could spend twenty-three hours a day in solitary. Even the ones who hadn't even been convicted of anything."

"Fuck."

"Yup. But the county did some big investment package a couple years back. Now it's all classes and workshops and psychologists." Suddenly I have an urge to tell him about Reynard. To connect these two kindred spirits. I know better to ask if one knows the other. But Brad and Reynard are probably the only two people left alive that I genuinely want to be happy. "That's until they run out of money I guess. Maybe then it will be back to lockdown."

"And now you gotta do wrestling or they'll put you back inside?"

"And my GED," I add, realizing I've gone and eaten the entire thing, minus the one piece Brad picked at.

"That's good. You gotta get your GED."

I shoot him a warning glance like I'm done being lectured at.

"Yeah, but Mrs. McKenna's the other half of my parole."

Brad bursts out laughing. "Girl, don't you worry. I'll send pizzas over to the penitentiary when they take you away."

"Girl?"

"Yeah," Brad says, his smile dropping. But I don't want it to drop. I want to see him smile. "Like, you know, sister. Girlfriend, queen…"

"I…uh…"

"What, they don't have queer prison gangs in juvie?"

"Not that I saw."

"Oh," Brad says in all seriousness, grabbing the ice cream tub again like he was about to use it to call the governor. "Well, I've been seriously misinformed about life inside then. Guess I better reevaluate my life choices."

I can see him grin at me. Frothy white ice cream covers his top lip, and fudge brownie on his bottom lip. It kills me he doesn't lick it off. I want to bite it off his face, and I don't know why.

"If you keep hogging the ice cream, I'll do worse than send you to juvie."

"Hands off," he shrieks, playfully slapping my hand away. "These are stolen goods you're handling."

"All right, I'm coming over."

I'm genuinely on the cusp of hopping over the counter but Brad crying out with anxious laughter like I'm about to smash a water balloon in his face makes me stop.

"No! There's cameras in here. Honestly, I'm not worth going back inside for."

We both settle back down on our stools, making short work of the final scoops from the tub.

"I don't know about that," I say with a smirk. "But till I fail my GED and get kicked out of wrestling, can I still get free pizza?"

"Sure," Brad says with the widest grin I've ever seen.

Chapter 5
Hector the Vanquisher

It's so hard to know yourself when everything in your life has been set up to deprive you of the very concept of having a self. Like, your ultimate, unique form of being sits in a pickle jar on a dusty shelf in a dingy shed out back in an overgrown garden of an abandoned house, and all you've got is the memory of who you thought you might be. That's the answer to Brad's question. That's what it's like going into prison at fifteen years old.

I walk past the shut-up Domino's early on Saturday morning, unready to face the destiny the fates have laid out for me. Qualify for a wrestling competition. It's not as easy as it sounds. First of all, you have to get into the right weight class, and I know I'm on the higher end for my age bracket. I know I'm going to have to work hard to get down to two hundred and fourteen pounds. Pizza and ice cream notwithstanding. And even once I'm there, the guys in that "heavyweight" category are tough as shit to beat.

Although it's eight in the morning the gym is busy. It already reeks of sweat. The sacred circle in the center is empty of course, but all around are boys of twelve, teens of fifteen, and high school seniors smacking punching bags, doing pull ups, or Zotos's particular form of torture, the weighted rowing machine.

"Good morning, Achilles," Zotos says from behind his desk in the corner of the large space. I hop over someone's runaway medicine ball and sit down by his desk, which is covered in accounting paperwork he's taken from the office next door. He's standing, staring at me through half-moon glasses too small for his face, the vein wrapped around his skull pulsing. I remain stuck to the chair, suddenly fearful of what I've done wrong. In juvie, when you enter a room, you sit until you're told otherwise. Zotos watches me sitting there. "Get the fuck up and start working out you fat sack of flab!" Zotos flings the papers he's holding at me and I jump up in shock.

Every station seems full. I don't know where to start. Groups of guys in twos swing across the monkey bars, while the smacks of the punching bags warn me against approaching them. Only the dreaded rowing machines are empty, three of them facing a large wall map of the Aegean Sea, the weights placed deliberately on the mat beside. I feel I'm about thirty seconds away from having to row from Athens to Troy.

I decide to jog on the spot. At least I'm wearing shorts and a hoodie. Sporty enough. Although not the official singlets we have to train in. Even though they're spandex, there's not a hope in Hades they'll fit.

"Achilles," Zotos yells, "what the fuck are you doing?"

"I'm…exer…cising," I say, already out of breath. Zotos stares at me like I'm a goat at a feast asking what's for dinner. And, unfortunately, more than a few of the dinner guests have stopped to watch this poor creature build his own funeral pyre.

"Hector!" Zotos screams at the top of his lungs, "get your ass over here."

From the volume I expected Hector to be three doors down, but he's actually about ten feet away, smacking the shit out of a punch bag. I can only see the back of his body as the muscles under the tight spandex rumble with every powerful punch, but instantly I recognize this guy. Hector finishes up the last of his one-two rounds on the punch bag, then, not even breaking a sweat even though he's clearly been here since seven in the morning, trots over to Zotos' side.

Hector is every bit the man I remember, just fifty percent more. Taller, bulkier, squarer. Like a tank that got an upgrade. His flaming red hair and fair complexion gives his jawline a smooth sheen, unlike my grizzly stubble. But he must wax his chest now, because I distinctly remember copper used to run down his torso. We all used to make fun of him and call him rusty.

"Cousin," Hector says, offering out his powerful claw. I shake it suspiciously, his smile like a flashing alarm that he's up to something. Or, more likely, has already sized me up and realized I'm not even a threat worth worrying about.

"Achilles," Zotos says beaming with something akin to pride, "Hector is now second in the state."

"Good for him," I say, not looking at his smug face.

"What position did you reach, Aki?" he snarks.

"Fourth," I say, dragging my eyes to him. "And I did it when I was fifteen, *second* cousin."

"If Hector wins at Regionals, he'll go top of the state," Zotos says, slapping him on the back. This chumminess confuses me. I always remembered Zotos calling Hector a shit-faced snot-nosed rug-rat. To me Hector still looks every bit the part. He folds his bare arms, the red singlet barely containing all the rippling muscles not normal on a teenager.

"Maybe you can hold my towel during the fights, Aki. I'd be happy to show you how it's done."

"Is that trash talk? 'Cause I'm used to dealing with gangsters and murderers, *Rusty*."

"All right, that's enough," Zotos snaps, even though I'd barely started. "Achilles, into the ring."

"But…I don't have anything to wear." The loose shorts and baggy hoodie would be grabbed and used by an opponent to floor me in five seconds flat.

"Then strip."

A crowd was gathering around the central ring. Kids who spend their Saturday mornings battling through the monotony of training left their gloves on the floor and punch bags swinging as they gathered around the mat. Hector snorts with pity-stuffed disgust and walks away, back to his punch bag. He doesn't need the distraction. But the kids are waiting for something. At least fifty of them, from the arrogant twelve-year-olds comparing numbers of armpit hairs to the boys of my age who'd once looked up to me. Now I am their spectacle.

"Uncle," I whisper, "I don't really feel comfortable fighting today. Like, I only just—"

I don't get a chance to finish my sentence because

Zotos shoves me toward the center of the ring. The boys don't fall in hushed silence like I'm some returning hero. Far from it, I'm the jester about to be laughed at.

"Get them off," Zotos yells, grabbing at my shorts and nearly pulling my underwear down too.

"All right, give me a fucking second."

This is worse than juvie. No one made you strip in front of a crowd of giggling pre-teens or guys jacked up on testosterone figuring out the best way to take you down. The Beasts at least ran their torture through a set of rules. It wasn't some kinda free-for-all Colosseum contest, as much as they might've enjoyed that.

All the eyes watch me, but Zotos is busy peering at his phone through his half-rimmed glasses, tapping away one button at a time. Hector keeps up a one-two-one thwack against the punching bag as a soundtrack to the public shaming.

Sucking in a deep breath and wishing I hadn't eaten an entire pizza and bucket of ice cream last night, I slip off my shorts. The new boxers from Target are a tight fit, so they might as well have been a singlet. I pull off the sweater but with a great deal more reluctance, turning my back to the waiting crowd, but exposing my front to the empty parking lot. And maybe even Brad out there, coming to gawk at the Greek gods before he starts the early shift.

Out of the corner of my eye I catch the statue of Ares by the entrance. Man-sized but hardly man-shaped. A carved image of a sculpted god is not a healthy benchmark for any of us, let alone these kids hastily whispering around the edges about my less-than-Olympian body.

They say the sport of Greco-Roman wrestling is the closest thing we have to the thrill of the ancient battlefield. That it's a sport for heroes where cunning and bravery are pitted against brute force and raw strength. That's how Zotos always put it: *Imagine yourselves running across the coast toward Troy. Priam's army rushes out of the gates to meet you. There's no space for weapons, no time for spears. This is man-on-man, Greek versus Trojan in the most famous battle there ever was or ever will be.*

In the practice bouts we were always divided into two teams: Greeks in blue singlets and Trojans in red. At the end of the season, whichever team had won most practice bouts was rewarded with a feast at The Athenian downtown, while the losing team washed the dishes of the victors. It keeps an unhealthy vein of competitiveness running through every interaction inside the gym, or outside of it. You follow the instructions of your team captain to the letter. You train together, eat together, and avoid the other side, whether at school or the mall, because this is war. Ancient and all-encompassing.

As I pad to the edge of the shock-absorbing mat and wait for my next humiliation, I can see from the whiteboard on the wall that Hector's red-singlet Trojans are currently leading by fifteen points. Not an insurmountable lead, but a significant one nonetheless.

"Strategos," one of the blue-singlet boys asks Zotos, for that's the name we all have to call him. "Will this count towards—"

"This is not a competition," Zotos bellows. He's a man born in the wrong time. An accountant in a washed-out tracksuit addressing a crowd of sweaty teenagers in a poorly air-conditioned gym in the flatlands of Southeast Texas. He should've been an Achaean general standing on the shore of the Peloponnese. "But before you stand Achilles, who was once the greatest fighter this gym ever had. Now look at him."

I glance down at my half-naked self; the image they were projecting was a lot worse than the reality I can see with my own eyes. But the kids snicker. I couldn't blame them, I would do the same in their situation. In fact, it's a testament to Zotos' discipline that they aren't more cruel.

"Fifty dollars," Zotos says, pulling a scrunched-up note from his tracksuit pocket, "to the man who can perform a takedown on the legendary Achilles."

A takedown is the highest scoring move in wrestling. There's a few different versions which will collect different points, but it's basically trying to get control over your opponent so three points of contact are on the mat; two arms and a knee or two knees and the head for instance. But this isn't the normal rule-based sixty-second bout or a match between equals. There'll be no shaking hands before or after, which Zotos religiously enforces. Withholding a handshake meant automatic disqualification when it came to competitions.

No, this was something far outside the normal. Like some lost chapter of Homer's story where the Greeks and Trojans call an uneasy truce to fight off a raging giant threatening to destroy both their camps. And here I stand, neither red nor blue but pink, like a bastard son of Cronus offering glory and riches to the next Heracles who can defeat me. I glance back at Hector still thwacking the punchbag. He's the only one not interested in the spectacle. At least not yet.

"Who's brave enough to try?" Zotos cries, waving the fifty dollar note in the air. He must've secretly offered them a maiden and a pizza-pie too because the bare arms of fifty kids shoot up into the air and they begin to jump and screech like there'd be no ice cream if they didn't. Zotos might as well have said *stay quiet if you sit down to piss*. No group of boys, not even the ones in juvie, are easier than the Greek boys to rile up into a bout of toxic masculinity.

"All right then," Zotos says, folding up the fifty and flashing me a wink. He grabs his folding chair from behind his desk and sets himself up in front of the circle like Zeus readying himself for an amusing conflict among the humans. Something to pass the time till lunch. "Nikos, you're up first."

I turn this way and that to try to find my opponent, worried Zotos is up to no good. I almost expect from the depths of the gym will emerge a terrifying titan who'll have me in a chokehold in three seconds flat.

But that's not Nikos. He's a scrawny kid, barely twelve and certainly the smallest in the gym. He rushes toward me from the crowd, screaming like a little lion cub as his bony arms flap around. He's so hocked up on Zotonic jingoism the poor boy doesn't even pause to acknowledge the ring. I'm Satan and he's a warrior running head-long toward a sainthood.

I bend down slightly and pick him up, my hands under

his hairless armpits as the kid writhes and kicks and punches the air.

"What do you want me to do with this?" I ask Zotos while Nikos continues to tire himself out by cycling punches which cast a gentle breeze across my chest. He doesn't even try to unhook himself from my grip or get into a vertical position where he could at least land a kick on my chin. It's not in the rules, but in Zotos' version of Hades, there are no rules but his own. He glares at me instead of answering.

"Fine, what do you want me to do with this, strategos." He shrugs. I shake my head, wishing there was some appeals process for the parole board to unhook me from this cruel and unusual punishment. I'll stay on parole till I have my bachelors if they want. Just not this.

I carry Nikos to the edge of the circular mat and drop him outside it, onto the harder mats which aren't so friendly if you land on them wrong. Nikos is fine, though. He falls on all fours then trips again trying to get back up. But the kids aren't laughing, not anymore. Even Hector stops punching the damn bag. Silence falls over the gym, and I can hear Nikos holding back a sob. It's the young boys who look most afraid. Before the bout, they all put up their hands and jumped up and down when the stench of bloodlust caught their senses. But like the dawning realization that falls across any front line of infantry, they know they're just fodder.

"Adonis," Zotos yells from his throne, "you're next."

I shake my head once again in silent protest as a boy is pushed to the front by his brothers already wearing the look of defeat. Adonis has a long way to go before growing into his name.

It takes two-and-a-half hours, but one by one, all the boys of Zotos' gym are soundly and sorely defeated. More accurately, they failed to defeat me, and thus failed at the one thing Zotos had expected. Well, all except Hector. By the time Zotos started calling out names of the fifteen-year-olds like a one-man firing squad, we all knew the entire purpose of this charade. And it had nothing to do with fifty dollars.

Quietly I started to enjoy the worry seeping across Hector's face with every kid I shoved to the ground, pinned, held, or even scared off with just a quick and sudden movement. This would be Hector's moment to lose. What kind of team captain, what kind of state champ, would he be if he couldn't perform one simple takedown on a guy, two years out of practice, who'd just used up every ounce of stamina fighting off every boy in the gym?

As for me, I could plead exhaustion or a problem with technique or simply brush it all off because I didn't care. But Hector, with all his muscles and girth, would not soon recover from a failure to vanquish Achilles, his mortal enemy since time began.

But before that, I need to get my breath back. I sit on the mat itself, my black boxers almost see-through with sweat, gulping down cup after cup of water from the machine which Nikos and the boys have taken to fetching for me like some sort of old-fashioned fire drill.

Although each and every one of them has been defeated by me, they all know the real fight is against Hector. And the boys, the Greek ones in their blue singlets anyway, want nothing more than a tribal victory over their hated Trojan enemies.

In the enemy camp, Hector is holding court by the punching bags. The second strongest boy, Giorgos, is using his own painful defeat I'd just inflicted on him as a teaching moment for his captain Hector. *"Don't make the same mistake I did and try to out-maneuver him, he's too quick,"* I can almost hear him say, desperate to deflect the embarrassment of me flapping his parry with one hand, knocking him off balance while locking his other arm behind his back and then using his unanchored weight against him so he just tumbled to the ground like so many decapitated statues.

"Do you want more water, Achilles?" Nikos asks, as he and the other blue singlet boys dance around like anxious fireflies, waiting for the brewing fight.

"No, thanks," I say, wiping a great wave of sweat from my forehead. "I'll piss myself if I drink anymore."

"You can do it," one boy says.

"Yeah, Hector's not so great," agrees another. "He just scares everyone into falling."

"Don't worry, boys," I say, offering out my tired hand for four of them to grab onto and help me back on my feet. "I don't scare so easily."

"Were you really in jail?" Nikos asks, his young mind trying to frame if I was worthy of this hero-worship.

"Shut it, Nikos." Adonis punches his friend in the shoulder. "Only bad guys go to jail."

"Are you a bad guy?" Nikos asks with innocent wonder as my heart pounds inside my soaking chest.

"Not all people in prison are bad," I tell the boys, as Zotos returns from smoking a cigarette outside. Hector's camp takes that as a signal to cease their strategizing and slip to bucking up their commander with slaps on the back. "But, yeah," I add, "I just got out yesterday."

I leave my fan club oohing at their new icon as I take up position on my side of the circle, waiting for Hector.

"Fifty dollars," Zotos says again, "and your parents will be coming to pick you up in twenty minutes so I'm putting a three-minute limit on this bout." He glares at Hector as he slowly sets up camp on his side of the ring. "Do you both understand?"

"Yes, strategos," Hector says, with put-on solemnity.

I, meanwhile, say nothing. I'm bent over, resting my elbows on my thighs and pretending to pant like a dog. Now we come to the psychological part of the battle, and the five seconds of eye-contact that will, almost without fail, decide the victor before the whistle has even been blown. I can see clearly in Hector's eyes the fire of indecision. I'm a wounded animal; a bull jammed full of knives roaring around the ring, the crowd quiet with shock that I've survived so long. Hector's smart enough to know he can't just cut me down with one swift blow. He can, but it will be a pyrrhic victory.

Hector needs the crowd behind him. He needs to draw me out, let me land a few blows to show off the spectacle. The struggle has to be poetic. No one remembers the straight defeats. No one writes epics about the conquering forces vanquishing enemies without breaking a sweat. No one would know the name of Hector if it wasn't for Achilles standing against him.

Hector launches the first move, dancing across the mat and we lock horns and pirouette around the ring. It's an overture. The orchestra is only striking up. The violins treble into tune with the twanging sinews of our arms. Then the brass, the meat of the music. Chests smash like cymbals. We twist and turn with the bass, trombones extending like his arms around my waist, but it's a false crescendo because I spin out with ease and bring with me the voices of the crowd. The note of song striking this band into full orchestral cornucopia. Our feet slam a beat on the pounding mat knocking us across the middle eight right as we ascend to the climax. Hector moves in to knock me off-balance to set up the take-down. But it's premature because I see it before it comes and spin away. This is only the end to act one.

We retreat to regain our breath for intermission. Zotos watches like a maestro. The boys are transfixed. The critics have all been proved wrong. This isn't going to close on the first night. Hector and Achilles are immortal enemies. And now his pedestal is crumbling, and I can just sit back and watch. I'm not the lyricist with a point to prove. This theater bears my name, my image, the profits from every miss-step go straight into my pocket. This is where the bell would sound, but the show is ready to go on, and go on it must. For it's written in our folklore which lives in our Greek veins.

Hector dives forward again and pulls me into an arm drag. It's fine. It will gather a point or two from the judges.

But the judges are the gods and the reward will come only after defeat. Hector screws up the transition to gut wrench. He's off his game. The boy has never had to work so hard in his life. The sort of guy whose jock body, blemish-free skin and suburban padding have insulated Hector his entire life.

We're cut from the same clan; my father is a henchman for his. But that's the difference between the son of a prince and the son of a warrior. Hector grew up in the palace of Priam while I was dragged up from the dregs of the sea-nymphs.

Now the drums clash. The entire cast is out on the stage, belting out each melody from every number; we throw all the moves in the book at each other. Hector is as desperate as a man who knows the war is already lost. He surveys the battlefield through sweat-drenched eyes and can see no path to victory. All he can do is cut down the opposing general and make it that much harder to come back and fight another day.

But Hector can't even manage that. He's got one move left, but I've already calculated every possibility open to him. Just like those tense stormy days in the juvie dining hall. You count who's there and who's not. Analyze the hotspots and potential outbreaks and sit strategically. Close to allies but far enough from the Beasts. You count the notes in your head. How long has it been since I threw a punch? Does an outright majority of newbies fear me on reputation alone, or have they first-hand evidence of Achilles the Great?

I've added it all up by the time Hector gets close enough to make his move. I twist, hop from one foot to the next and the watching crowd lets out a bated breath. Two leading roles, but only one can get the loudest round of applause. One's the lead, the other supports. And Hector has failed to prove to the gods he deserves a leading role.

"Time," Zotos yells. But Hector chooses not to hear. I retreat, but he wipes the sweat from his brow and leaps forward once again. "Time!" Zotos screams again. Hector's not playing by any rules. He strikes me in the back of the leg, with his foot, an illegal move and I fall to my knees. "Enough," Zotos screams, sliding into the ring and knocking Hector away. I'm on the mat, wounded and sore, but I've won more than I gambled. Hector's face flares redder than his hair. The sweat soaks his singlet, maybe for the first time.

"Go get showered up, Hector. We'll talk about this later."

I sink into the cool mat, knowing full well my body is sticking to it. I'm the fallen soldier on the battlefield, but in the fall I've become the hero. The boy's step over and around me, sitting in assigned places to hear Zotos' last oration before the day is done, like he's a preacher telling stories of a long-dead faith. I close my eyes. This battle might be over, but the war is far from won.

"You've still got it, Aki," Zotos says. I peel my eyelids open, cheek stuck to the mat.

"You made me fight the entire gym," I say, safely now we're alone. All the boys have been picked up by their parents. The Saturday morning Greco-Roman wrestling crowd has departed. I can already see the taekwondo teacher setting up for the next group of kids from a neighboring culture in the melting pot.

"And you're undefeated. Fifty wins and a draw."

"I'm close to death."

"But you survived, Aki." Zotos leans down, stretching his polyester tracksuit to the limit. "You didn't survive two years inside on reputation alone, did you? Now you've put the fear of the gods into all these pube-less little shits." Hector included. That crafty strategos.

"Come on," Zotos pulls me up. "Go get showered and I'll drive you to school."

The once-familiar locker room is still lined with the same poorly-lit rows of rusty lockers and never upgraded benches that bear the initials of my father, who scratched them in as a boy. No one should be left inside, so I peel off my underwear at the entrance and drop them on the floor beside the dry clothes I came with, flipping a scratchy gym towel over my shoulder and padding to the open shower block.

"Stop, you're hurting me," I hear a voice drift from the shower block. I step back from the tiled entrance. Inside is one big room with two dozen open pipes, some with shower heads, so there's no hiding from whatever's going on inside.

I've never heard of a single juvie in the state with an open shower block, so how this gym, that is used mainly by kids, could get away with it was a testament to Zotos' tightwad attitude against spending a cent he didn't need to.

"You said you wanted it," another voice adds. A familiar one.

"I do but it's too sore."

"Just relax." It's Hector.

"I can't," the other voice says, more pained than before, almost through tears. "Please, Hector, just stop, I can't take it."

And neither can I.

"What the fuck's going on in here?" I demand. But it's perfectly clear. A naked Giorgos is pushed up against the tiles, slightly bent over, with Hector standing behind trying to stuff his ample self inside his friend. Giorgos jumps up when he hears my voice. He scurries off, almost slipping on the wet floor, and pushes past me, avoiding eye contact.

"Care for another round?" Hector asks with a broad, callous smile, his hard-on now pointing directly at me.

"I'm good," I say, hanging the towel up on a hook and stepping under a searing stream of water, but I stay transfixed on Hector, my gaze warning him to not creep up on the hastily-dressing Giorgos, or *me*.

"Scared?"

"Me?" I scoff, "No. I just don't want to break your neck on this wet floor. You see," I say, flexing every muscle I have left under the scalding shower. "In juvie the one place to settle a score is the shower block…because they know you can't come in with any weapons. This is the place we fight, Hector, not fuck."

He shrugs, re-opening his own waterspout.

"Any hole's a goal, eh, cuz?" I ignore him, but the stench of his failed victory is now swirling down the drain. He's angling for another go. If I was in juvie, this is the part where I'd run a mile. Only a fool gambles away his life for the sake of dignity. "Funny how they let an animal like you out after two years."

"It's parole, Hector."

"You mean pussy release, Aki?"

"What the fuck are you talking about?"

"I heard they let you out early for good behavior. Sitting in juvie sucking dicks, I believe I overheard your father say. He was so disappointed in you when they said you were eligible for early release." I laugh at the naked attempt to rile me up. "Maybe you're a better cocksucker than a wrestler."

The water keeps running. I massage the chlorinated soap through the hair on my head, and face the tiles to let it course down my back to have two seconds without staring at Hector's unreal body.

"Ah," Hector says, as I wash the sweat and grime from every crevice. "I guess you survived being a faggot, not just sucking cocks."

"What?" I say, turning around to see his smirking face through the prison-bar water. He's not even pretending to be under the shower – standing in the center of the shower room, arms dangling by his side.

"That's a mighty fat ass you've got on you. Must've seen quite a bit of action."

I don't even feel myself slide across the tiled floor. It just happens. The only thing in my head is the fact there's no Beasts waiting in the wings. No one to come and throw me in solitary for days, weeks, months on end. No prison director to explain myself to.

Hector stumbles backward, blood and spit flying out

his mouth and staining the water pink as it rushes down the drain.

"So the myth's got a heavy dose of truth, does it?" Hector says with a bloody grin. "Maybe give me a turn on it." He grabs his cock and smacks it off his hand like a weapon. "And I'll think about letting you win next time."

"What the fuck's going on in here?" Zotos yells from the shower entrance, staring at us both through steamed-up glasses. But he knows we're both at fault. I wouldn't be standing with a raised fist for no reason, and Hector wouldn't be spitting blood if he didn't deserve it. But now my stomach drops. It's not just Uncle Zotos watching, he's my parole officer.

"I was just…uh…"

"It's nothing, strategos," Hector says with both eyes on me. "We were just catching up on old times."

Zotos doesn't look convinced. He dismisses the smart-talker and addresses me directly. "Get some fucking clothes on, son. It's time I dropped you at school."

I can see Hector grin as I follow Zotos out. The walls of Troy might be a little bruised, but they stand as strong and abhorrent to me as always.

Chapter 6
Jesus the Teacher

Mrs. McKenna is staring me down, standing behind her principal's desk like she's captain of a starship, dreadlocks folding over her canary yellow suit.

"You know how many inmates don't have a GED?"

"You don't need to tell me; I've already been inside."

"Eighty percent," she says, drawing out a big eight-zero with a sharp, colorful nail across her desk.

"You know how much less likely you are to return to jail if you get your GED?"

"A lot less likely?"

"Twenty-five percent." She bangs her fist on the desk with each syllable. I sit back, a little startled. Every muscle in my body aches, and she's not doing my ears any favors either. "You're a quarter less likely to go back to prison if you get your GED."

"That doesn't seem like very good odds."

"Oh, it's not for my benefit, Mr. Konstantinos. It's for yours. Because if you do go back inside, then you're going to want to be in there forever 'cause I'm going to be right there when you get out, booting your balls until you get your goddamn GED, do I make myself clear?"

"Yes, ma'am."

"I don't know why you were in there in the first place," she says, turning away from me to look out the window at the trees waving in the early-evening wind. School on a Saturday is a strange place. Like juvie when everyone's out in the yard, but they make you stay inside to slop out the toilets. "You are not going back to prison, Achilles. If there's any justice in the world your record will be wiped clean and that piece of shit father of yours will rot away inside."

I'm taken aback, but unsurprised. Given the amount of time she's spent with both my mom and Uncle Zotos it's no surprise she knows the full story. Or probably just guessed it. Every two-bit reporter who wrote even a single line about a fifteen-year-old going away for shooting dead a gang leader inside a meth lab knew there'd been a miscarriage of justice. Hell, even the damn brothel keeper knew it.

"I'm a Black woman in America, Aki, I've got no time to wait for justice. So, we are going to put everything in your corner, every statistic we have, to help you get your life back, do you hear me?"

I nod, but she seems unconvinced. She leans across the desk, one sharp-nailed finger pointing dangerously close to my throat as if it's a screwdriver. "You're lucky to be a white boy…well, white-passing, anyway, to get this kind of opportunity from a Texas judge, you understand? But if you screw this up you make it twice as hard for the Black and brown boys still inside to get the same kind of chance."

I swallow hard. "Mrs. McKenna, I know that, but—"

"But nothing. If you even think about putting one foot wrong, if you even come within two whiffs of a joint or a bottle of beer, I don't care if you gotta call me or your Mom or the goddamn Greek mafia, you stay the hell out of trouble, you hear? Or I swear to Jesus, Achilles Konstantinos, I'm gonna—"

A knock at the door startles us both.

"Come in," she says, her tune changing like the weather. But I keep my eyes straight ahead, not wanting to know what the next circle of Hell was about to toss my way.

"Ah, Jesús, thanks for coming."

I turn to see. "Brad!"

"Hey, Aki."

It's him. Brad from Domino's, carrying an overstuffed backpack by the strap and another armful of books under the other arm. He couldn't look more different. Like the red and blue uniform was his superhero costume and now he's back in his regular disguise.

"Who the hell is Brad?" Mrs. McKenna asks, her tractor beam gaze now falling on Brad / Jesús.

"Just my manager…he, you know, wants us to have 'Texas names.'"

"Ah-ha," Mrs. McKenna responds, holding her suspicion closely as if there's some sorta wrongdoing hiding beneath this story.

"Sorry," Jesús says to me as he takes the chair beside mine. "I should've said."

"Hey, no. Of course not. What does it matter?" Why Carla called him a chimp I've no idea. I stick out my hand with a grin and he shakes it.

"Jesús and Achilles," Mrs. McKenna says, eyes rolling. "Worlds colliding. Now I know Jesús that you weren't happy about me forcing you to do this tutoring program."

"No?"

"What do you mean, 'no?'"

"I mean, no, I wasn't unhappy."

"But you sent me emails, several of them." She swivels her mouse around, trying to wake up the aging desktop computer as Jesús shakes his head vigorously again.

"Maybe you're thinking of someone else, Principal McKenna."

"Thinking of someone… Jesús, you're the only kid in the goddamn tutoring program."

"Like I said," he says, shooting me a quick glance, "happy to be part of it. No trouble at all."

"Well…good. Because you need social justice credits for CalTech—"

"CalTech," I say, slapping my leg. I've been trying to remember where Mrs. McKenna mentioned Jesús was planning to go to school. "That's awesome, man."

"Yeah, *man*," Mrs. McKenna says mockingly. "And you, sir," she points at me again, "aren't going to do a thing to screw that up. Jesús's time is precious. He has to work and study and keep your sorry ass out of jail. So, when he says jump, you say…" I stare blankly, trying to figure out if she wants me to jump or… "You say *how high?*"

"Oh, right, yeah. Sorry."

"Here," Mrs. McKenna says, chucking a keychain at Jesús who catches them with his one free hand. "Lock up the library when you're done."

"Thank you, principal—"

"Now piss off so I can get this goddamn letter of recommendation done." She bangs the boxy monitor to wake it back up. I grab Jesús' heavy bag for him before he can, and he nervously nods a thank you as we head out into the corridor.

"Didn't expect to see you so soon," I say after a few long minutes of silence as we walk down the empty hallway to the school library.

"Yeah," he responds with only a nervous laugh. I feel odd, too. Almost like…we're nothing but two strangers who chatted once and bump unexpectedly into each other again and now find themselves with nothing to say. He's different inside school than out. The superpowers are subdued. The over-the-top Reynard style personality which gave me my first decent laugh in two years was replaced by sullen, stamped-upon teacher's pet trying to hold up the weight of all the expectations placed upon his shoulders like a five-foot-six Atlas.

We make it to the dark and empty library but every step drags. Jesús knows exactly where the light switches are, and he spills his books out over a table as I take a seat across from him, my chair squeaking in protest like it's going to break.

"Why didn't you want to do the tutoring?" I ask.

"No, no. No…no, it wasn't that," Jesús says, not looking at me but busying himself with the books and notepads, taking some out of his backpack then putting some back inside. "I'm just busy, you know. I gotta work and stuff."

"I'm sorry. I don't want to make things harder for you."

"You're not, Aki, I promise. I just didn't expect to see… *you.*"

"Yeah," I smile, and he smiles back. "But maybe we can study over pizza, too."

"I'd like that."

"You know I was at the gym this morning. First time back on wrestling."

"How did it go?"

I think the grin told him the answer. But it was a complicated grin. It had gone badly, terribly, or so I had told myself. Sweating out of every pore in my body as I knocked back kid after kid, then the final dance with Hector which I thought would end in yet another humiliation for me had actually been…sort of fun.

"I think it went all right, in the end. My Uncle Zotos is a sadistic monster though. He made me fight every kid in the gym. Well, not really *fight*. He offered a fifty to the first one which could do a take-down on me, like get me on the mat."

"Holy shit."

"Yeah…although come to think of it he never gave me that fifty."

"Gave you?"

"Yeah," I respond in surprise. "None of them managed to do it."

Jesús looks like he's just choked on a piece of stuffed crust.

"You…beat them all? Every kid in the gym?"

"Sure. Although the last one was more of a draw. But Hector is one place away from being the state champ, after all."

Jesús stares at me like I'm a ghost and monster and god all rolled into one.

"That's…impressive."

"Meh." I shrug. "I wasn't prepared *at all*. I don't even have a singlet, I had to fight them all in my underwear. I was drenched by the end of it. They were practically see-through."

Jesús now looks like he might faint. His eyes drift a hundred miles away and his cheeks start to flush.

"Are you okay?" I ask, slightly worried.

Jesús clears his throat and shakes his head, slapping open a big yellow GED textbook and staring at the words, but I can see the red rise up his neck and flush his dimpled cheeks. I reach over and flip the book around. "You're looking at it upside down."

"Oh, ha!" His laugh is nervous and high-pitched. "Well, you won't fail phys-ed, at least we know that."

I return a wide smile, the chair groaning as I lean back and wonder what I can do to help him loosen up.

"How about Pythagoras, let's start with that."

"Okay," I nod, taking a breath. "Pythagoras of Samos moved from the Aegean to Magna Graecia, what's now Southern Italy, around…530 BCE…yeah, 530. He set up an academy in the Achaean city of Kroton where he taught that each soul is immortal and, upon death, enters a new body. He also discovered the movement of the planets is controlled by mathematical equations. Oh, and he proved the earth is round. Aristotle thought he was supernatural, and apparently a priest of Apollo gave him a magic arrow which allowed him to fly. Once a deadly snake bit him, but he bit it back and the snake died. He also taught Plato and Pythagoras' community on Krotos was the model for Plato's *Republic.* The pantheon building in Rome is also based on his mathematical models of architectural beauty."

Jesús sits in stunned silence. Nothing, not even his face moves under the flickering luminous light. I start to wonder if everything I've said is wrong. If I confused the world's first philosopher with someone else. Archimedes perhaps. No, I'm sure I remembered it correctly.

"I…uh, meant Pythagoras's Theorem…you know, the square of the hypotenuse of a triangle is equal to the sum of the squares of the other two sides." Jesús hasn't just seen a ghost, he looks at me like Pythagoras himself has just walked into Domino's.

"Oh, right. Yeah, I know about the triangle stuff."

Jesús hesitates, like he's desperately afraid to ask me his next question.

"Did you…read the original Pythagoras?"

"Actually, none of his original writings survive. Most of what is known about Pythagoras comes from writers during Roman times, and their Greek is way easier to understand than, let's say, Homer."

"You…" Jesús swallows hard like I'm about to thump him. Although, I don't know why. "You know ancient Greek?"

"There's not really one ancient Greek. Mom insisted on using Attic Greek at home. It's way more complicated than modern Greek. It has all these different tenses and cases, like in Attic you've got this dual number when you want to talk about two of something, not just singular and plural."

"Uh-huh."

"But I read Aristotle and Plato and Xenophon and all that stuff as a kid so actually for me modern Greek is the one that seems weird. Like, smaller, you know? There's less room for expression. Aristotle was talking about all these big ideas, but they've got to be talked about so precisely otherwise the meaning gets lost."

Jesús slams the textbook shut, making me jump.

"And I guess your mom read you the *Iliad* and the *Odyssey* as bedtime stories?"

I grin. "She did, actually. But Homeric Greek is way harder than Attic. The pronunciation is so different. It's like, you know the *Canterbury Tales* in old English?" Jesús just stares blankly. "You know, Chaucer?" He nods, but I'm unconvinced. "Well, anyway, it's like old style literary Greek. Mom always read it to me so I knew the stories by heart practically. But no one talks like that of course. I read Homer by myself in juvie though."

"Really?"

"Yeah, the librarian, man, she was so nice to me. She went to all the libraries around Houston, to the college libraries as well, and borrowed the books for me. I had to basically read it aloud the first few times, but I got there."

"That's…so nice of her."

"Yeah." I smile, remembering how I'd sit in the hallway outside the library, chained to the seat, waiting for eight AM when Anna would come unlock the door, her bag full of a new surprise for me. "Anna, the librarian, also used to bring me the modern Greek translations of books banned by the State, 'cause the guards didn't know any better. The

English teacher in juvie assigned me an essay on Shakespeare, and Anna had to bring me the Greek translation of the *Sonnets* because it's banned."

"You can't read Shakespeare in prison?"

"Not the *Sonnets,* anyway. And she brought me the Greek versions of other banned books too. Dante's *Inferno. The Vagina Monologues. Game of Thrones.* Gore Vidal's autobiography. Dan Brown's *Digital Fortress. Memoirs of a Geisha.*"

"Those are all banned?"

"Yup."

"Why? I mean I can maybe get behind *The Vagina Monologues* but *Game of Thrones?* Why would they ban that?"

"No idea. But on Sunday's I used to read out loud and translate a chapter of *Game of Thrones* from the Greek version I had to some of the other guys. We figured out where the TV show was up to from the newbies, then for the rest of the day whenever we'd be in earshot of the Beasts we'd be like: 'Wow I can't believe Joffrey gets poisoned' and they'd get so mad. They couldn't figure out how we knew what was gonna happen. Although, it didn't really work for the last seasons. We'd just try to make stuff up though, to see if we could guess it right."

"Who are the Beasts?"

"That's what we call the guards in juvie. It's a pretty accurate, generous, even, description."

"Sounds like it if they sit around watching *Game of Thrones* but don't let you read it."

"Sometimes they'd just ban a book for no reason at all.

Just to be dicks. One kid had to read *Fried Green Tomatoes* for college credit and then they decided it was banned. So I got Anna to order it in Greek and I sat with him in the library every day for two weeks reading and translating it for him so he could write the book report."

"That's insane."

"Yup. And there was this one kid who was really messed up. He'd been abused in every foster home he'd ever been in and used to scream all night when he first came in. Like he kept the whole block up. Then we found out he loved Disney, and the only way he'd fall asleep was to put a Disney movie on for him in the TV room and he'd relax enough or fall asleep watching it and we could carry him to his cell."

"Poor guy."

"Yeah he really had it tough. Anyway, when the Beasts found out what we were doing they smashed up the TV and blamed us, and he went back to screaming."

"God that's awful."

"Yeah but then, get this, we'd start to sing Disney songs. The whole block through the cell bars. Dozens of us. Someone would start, no idea if it was the right words, but close enough, and we'd all join in, singing these songs from *The Little Mermaid* or *Lion King* at the top of our lungs until he fell asleep. But we couldn't keep singing every night, so Anna tried to get him some Disney books, for kids, you know, see if that would help him."

"Did it?"

"He couldn't read."

"Ah."

"Not a word. He didn't even know the alphabet. So a few of us decided we'd teach him. Anna bought him this really beautiful book, *ABC Disney Pop-Up*. You lifted up the pages and this character would spring out. Like Kaa the python from *Jungle Book* would slither out beneath the letter K. Man he loved that book. But he was enjoying it so much the Beasts came to figure out what was up with him. They saw the book and banned it.

"No way."

"Yup. *ABC Disney An Alphabet Pop-Up Book* by Robert Sabuda is banned from Texas prisons by the Department of Public Safety."

"So he never stopped screaming?"

"I don't know. After the Beasts took away his pop-up book he really went downhill. They moved him to a psych ward that afternoon. Aesop's *Fables*, that's another pop-up book one kid got sent for his birthday. They ripped it out his hands and got the State to ban it. They did the same thing with a Jewish kid's *Chanukah Fun* coloring book. A coloring book. Not even with the pencils."

Jesús' eyes flare red, tearful, like he doesn't know what to do with the weight of all this sadness I'm pouring out onto him. Atlas weeping under the great big thing he's just been given to hold onto for the rest of his life. These things roll off my tongue because I'm only relying facts. These things happened and I saw them. I heard them. I whispered about them as hot days simmered with tensions, The Beasts did one thing, and then another, and then another. Always coaxing us, squirting vinegar into the eye of a chained tiger knowing fine well they've got the keys and the gun. I don't know what I expect him to do with this information either, I just have to tell the stories.

Just like in juvie, certain books I read in smuggled Greek I couldn't keep to myself, I had to sit in the corner of the library, a few ears gathered around and turn the Greek on the page back into the English it once was. I had to tell the stories like Homer himself was moving through me. No wonder Mom kept praying to that damn statue of Thamyris in my bedroom, the singer who could out-sing the muses.

"One kid wanted to keep up his programming studies," I say, rolling off another banal example of evil. "Then they banned his C++ textbook. Jon Stewart's book from *The Daily Show*: banned. Encyclopedias: banned. The fucking *AAA Road Atlas of the United States*: banned. But *Mein Kampf*, *The Protocols of the Elders of Zion*, David Duke's *Jewish Supremacy*, and even *The Hitler we Loved and Why* all sit on the shelves. Anna even had to order *The Color Purple* all the way from Greece for me after she found out it was banned. That one I also did readings of and translated as I went. Remember when that movie *Alita Battle Angel* came out?"

"Yeah. I never saw it, but I remember."

"Couple of kids asked to read the comics, they banned it. We got a new civics teacher at one point who tried to give us a civil rights lesson. He couldn't bring in books by Juan Williams, or Henry Louis Gates, or even Harriet Beecher Stowe and Sojourner Truth. Banned. Although they never banned my favorite."

"What was that?"

"*Les Misérables*. You read it?"

Jesús shakes his head, still stiff with shock. I guess opening up to him like this was a bit of a revelation.

"I saw the *Glee* episode where they sing a couple of the songs from the show though. It didn't much suit Lea Michelle's voice."

"I haven't seen the show and I don't know who Lea Michelle is, but I love that book so much. Just makes me think about how easy it was in the past for people to rise up and fight against tyranny, you know? Like…they'd take a stand and they'd fucking make a revolution happen. God I'm still surprised they never banned that one."

"Start a revolution and see if they do," Jesús says. It's one of the nicest things anyone's ever said to me. Like a stranger complimenting you on a job well done, or coming across a crowded restaurant just to comment on the color of your eyes.

I want to tell him about those dreams. Well, sometimes dreams, but more often the epic fantasies I play in my head as I try to fall asleep on a prison-issued pillow. The ones where I'm a great revolutionary. Sometimes chasing Red Coats in colonial Philadelphia, but more often than not climbing the barricades in Paris like Marius, or back in nineteenth century Greece awaking from half a millennium of Turkish domination. That's my dad's favorite time anyway. It makes it so easy to spew racist bile at Turks when he can innocently lift his hands and say: *'it's just history.'* I want to tell Jesús, but he's staring down at his cell phone screen.

"Oh my God I found the list."

"Are you serious?"

"Yup. Texas Justice Department list of…fifteen thousand banned books. Holy hell."

I watch as he scrolls, thumb frantically spinning the screen, stopping for a moment or two to take in a title, screw up his face, shake his head and keep on scrolling. But he does it without the sad note of pity, it's all in good humor, gallows humor. Once you've been there, there's not much else which will make you laugh. And the indignity of injustice suits him.

"*Drag Queen Baby Names*," Jesús says like I should know it. "What the hell are they banning that for? Scared a bunch of inmates are going to start a drag show? *Ernst and Young Tax Guide*. Well that makes sense, you don't want prisoners committing tax evasion I suppose. *Girl with the Dragon Tattoo. Spanish English Bilingual Dictionary*…sorry, *visual* dictionary. A Beatrix Potter pop-up book of *Peter Rabbit*. What the fuck do they have against pop-up books?"

"Anna said they gave some excuse about hiding stuff inside a hardback cover, but there's plenty of other hardbacks, plus it's not like a visitor just hands over a book during family time."

"Yeah and they can search your butt cracks but not books? Huh," Jesús is still scrolling. "They banned *Letters from Prison* by Marquis de Sade. Well that makes sense since it's about horrific injustice… Oh no! Not *Fun Home*!"

"What's that?" I ask.

"*Fun Home*! Alison Bechdel?" I return a blank stare.

"I saw the musical in Houston. It's *a-mazing*!" Jesús' starts to fan himself with his free hand, his neck and cheeks turning red again in a way that's too cute to handle. He excitedly flips the phone to YouTube and starts to play a video of a song I don't know. "This won five Tony awards."

We listen and he sways along, mouthing every single word, every single note and pitch and tone of the actors on the stage. I have to laugh. In the cone of aloneness of the school library on a Saturday, Jesús is miming with every theatrical bone in his body, utterly and unashamedly himself. I watch in awe, smiling so wide my cheeks begin to hurt. Just watching. I feel he wants me to join in. He's mouthing the words to me, singing silently as if I'm the only one in the audience and he's up on a Broadway stage giving the performance of his life. But I don't know how to sing, or to mime, or to sway, and especially not how to react to any of those things. So I sit back and watch and smile, and that's enough.

"Fuck, man, I can't believe they banned *Fun Home.*" The song over, he flicks away from YouTube and, phone flat on the closed textbook, opens a search bar and types something in.

"What are you searching for?"

"Yup," he says, "they banned my favorite book too." He sighs and flips the phone down, the shattering pettiness of it all that bit too much. I appreciate his frustration of solidarity. I really do. Because no one else, save for Anna, ever understood what it was to live your life censored.

I take in a breath to ask the question, but he's already telling me.

"*Before Night Falls* is this mind-blowing autobiography by this Cuban exile, Reinaldo Arenas. It's all about his early life and how they put gay people into concentration camps in Cuba—"

"What?" I say, shocked to hear about some new injustice in the world. I thought after two years in juvie surrounded by boys who should never have been there, I'd heard it all.

"Yeah, for a long time the Communists put gays into camps. Anyway he escapes to the US eventually and dies young. But it's just the most beautiful story. Javier Bardem plays him in the movie version." I see a tear forming in his eye. I thought only I cried at the memory of books, but apparently so does he. Now he sees me looking at him funny, like I want to ask him something that I'm afraid to ask, as he was before. But I'm not afraid.

"I guess you're gay," I say, realizing that my mouth has never before formed that word. Jesús leans across the table, pulling me in like we're two inmates planning an escape.

"No shit, Sherlock," he says with the widest smile. "I'm the modern American queer. A Tequila twink, a south-of-the-border rice-and-bean queen. A teenage Mary longing for a big strong Okla-homo to take me away, but instead all I got is a Grindr Extra account I blackmailed Mr. Pierce the cute history teacher into paying for."

"Hey, I remember him."

"You wanna see a pic of his hole?" Jesús asks, phone at the ready.

"Umm…no. I'm all good."

"So," he asks with a mischievous smile, reminding me of a statue of a drunken Dionysus that used to stand in the entrance to my aunt's Greek taverna downtown. "What kind of *unspeakable* things do they do to fags in juvie? And, please, I beg of you, be very specific."

"Eh…nothing." I shift in my seat and my uncomfortableness screams louder than a fire alarm.

"Nothing?"

"I mean, there wasn't, uh, any gays. Queers, uh, LGBT—"

Jesús cuts me off with a cackle.

"None?"

I shake my head.

"Well, you know what that means, don't you?"

I shake my head again.

"It's probably you."

My heart grinds to a screeching halt. I feel the world slip away, the library, these books, this chair and table, myself, it all dissipates into a black hole. I don't understand a thing yet understand all at once. My legs start to tremble like I need to get up and run. Run up to my cell to hide. To hide with Marcus. To sneak into his bottom bunk, to cower in the smooth part of his neck as his hairless shoulder sits firmly against my lips. To feel safe by his side. Comforted by his scent. Smell his pillow when he's not there, and even when he is. To just lay on my top bunk and watch as he does his pushups. To watch as he *knows* I'm watching. To watch as he does it topless, then short-less, then…

"Ah-ha I'm just messing with you!" Jesús shrieks, slapping the table and me back to life.

"Oh, uh…ha. Got you. Anyway," I say quickly as Pythagoras stuffs my escaping soul back into my body. "I think you're the bravest person I've ever met."

"Me? Because I've got a patch on my bag that says *Fuck ICE*?"

"No, well, not only that. Because you're…you. All of you. Like, right here, in my face."

"Well," he says proudly, "I do enjoy being in your face."

"I like talking about books with you."

"Aki," he says, winding his smile down to seriousness. "I think you're incredibly brave as well."

"Me, no…come off it. I'm just—"

"Stop." He places a hand on mine. It's like a bolt from Olympus, but stronger. "I know you've told me things you've probably not told anyone else. And I need you to know you can trust me. There's nothing you can't tell me, okay? Nothing in the world."

I nod, and swallow back what threatens to be a flood. I've not cried. Not for a while. Not since… No. Not even then. The trauma of that was too drawn out. Too long to sustain a cloud of sadness when I couldn't afford to be anything but Achilles the Great. Jesús senses it too. How my top lip trembles, and my teeth chatter just a bit even though it's perfectly pleasant. He pulls back his hand. Gently though, not in fear of it being ripped off, but in acknowledgement that we've had our moment. Whatever *we* are, it's started. The sinews of trust are knotting themselves over a deep wound that cuts through me and him. I know the feeling. It happened the first night I spent with Marcus.

"Now," he says, opening a different book altogether. "Will we do some quadratic equations?"

Chapter 7
Achilles the Savior

A week later, I'm hanging out at the parking lot of the strip mall with two dozen kids, most of whom I don't know and even less of whom I trust. The gym is shuttered, but one late-night light still shines from inside Zotos's accountancy practice. And at the corner, next to the boarded-up nail salon, the blue and red sign from Domino's casts an inviting glow across the puddles and potholes of the parking lot.

"Carla, I really don't want to be here."

I know Jesús is working tonight. He told me earlier that day during his three-hour gap between school and work—our tutoring time—that he would be working the closing shift tonight. That means Lynette, the woman who apparently calls herself the manager because she'd been there six weeks longer than him, would lean her big boobs over the counter for every pubescent boy and white-collar Dad in the county to come along and slip singles in between her tits while waiting for their pizza. Or so Jesús described it anyway. What a fun way to spend a Friday night, for a queer teen. Not.

I'm anxious to stay out of sight, but keep the store in my line of sight. Peering between two parked Range Rovers, that I can't believe parents buy for their kids these days, I can see Lynette flirting with one of those red-hat guys. Jesús will be slaving away in the back. I can see movement, and I skip behind one of the cars. I can't let him see me wasting my time, more than that, threatening my future with these lowlifes. Zotos to the front of me, Jesús to the back.

"Have a drag," Carla says, ignoring once again my complaints and swinging from the beanie-hat-wearing stoner to me like she's the chimp dancing between trees. She tries to stick the blunt in my mouth. Reflexively I knock it away, harder than I mean to, and it falls into a puddle, sizzling out.

"Hey, man, not cool! That's my mom's weed," the stoner complains.

Carla shoots me a death stare, banging her mitten-covered hand against someone's car door. Her car door, I realize. When we were fifteen, hanging outside the Walmart or inside the twenty-four-hour McDonalds off the freeway was cool. Going to a place we couldn't get to without some big brother or older cousin giving us a ride. Now she had a car, but yet we chose to be in a mini-mall, only a fifteen minutes' walk from my house, hanging out with a bunch of loser nobodies.

"What the fuck is wrong with you, Achilles?"

"I told you Carla," I say, shivering even though it isn't cold. "I don't want to be here." There's no point in hiding what I say from the stoner, he can hear. But now he's crouching over the puddle, trying to salvage whatever weed he can, dabbing it dry with the edge of his checkered shirt.

"Why don't you talk to some people? Everyone's been asking for you all week, they're all, *Carla, where's Aki? Carla, why is Aki not coming? Carla, tell Aki this, tell Aki that.* I'm not your fucking secretary. Get a fucking cell and talk to your fucking friends because I'm sick of it."

Her raised voice perks up a few ears. There's no hiding by the side of her car anymore.

"Brah!"

"Adam," I shudder, nodding as Adam saunters over from the other side of the car.

"Didn't see you there, brah, good to have you back." He grabs my hand like he's running for president and pulls me into a back-slapping hug. It's funny—some people I don't recognize at all. But Adam, he's just become more Adam. The Ralph Lauren polo shirt underneath a Uniqlo puffer. The blond hair swept back over his square face. The all-American, white-boned boy who, in any other city, in any other state in America would be top of the school food chain. But in the outskirts of Houston, this WASPy kid is in a minority of not much more than one.

"Yeah, man, it's been a while."

"You know, my brother's been working on your case at Columbia."

"Oh yeah? Anything new?"

"Maybe, brah. He's doing an internship this summer at one of the big Manhattan firms. He's taking it straight to the *pro bono* department to look into. You know, it was his essay on your case that got him into pre-law in the first place."

"Wow. I'm so glad someone's profiting off it."

Adam doesn't pick up on the sarcasm. In fact, I'm not even sure I do. What do I care if his brother starts his career on my behalf? Get me off and I'll get on my knees for him and his brother… Oh fuck. Why am I thinking that? Suddenly the image, the idea of Adam and his brother in nothing but matching polo shirts lodges in my brain.

"Come grab a beer, brah."

"Yeah, man, I will soon… Carla," I hiss, pulling her close once he's out of earshot. "There's fucking beer here?" The stoner is still standing there, watching the two of us while picking at the damp bits of his weed, a sour face on him like a kid whose ice cream I've ruined. "Can you, like, fuck off for five minutes?"

"Oh, uh, sure, man. Yeah, sorry. No trouble, okay? No trouble." He scurries off like I've just threatened to screwdriver him in the throat. He wants my Dad for that. Carla just giggles.

"Why don't you relax, Papi? Have a drink, loosen up, baby. I wanted you to have fun."

"Fun? The second a cop drives by, what you think he's going to make of me standing here with you lot and your weed and beer in cars? Not even a cop, my uncle's still working inside. Carla, this is fucking serious."

"All right, all right. Jesus, Aki. I never thought prison would turn you into such a narc." She pulls open the back door of her SUV. "Get in."

"You are not driving."

"Of course, I'm not driving. Get in the car, dumb ass. The windows are tinted."

She's not wrong. I can't see a thing inside. Plus it's dark. But sitting in the leather seats in the back, the hazy lights of Domino's pizza are very visible, as are the headlights behind us with Adam always trying to buy his way into hanging out with the cool kids.

Carla's already lost her denim jacket, and her hands are attacking the waistband of my sweats.

"Carla." I try to pull her arm away, but she snaps right back. "Carla, baby, what're you doing?"

"Come on, Aki. Let's try again."

"Carla, you can't be serious. There's twenty other kids out there." On cue, their laughter cuts through our hushed conversation. "We're in the back of your car. It's hardly time—"

"When is the time, huh? Cause you've been home for eight nights now and you've been as soft as an under-baked pretzel, Achilles."

"You really want me to get naked in the back of this car? Fine." Coat still on, I yank down my sweats and underwear. Soft as a pretzel indeed. "This is what you want, right? It's about the only thing you seem to be interested in from me. So, here it is. Thanks for making our first time again so fucking special."

She says nothing, just looks at it, then me, and my miniature tantrum hangs in the air between us. Suddenly I'm intensely aware of being in a fairly busy parking lot with my balls sticking against her leather seats. But I feel that pulling up my pants now would give away my wider point. This wasn't the time, nor the place.

"Are you gay?"

"Wh-what?"

Carla asks it with her stoned face. She's not out of it, but she's part of the way there. "I'm just asking. You know, prison, guys together, lonely. I'm not judging, I'm just asking."

"Carla, you're being ridiculous."

"Oh yeah? So, fuck me now then." She starts to unbuckle the belt on her white pants, pulling the button out, unzipping... I immediately pull up my sweats in response.

"Quit that right now."

"'Cause I could ask any single one of those guys out there to come here and they'd fuck me without any problems. Threaten to put them away for two years, hell, even two weeks and they'd fuck me twice just to make sure."

"Fine then, fuck them. You already have been, so why stop now?" I twist my fingers on the door handle, ready to dive straight out. "Who do you want first? Adam?" She says nothing in response. But her face changes, deepens, like she's no longer putting one hundred percent of the blame on me. Just perhaps, I can see her think, having it off with Adam and fuck knows who else while simultaneously expecting me to slot right back in to where things were two years ago ain't the smartest idea. But I'm in no mood to understand. "Go on, Carla, get on your back. I'll send Adam in and tell the rest of them to form an orderly line."

"Fuck off, Aki."

"Gladly," I say, slamming the car door shut. I take a deep breath, sucking in the cool night air. The brazen laughter of teenagers drinking publicly not ten feet away drifts over on the overcast sky. I can smell rain coming. Not just rain, a storm. I can smell it bouncing off the metal. Like the air that would seep in between the bars in our windows; particles interacting in the sky, swarming together like they're stuck in a washing machine; the scent of a coming storm tanging the air.

I don't want to go anywhere near Adam or the meatheads. But I don't feel like going home. Not on a Friday night. I'm free. I want to live. I should want to live. But all I want is to be back in the confines of the school library, pouring over books with Jesús. Or even back in Domino's, recreating the magic of that first night out.

Despite the knowledge of big-breasted Lynette behind the counter, only moments later I'm opening the glass door of Domino's Pizza.

"Hiya, darling," Lynette says, not looking up from a set of printed spreadsheets. "We're closing soon, so order up quick."

I can hear Jesús in the kitchen, even if I can't see him. There's music in the background, music I don't recognize, and it sounds like he's cleaning.

"Actually, I'm here, uh, to see Jesús."

Now she looks at me. She stares with all her body, figuring out what my deal is. To be honest, I don't know either. The noise outside is all-encompassing. I never noticed it in the back of the car with Carla, but it pings off the glass door like we're under attack. The shrieks, the laughs, the yells, the bangs, the smashing of bottles. I've come from there, but I don't want her to associate me with this outside.

"Aki!" Jesús rushes out from the kitchen, wiping wet hands on his apron. "What're you doing here?"

"I wanted to know if I could walk you home?"

Jesús stares at me. Lynette stares at me. She grins. He's shocked.

"Yeah…sure. I mean, I have to close up first, so like, in about twenty minutes?"

I smile and take a stool.

"Well," Lynette says, grabbing her bag off the counter like a dead racoon and swinging backward through the counter as if she's walking out of an old-fashioned saloon house. "I'll leave you boys to it. Jesús, put the trash in the dumpster this time, not just out back."

Jesús nods, but he's not really listening. Lynette's gone, but she could easily have been sprawled out on the counter for all Jesús cared. I'm the only thing he's interested in.

"What're you really doing here?"

"I told you, I wanted to walk you home."

"Ain't those your friends out there? Don't you want to be with them?"

"Eh," I glance back at the banging and yelling like it's *Mad Max*. "Not so much my crowd these days."

Jesús dances around, picking up a brush and putting it back down, going back into the kitchen, filling a bucket and coming back out. But he talks, too, and I listen to all the things that have happened in the few hours since we last met. But it feels like an era has passed, and an epic can be spun between us. The only thing I want is to hear the words he has to say, all of them. Jesús picks up some of the many threads of conversation that eke out in our meetings that must be dropped, half-knit, because I've solved the problem, or he has to go to work. Just as Homer might stand in an Athenian square and know all at once where Priam and

Hector and Achilles are at any point in the story, Jesús pulls all those threads together and wraps me up in the story.

"So, Taylor posted this response," he says, only briefly glancing at the till as he folds up a roll of receipts and counts out the remainder of the cash inside. "But it was a screenshot. She'd gone into her notes and searched for this. Why was she searching for something she allegedly wrote the night before? And Kim was all 'oh, this proves she knew it was coming.'"

"So that's why they hate each other?"

"Honey," Jesús says with a wink that causes an involuntary smile to split across my face. "That was back in 2016."

"There's more?"

"*So* much more," he says, slamming the cash register shut. "But I have to take the trash to the dumpster. I'll be back in a few, okay? Then we'll go?"

"Sounds great."

Jesús grabs two large trash bags and heads out the back through the kitchen. I get off the stool to help, but it's too late. He's already gone. I only notice in the silence of the buzzing fluorescent lights, but the parking lot is quieter now. But I can still see Carla's SUV parked across the way. Suddenly I'm struck by guilt. Like I'm cheating on her. She's out there and I'm in here. But we're not together, I remind myself. I've been out for eight nights, as she pointed out, and we're still nothing but two people who can't seem to have sex.

I play with the laminated menu, running the sharp edge along my finger and wondering if I'll get cut. What would

Jesús do? Would he pull out the first aid kit tucked away in the kitchen, clean off the blood and wrap it in one of those blue restaurant-edition band-aids? I think about his face, concentrating on putting two slices of skin back together. I think about his hands, holding mine tightly as he makes it all better. Checking he's not around, and no one is watching from outside, I rapidly slice the hard plastic along the tip of my index finger, hoping for blood. But it doesn't take.

Far more than five minutes have passed, and he's still not back. I lean over the counter; the back door is open into the night, but there's no sign of him having returned. No sound either.

"Jesús?"

I haul myself over the countertop without a second thought. In juvie, there's no time to hesitate. If someone's in danger, they need help now. My shoes skit across the still-damp tiles in the kitchen and I slide straight to the open fire escape door. The restaurant backs onto a high wall separating the strip mall from the homes beyond, but in the concrete space marked "keep clear" there's only a scattering of rusty tins to cook pizzas stacked up. No dumpster. No Jesús.

"Fucking faggot."

I hear the words like a far-off crack of thunder. I run down the alleyway behind the other closed stores, closer to the road where I can see the dumpsters. I can hear a hard boot connecting with the soft tissue of a stomach, and someone coughing as they are smacked again.

"Piece of shit joto," another voice says, accompanied by a hocking great wad of spit.

I turn the corner and at the end of the alleyway, hidden from street view behind the dumpsters, Jesús is lying battered on the ground, surrounded by ripped open trash bags and two kids—they must have been hanging in the parking lot—standing over Jesús, taking turns kicking him in the stomach. They laugh, hard. The one on the right readies his foot to stamp on his head. This isn't a schoolyard fight or a casual mugging. They're in it for the kill.

But I don't stop to think about any of that. Not as I emerge from the darkness, taking it step by step, not giving myself away till I'm close…close…close enough to act.

I grab the one on the right's leg as he's about to stomp Jesús' face. There's enough force there to smash a skull. All the easier for me to lean in like I'm going for a takedown. His knee shatters with a blood-curling crunch as I snap it hard in the wrong direction. But he doesn't have time to even cry out. I've got one arm wrapped around his broken leg while my other hand flies upward, permanently crushing his balls and giving me the leverage to lift his entire body up, and turn it into a dangerous weapon to use against the left attacker.

Their skulls smack together and the one on the left falls instantly to the ground as his nose explodes in a dimly-lit rainbow. He's down, but not out. I spin my human weapon around so hard the bottom half of his leg is hanging on by mere sinew alone. But now he sees my face.

"Fuck!" he screams as I slam his body directly onto the one lying on the ground. He lands on top of him with a rib-snapping crunch, and they both cry out in bloody agony. "It's him. It's Achilles."

"Oh man," the one with the busted nose says, laughing like he's not just bought himself weeks of reconstructive surgery. "De verdad, te has vuelto loco, güey."

I drop down to check on Jesús. He's battered, bloody. His face is cut in ten different places and I can see scuff marks snaking under his shirt. Through his pained face fear screams from his eyes. But not for himself, for me.

"Aki," he whispers through swollen, bloody lips. "They're from school. They know you. They'll put you away forever." He groans hard, trying to turn onto his back. On the other side those two cackle away like hyenas.

"He's right, güey!" The one who's knee joint I shattered says while painfully coughing

"It's a hate crime, attacking us two Mexicans," the bottom one says.

"Yeah, yeah, hate crime," he laughs with his buddy. "¡Vas a pasar el resto de tu puta vida tras las rejas por esta mierda!"

That Spanish I know. *You're going to spend the rest of your fucking life behind bars for this shit.*

"Jesús," I say, "don't move a muscle." I shift his body closer to the dumpster as he cries out in pain. I suck in a harsh breath; hurt I've caused him more pain. But I need him out of the way. I need space to work.

I grab the one on top's foot, the one on his good leg. In one quick move I stamp hard on his knee and yank his leg upward. He howls at a pitch only heard by dogs as both his legs now dangle away from the knee. His friend pushes him off, one hand assessing the damage of his bloody nose as he scrambles to get up. But he's not running anywhere. I grab him by the waist and lift him straight up in a textbook move. The wall is calling me, asking to hurl his body across it.

"Aki!" Jesús cries out while coughing. "No, they're not worth it."

"If I'm going back inside," I say, cracking the guy's back over the corner of my knee instead painting the wall with his insides, "then I'm gonna make it worth my while." I let him drop to the ground as he spits up blood. His face rests on the concrete next to my shoe. I take a half step back like I'm about to kick a football. "I can kill you both and still only get one life sentence."

I pull back my foot, rub my hands and lunge forward with enough force to kick a head clean off its shoulders.

"No!" the attacker screams, and I pull up, just grazing the top of his forehead. "Por favor!" he cries, tears and phlegm mixing with blood on the ground. He pulls up his hands to cover his face, but I don't think they've got the message yet. I kick him onto his back instead, knocking onto his friend who's passed out from pain.

"I don't see any reason to let you live."

"Aki, no!" Jesús cries out, snaking forward to grab my leg. He hangs onto it, eyes staring up at me, blood-shot and bruised. I stop. The anger dissipates from my body, and suddenly all I want to do is get him out of this stinking alley. I bend down and pick Jesús up. He moans with pain.

"I know it hurts, hang on to me. I'll get you out of here." The attacker with the busted legs is unconscious. "The Greeks still run this town," I tell the one sobbing blood into his hands. "And our vengeance is long, slow, and eternal."

I carry Jesús carefully but quickly back inside the restaurant.

"Let's get you back inside and I'll call an ambulance."

"Don't you dare," Jesús replies like he's more fearful of that than anything else.

"What? Why? You're badly hurt."

"It's thousands of dollars. You think I can afford an ambulance? My phone's inside, call an Uber."

"A what?"

"Just put me down here," he says as we reach the back door.

"On the ground?"

"I don't want the cameras inside to see. The front door is locked, just grab my bag and hit the lights then come back out. It will lock itself."

Shocked he doesn't want an ambulance, I do what he asks, grabbing a bottle of water for him as well.

"Thank you," he says, spluttering as I lift his head off the concrete and hold the bottle as he drinks.

"How do I get Uber on this thing?"

"Give me," he tries to hold it, but he's too weak. He unlocks it and gives it back to me. "Just swipe to the next screen," he says with great effort. He sips water but spits out more than he swallows.

"How do I get it to take us to the hospital?"

"No! No hospit—"

"Stop yelling, Jesús, you're hurting yourself. You need a hospital for fuck's sake."

"Aki, no. No hospital. I'm serious."

I've found the address of the nearest hospital. My

thumb hovers over it, ready to order. His body is mangled, like he's been put through one of those pizza dough makers. Nothing looks right, not his face, not the way his bruised neck is unable to keep water down. But this is not my world. It's his. Every time I felt sick or had a headache or was recovering from making sure everyone inside never forgot I was Achilles the Great, I took myself to the nurses station. The world was not like juvie. It was far more terrifying.

"Fine," I say, typing in a new address. "I'm taking you home."

Chapter 8
Saphie the Aeschylus

"There we are," Mom says, dabbing Jesús' cuts with a cotton ball dipped in Greek-strength Bactine. "It looks much worse than it is."

I pace, biting my nails, unable to sit or stand or walk. Anger and fear, diffused in equal measure, course through my veins. I want to go back and kill the two monsters who did this to him. Even though he seems all right, I can't bear the sight of him lying on the couch, bruises popping up like mushrooms after a heavy rain, with Mom sitting on the coffee table cleaning and dressing his wounds.

"Sit down, Achilles," she says sharply, "or go check on the meat I put on for you both, just stop pacing around behind me like a damn goat." Goat? Did she really say goat? "You were right not to take an ambulance to the hospital," Mom says to Jesús, pulling his shirt up to rub antiseptic cream onto his bruises. I can't help but stare. His frame is so slight, tightly packed like dusty sardines in a soft skin can, but red and blue and purple swirls around his abdomen like a dark and stormy sky.

"Oww…ow ow ow. It stings."

"Nearly done." She wrings a flannel of Jesús' blood into a bucket, then dabs it just under the rim of his black polyester Domino's-issued trousers. He sees me looking. I turn away.

"Thank you, Mrs. Konstantinos."

"No thanks needed, dear. Not at all."

"Are you sure he doesn't need a hospital, Mom?"

She ignores me. "I studied nursing in Athens. You're in good hands, dear." She wrings out the flannel once again. "The state of the hospitals these days, it's appalling. I went back to Greece to have my eyes done last year, remember, Aki? When I was away for a month?"

"Yes, Mom."

"Do you know how much my insurance wanted me to pay here?"

Jesús shakes his head.

"Eighteen thousand dollars! What with the nights in hospital and the tests before and after. Highway robbery! They said, 'Well, Mrs Konstantinos, if you only want one eye we can do it for twelve.' No thank you, I said. I bought myself a direct plane ticket and three weeks in the Aegean for half as much."

"How much does it cost in Greece?" Jesús asks, turning on the couch as Mom wraps a large plaster over the bottom part of his rib cage.

"Oh, it's free."

"Free?" he says, spluttering loudly.

"If you'd been beaten up any worse Aki would be better taking you straight to Greece for a doctor."

"Sounds nice."

"Jesús," I ask, "aren't you on your parents' insurance?"

He glares back at me, as does Mom, as if I've said something horrendously offensive.

"Achilles," she says with her warning tone.

"It's okay," Jesús adds, finally lying flat on the couch as Mom pulls his blood-stained electric blue T-shirt back down and dabs his forehead with a clean cloth. "My parents aren't here."

"Oh my God…Jesús I'm so sorry, I didn't—"

"They're not dead! My Dad's in Honduras and my Mom…well they took her two years ago so nobody knows."

"ICE?" Mom asks.

Jesús nods. "Technically, I live with my aunt, but she's in Vegas so…"

"So a hospital is the last place we want you to be." The room sinks into quietness, with only the sound of Jesús' labored breathing and the oven heating up the meat Mom insisted we eat. The typical Greek response to tragedy. "You always have a home here…Hay-zeus. What you're doing for Aki is wonderful. I can never thank you enough."

"Don't worry, Mrs. Konstantinos, he's smarter than me."

"He *thinks* he is, and it's Saphie, dear, please."

But these shards of conversation are as out of place as a rose in a prison yard. The silence needs to sit. I see a tear drip down Jesús' closed eyes and stain the sofa. Water from the flannel falls drop by drop into the bucket.

"Even in our sleep," Mom says quietly, dabbing his forehead and wiping away his tears, "pain which cannot forget falls drop by drop upon the heart until, in our own despair, against our will, comes wisdom through the awful grace of God."

"That's…beautiful," Jesús says. His smile births light back into the room. I finally stop pacing and come closer. "Who is that?"

"Aeschylus," I say, so in love with my Mom that she knew the right thing to say to make Jesús feel better.

"No, actually," Mom says. "It's Robert F. Kennedy's take on Aeschylus. In Greek it's more like 'Zeus, who guides mortals to be wise…blah blah blah, favors come to us from gods, seated on their solemn thrones.' That's a more accurate translation, but I do like Senator Kennedy's interpretation."

"Mom says she was the one who told him what to say."

She smiles at me as I join her on the coffee table, and Jesús settles in for a story.

"I practically dropped out of high school to follow Senator Kennedy. My father was so angry he threatened to pack me off to Greece to my uncle's goat farm! But then Athena showed him the way and I went with his blessing. What a time that was, 1968. It felt like the whole world could change on the wings of a butterfly. I was only stuffing envelopes and answering the telephone, but still I felt this close to the center of it all."

"And you drove him through a cornfield," I add.

"Well, the Senator was going to miss his plane. And no one else could drive a combine harvester."

"Neither could you, Mom."

"They didn't know that. They all thought I was a farm girl for some reason." Mom explains to Jesús as she folds up a flannel and leaves it to rest on his forehead, dries off her hands and pulls herself up off the coffee table. "We were in Indianapolis when we heard the news that Reverend King had been murdered, slap bang in the heart of the black neighborhood. The suits wanted to get the Senator out of there, they were afraid no white man would be safe in the coming riots. Senator Kennedy said he would riot with them if it came to it, but that there could be a better way. He stood up on the back of a flatbed truck and told the crowd the news, then looked over at me, winked and quoted from his new favorite poet Aeschylus." Mom goes wistful, silent, but smiling into the kitchen. "Achilles, go bring your friend some clothes. *Hay-zeus*, do you eat goat?"

Jesús stares at me with a horrified look.

"Just say yes," I whisper.

"Of course, Saphie. It's my favorite."

I never expected the night to end like this, Jesús lying in my bed, wearing my old training shorts and state championship T-shirt about eight sizes too big for him, while I lay on the floor under an old and scratchy blanket and on top of an even older one. But in the darkness, despite the pain in my shoulders from the unexpected street match which I know is worse times ten for Jesús, I can't help but smile knowing I can't be seen.

"I never said thank you, Aki," Jesús says softly from the distance of my pillow. I'm on my back, one arm reaching behind my head and staring up at the ceiling, just like him.

"You don't need to thank me."

"I do. I really do. You put your whole future on the line for me, without even a second thought. Your life even, you don't know what those guys could have been capable of."

"Have they been bothering you for a while?"

"They say stuff at school. They hate that I'm also Hispanic and so, well, you know, me."

"They're monsters."

"No, they're not, Aki. They're just two guys jacked up on more machismo than they know what to do with."

"The school doesn't do anything?"

"Mrs. McKenna once told me to be less obvious. That was in ninth grade."

"I can't believe I don't remember you."

"Achilles," Jesús turns to peer down at me from the bed. "You were like…the ultimate jock back then, even as a sophomore you were the most popular, the most athletic, and you had Carla Gonzales on your arm acting like she was Grace Kelly."

"I don't know who that is."

"Meghan Markle."

"Ah. What was high school like for you with me being…a jock."

"*The* jock. And it was fine, I dunno. It's not like you bullied anyone."

"I'd never."

"I know you wouldn't. That's what it was like…like having a just and good king sitting on the throne and all of us were the peasants. But no one bothered me back then, not really. Not till you left."

"Why did that change things?"

"It was like a power vacuum opened up in the school. There was not one jock, but a whole bunch vying to take your place. Each with their gangs trying to gain popularity and reputation and…well, it's never really changed since then. There was no one to come and keep order."

I let his words float in the darkness, paying them attention as if they hover in illuminated light. Of course I *knew* I was popular back then. You know you're top of the food chain when you're not afraid of being eaten. It's an absence of something, privilege. An absence of fear; a race track without any hurdles to jump over.

"I'm sorry I left," I say, looking up at him looking down on me.

"Don't be stupid, it's not your fault."

"Still, I'm sorry."

The room falls quiet again. I still can't get over the silence. The peace. Not peace, because outside these walls I know the world is terrifying and exhausting and soul destroying. I know it's a place I don't want to live in without Marcus. But I know that Jesús makes me smile, so there's that. I feel like Prometheus sitting quietly in a cold, dark world, all alone, with only the man I made out of clay to be my friend.

"You know," Jesús says as softly as if he's talking me into stealing fire from Olympus, "you don't have to sleep on the floor. I…I can't imagine it's very comfortable."

I say nothing, wondering if I can pretend to be asleep already.

"I'm only one small person," Jesús continues, "I don't take up much space."

I close my eyes. How strange it is to hear those exact words said back to me, the magic phrase I'd said to Marcus. Compared to him, yes, I was a small person, and he agreed to welcome me into his bunk, into his bed. Even though it feels like a bad idea, I can't stop myself, or say no to this poor boy. He's the innocent victim of a fascist state and the thugs who live in it. The least I can be is his protector. I'd done more for boys in juvie than just sleep next to them.

I slip in beside Jesús, and he dutifully moves up. He smells like me, it's strange. Although it makes sense since he's wearing my old T-shirt and shorts. All the times Carla was in my bed, I was highly conscious a girl was beside me. Her cheeks left a residue of powder on my pillow. I could always smell her cherry lip gloss and her lavender deodorant. And she left behind a woman's scent, one that always made me remember I'd shared my bed with my opposite, not my same. Two opposing forces, was that why it was so hard for us to slot together? Is that not what should make it work?

Only hours ago, I thought I could overcome this burden. The failure to be her man, not even that, the failure to learn the lines for an audition I was supposed to have been waiting two years for. I remember her face, her disappointment, and the veil of accusation falling over me. How easy it is for her, or anyone else who stands outside the prison walls to exhort and teach the one who suffers.

"What was that?" I say, responding to the burp I know didn't come from me.

"Oh my God," Jesús says, covering his face. "I can't believe I just did that. Kill me, kill me now."

"You invite me into my own bed just to burp in my face?" I say, grinning so wide but he'll never know.

"Stop that, it's not funny. I'm so embarrassed."

"Oh grow up!" I say, and pull my stomach in tight to let out one great mighty burp.

"Achilles!" He smacks my bare arm, still hiding behind his fingers. I flip around and blow in his face. "Eww! Stop being disgusting." But then he burps again while trying so hard to hold it in. "Okay, I'll be going now."

"Get back here," I say, yanking him back onto the bed by the giant neck of my T-shirt. But he lands on his bruised cheek. "Oh, I'm sorry, sorry. Hope that didn't hurt."

"Not as much as my stomach. God, it feels weird."

"Yeah," I say, pulling down the covers and rubbing my own bare belly as it pings and dances. I can see Jesús is watching me intently, following every circular motion my hand makes over the black hair across my stomach. "Oh fuck, it was the goat from last week."

"What, goat goes bad after a week?"

"No," I say, flipping onto my side to lie almost nose to nose with Jesús. "The meat's fine, but it's the goat Mom sacrificed."

"Sacrificed?" Jesús doesn't seem amused.

"Yeah, to Zeus and…a few other gods. You feel like this because it's working."

"What's working? Achilles stop laughing at me, it's not funny!"

"When your belly feels full and funny after such a meal like that," I say, parroting years of my mom's words, "it means the gods are listening."

"Fine then," Jesús says with a huff like a cute baby dragon and flips around to face the wall. "I'm going to sleep and I'm not responsible for anything that happens in this bed. You can blame the gods."

Chapter 9
Achilles the Odysseus

From the place of tears I travel. In this dream I am at the end, I exist no more. By the grateful dread of things I am compelled. I know that. I see the trap closing. I know what I am. Oh, who of my friends is there to comfort me? Who understands? Leave me be, let me go, do not soothe me. Do not touch me, Achilles, said Marcus, and then departs the stage. The Greek tragedy of his life has come to a close.

The audience cheers, the muses congratulate themselves on a job well done. But I, the player, have been told no lines, nor paid no dues. This is a knot no one can untie. No number exists for a grief like this; trapped on a stage, unable to get off.

But nothing is fixed, I know that. And nothing abides. Everything gives way, sooner or later. For what we leave behind is not what is carved in stone, it is woven into the lives of others. Crowds of strangers may scream my name, they say I will be remembered for centuries, that no one will forget who I was. Who I am.

Yet all I can care for is how to make you smile, meet your next kiss, return your next touch, lest I die, and you forget. What good are these wings if I am too afraid to fly?

• • •

I wake on my side, my arm wrapped around nothing but empty space. Jesús is gone, but I know not far. I hear the tinkling of voices in the kitchen; him and my Mom. The pain across my shoulders from the previous night has gotten worse, but it's manageable. It's the sort of pain I feel proud to hold onto. Although Ares knows how I'm meant to wrestle all this Saturday.

"When the fuck did that happen?" I say out loud lifting the covers off me. My once black boxers glisten with the silvery crusted remains of a good dream. I cycle back through the memories, slipping away like an echo. Someone…something…not Marcus. Not Carla. But someone I dreamed of; their lips touching mine, my body moving against their soft, sweet smelling back.

I wriggle out of my boxers and quickly stuff them under my pillow just in case Jesús decides to wander back in. I pull on a new pair from the drawer, along with a pair of loose sweatpants and a T-shirt from the stack Zotos gave me. It's spattered in the garish blue and white of the Greek cross with *Zotos's Greek Wrestling: Harris County* emblazoned on the front in case we ever forgot. Mom and Jesús are sitting at the dining table, laughing at something unspoken and drinking coffee from a French press. I've never known Mom to do so before. It's striking to see Jesús sitting in my clothes, in my house in the morning light, stealing a secret inside joke. Striking in a way that chokes my throat with memories of a dream I never knew I had…or remembered had happened. But he glances at me differently. It's long and overwrought, like he knows a great truth, or a terrible secret.

"Aki," Mom says, pouring coffee for me. "Zotos is coming over to give you a ride to practice."

I take a seat and add sugar. Two, three, four, then stir and sip the steaming black ambrosia.

"They never gave us real sugar inside," I say to their perplexed faces.

"I think we've found our next diet, Saphie, and it's approved by the Texas Department of Criminal Justice."

Mom heaves with laughter, her night-dress bouncing as she wipes a salty tear from her eye.

"You're looking better," I say, inspecting the cuts on his face. Only one eye is black and swollen, along with his bottom lip.

"So are you."

I don't know what he means, but his lips part around the coffee mug to hide whatever meaning might hide behind those words. He's still wearing my old clothes. Carla never did. Even when Mom was out, she never sat in the kitchen in my old T-shirt, even when I offered, almost begged. The scene of a fantasy I wanted more than anything she offered to do to me in the bedroom. Why I'm comparing Jesús to Carla creeps up behind me. What kind of comparison is this? She's Carla. Carla. The most beautiful girl in school. Fine, we're not *together*-together, but it's an adjustment. Yet, try as I might to think of her, all I can see is Jesús in front of me, knees tucked under the T-shirt, stretching out the faded material, sharing syrupy baklava, peeling back layers of nuts and filo pastry while laughing with my Mom.

"Morning, all," Zotos says. I don't even hear the front door opening, or my cousins thundering in with him.

"Uncle Aki!" the twin nine-year-old boys yell at the top of their lungs, making Jesús jump out his skin. They both run at me, wrapping their arms around my neck as I roar, making them giggle as I try and lift them both up at once like I used to.

"Phil, Dean, get down from Uncle Achilles… what's wrong with you?" he says as the boys pull my shirt down and the mighty bruise across the length of my shoulders comes into view.

"Phil and Dean?" Mom cries out, almost as loud as the boys. She smacks Zotos' hand away from the coffee pot. "Phil and Dean?"

"They're in middle school, Saphie. What do you want?"

"Phobos, Deimos," she says, standing up and distracting them with the rest of the tray of baklava to get them off me. "Come outside now, who wants to build a pyre?"

"Me!" they both shriek, and rush outside with Mom following in her nightgown billowing from the wind outside.

"Good gods," Zotos says, sitting in Mom's seat and staring at Jesús. "What in Hades happened to you?"

Jesús shrugs and tries to disappear under my shirt. "Kids…" he mumbles.

"Jesús works at the Domino's," I tell Zotos. "And he's tutoring me for my GED."

"Ah of course. What happened, were you robbed?" He spits out the question like an old-time detective, one for whom injustice of this sort makes him angry. What a world when police used to fight injustice.

"I got attacked in the alley where the dumpsters are, but Achilles was there to help. If it wasn't for him I'd be in a much worse state."

"I'm glad you're okay. But that place is not safe at night, with all those damn kids hanging around. I have to keep a light on in my office so they think someone's still inside. Adds an extra three dollars to my electric bill." Zotos takes a bite of unfinished baklava from my plate and I can see him thinking as he chews. "How about this? I've got a whole bunch of unaccounted books from…business associates," Zotos glares at me, and Jesús does too, not following.

"I think he means business associates of Dad."

"You said it. Anyway," he takes another piece of the layered pastry and swirls it around the syrup displaced on the plate, "my employees won't touch it because they could lose their license, but you, son, don't have a license."

"A license for what?" Jesús asks, wrapping one foot under him on the chair. But Zotos is already grinning at the mastery of his own ingenious plan.

"All you need to do is sort through the handwritten ledgers and put them on a spreadsheet. I'll pay you thirty bucks an hour, you can quit that damn pizza place and work out of my office on the weekends and an evening or two during the week. Whenever you want. Then after Aki has finished practice you guys can study in the office. There's plenty of work to keep you occupied till you graduate. Aki's father has a lot of…business associates."

"Thank…thank you, sir," Jesús says, flabbergasted and continually glancing at me for reassurance.

"Great," Zotos says, holding out his hand for Jesús to cautiously shake. "But don't call me sir."

"But," Jesús says, swallowing hard and still holding onto Zotos' hand. "Why would you help me?"

"Do you know what solidarity means, son?"

Jesús shakes his head, but I have no doubt he knows exactly what the word means. Zotos strikes his hand out and shakes mine to demonstrate. "It means one person helping another. One hand reaching out to shake the hand of someone else, blind to creed or religion or place of birth. When my family first came to this country, we didn't survive on our own. We survived because we got help from others unlike us. The Indigenous people who know the land; Jews, Blacks, Spanish, Chinese." Zotos now clasps both his hands together. "One hand helping another. We've built our lives here for three generations on the backs of those who came before." He stands up as proud as an orator, the chair scraping back on the linoleum floor as he holds out his hand again for Jesús to shake. Slowly, Jesús unfurls himself from my T-shirt and the chair, and stands up barefoot. Zotos' hairy hand—as thick as a shovel—clasps around Jesús'. "And now I help you, just as you'll help someone else one day. That's how we build solidarity. Between immigrants, between struggles, between human beings. One hand helping another."

Zotos has talked himself into tears of pride, but Jesús only looks afraid, probably wondering when this weird man will let his hand go. Eventually he does, and uses it to root around in his pocket for a key.

"Here, Aki," he throws the keys at me to catch. "Take the dirt bike. The books are up in my cabin in the woods near Coldspring. You remember where it is, right?"

How can I forget? The amount of times Dad had driven me up there to the Sam Houston National Forest, along the narrow lanes and scattered roads to dispose of something unseemly in the back of his truck, or pick up something worse that Zotos had left for him in the cabin. The route was burned in my memory, part of my very soul. Like a lamplight-lit pathway to the Underworld.

I sigh. Transporting the accounts of criminals and roping Jesús into what surely must amount to a felony doesn't seem like the best way to stay out of juvie. Or jail.

"Good man," Zotos says. "Take the weekend off from the gym. I'll mark you down as attended."

"Really?" I spring up, suddenly full of life.

"Yeah, why not. Precious Hector needs some time to recover, and it looks like you got some good practice last night, given the blood I saw spattered across the back alley when I drove past the dumpsters this morning." His words leave us both cold. I had no idea of the damage I'd caused. "Well, boys, I better go save your mom from the twin terrors. Jesús, come by the office the next time Aki is at the gym. I'll set you up on payroll and with a laptop. And I'll pay you for today of course. It will take all day to get there and back. Aki, the ledgers are on the shelf in the office, just remember don't—"

"Touch anything, yes, I know."

"Good, well get yourselves ready and I'll drop you both at the bike." Zotos heads out to the back garden where I see Mom has the boys chopping wood with one ax each while she sits on the deck smoking and giving them instructions in Greek. Jesús stares at me like he's just played chess with Zeus and won.

"Come," I say to the still shell-shocked Jesús. "I've got some clothes you can borrow for your first day at your new job."

"I think we're lost," Jesús complains again as the bike rumbles slowly through thick forest. I ignore him, pretending the bike helmet prevents me from hearing. But he knows it doesn't, because we talked here and there before with the helmets on during the hour-long drive west to the park. I thought it was because of the constriction of the helmet or the awkwardness of having to hang onto my waist for dear life as we soared up the highway, but now I know there's words on his lips he isn't saying.

"We just need to get out of the forest, then I'll find it." His grip is still tight around my waist, even tighter now as the bike chews through branch covered pathways and sodden leaves.

"Achilles, this whole place is forest. You really came through here in a truck with your Dad?"

Again, I didn't answer, because again he's right. I am lost. Or if not lost, unsure of how to reach Zotos' cabin from our current location. The trees are only getting tighter, blotting out the mid-morning sky more often than not. And the bike revs harder and crunchier with every obstacle we knock by. Getting stuck out here would not end well.

Soon the vague pathway I'd been following disappears completely, and we're left with only the hard shrubbery of the forest floor.

"That's it, Aki. Stop the bike."

"I think it's just a bit further. Look, if we get up that hill, I'm pretty sure that'll lead us out. The cabin was definitely up a hill."

"Now. Stop the bike now." He smacks me hard in the side, and I'm left with no choice but to bring us to a firm halt so as not to fall over. Jesús jumps off the back like he's been shocked and pulls off his helmet while I lift up my visor.

"Fuck me," I say, looking up at the shards of mauve sky still visible through the trees. "When did it get so dark and stormy."

"Turn us around," Jesús demands. I look behind us, and to each side.

"Around to where, exactly?"

He stumbles over a root while shaking the pins and needles out of his leg in this fading light. I look up and try to see any semblance of sun, but it's like it's set forever.

"Are you sure you know where it is?"

"I'm telling you, Jesús. If we get the bike up that hill to the clearing beyond, it'll be a piece of cake. Zotos' cabin is right up there."

"How can you see anything in this dark? What the hell time is it?" He fumbles in his pocket for his phone. "Fucking hell, what's this?"

Branches snap under Jesús' feet as he pounds the soft ground towards me, phone first. The screen is a garbled mess. Numbers and letters and dots and dashes, swirling around the screen like nothing I've ever seen before. And seemingly neither has he.

"Did it get damaged along the way?" I ask, examining the phone. It looks faultless under the case and screen protector.

"I don't know how, it's been sitting in my front pocket the whole time."

"I'll try to restart." I hold down the off button as Jesús swivels beside me to rest against the bike. The swirling characters disappear from the screen. I try to turn it back on. It flashes as normal, but then something weird happens. Something that makes my stomach churn, and not just because I'm still recovering from the goat. I hold the phone in my hands and watch, Jesús too, as screeds of minuscule letters rush across the screen from the top corner. The top right, not the top left.

"What the fuck is that?" Jesús says, grabbing the phone from my hands. "Are those ones and zeros? What kind of Matrix spyware shit has gotten into this thing?"

Shoulder to shoulder with Jesús, I stare at the backlit screen, the tiny white text rushing from side to side like a code gone wrong.

"It's not binary," I say, swallowing hard and suddenly feeling the promised chill from the darkened sky. "It's Greek." Jesús stares at me like I owe him a new phone. "Ancient Greek…" I try to sound out the words in my head, but they don't make much sense. And then aloud. "Doric Greek. It's even older than Homer."

"Achilles," Jesús says with all the calmness of a coiled snake. "Why is my phone spewing—"

"Orpheus."

"I beg your pardon?"

"It's the lost story of Orpheus." I grab the phone back and follow the lines appearing on the screen. "Orpheus," I say quickly, reading this story I've never read directly, only heard recanted by other poets and storytellers writing centuries later. "Orpheus was the greatest poet and musician who ever lived, and traveled to the Underworld, to Hades, to reclaim his wife. This is incredible. How do I take a screenshot?"

"Screenshot?" Jesús yells. "One night with you and my phone's a fucking ancient DuoLingo. Fix it."

But I keep scanning the screen, the text never ceasing, the story of Orpheus comes alive with more details than anyone's ever seen. Suddenly a crack of thunder wakes me up from the discovery, and I see our situation as Jesús sees it. Lost in the woods, daylight overtaken by darkness with a phone possessed and…rain starting to fall hard on the treetops above.

"Okay, put this away, we'll deal with it at home. I'm sure it's fixable," I say, not sure at all. Jesús reluctantly stashes his phone in the backpack we brought to transport the ledgers, and I hop back on the bike, helmet on and visor down. He does the same. I rev the bike hard and ride straight up the small but sharp incline in front of us covered with the knobbled roots of wild trees. The bike hops over the crest and out of the tree line, and I notice we fly over a bubbling brook. It seems to flow free of physics, like it's floating around the edge of the wide grassy field we're now in.

If Jesús held on tightly before, now he does it like he might fall off the edge of the earth. And, secretly, I don't blame him. The way my stomach is bubbling like a cauldron I'd say every god on Olympus is screaming my name. Thunder cracks, but there's no lightning. It cracks again. And again. Atomic bomb-sized booms shake the heavy sky, vibrating through the earth. Jesús digs his hands into my chest as the bike roars out of the tree-covered forest toward the promised hill in the clearing.

"See!" I yell back, pointing straight in front of me through thrashing rain covering the black sky. "There's the cabin." I shout it loud, hoping to convince myself that this is the right one even though I know I've never seen this building in my life before.

We're in a wide clearing; grassy plains, an unending field, rolling downward toward the edge of the tree line that circles wide and round the back of the hill we're driving toward. Where the cabin stands watching. Jesús isn't looking. His helmet is pressed hard against my back, his knees squeezing into my thighs as if he wants to knock his heels together and be whisked away home.

But I keep biking through the storm, the wheels bouncing over wild grass and soft ground, upward through the slicing rain. The thunder is ceaseless. I'm sure Jesús has his eyes closed, but mine are wide open, darting across the horizon for a flash of lighting. I've watched countless thunderstorms in my life, and never once seen one without lightning. It's the lighting itself that causes thunder. The rapid expansion of air surrounding the path of a lightning bolt creates the booms which echo in our helmets and thump in our chests. But still surrounding us is only darkness and noise. No bolts of lightning from Zeus come to light the way. It's as if Zeus and light don't exist on this plane of existence.

Night speeds by as I hit the bike hard, trying to get closer to the cabin which seems to keep getting further away. I drive harder, faster, pushing the bike to its very limit through the soaking grass, the howling rain and unending thunder. But it's no use. The faster I go, the more the rain smacks off my helmet and the deeper Jesús' hands dig into my rib cage. The hill, and the promise of shelter, only get further away.

Despite the fading light I see two paths cut through the grass. One veers left, away from the hill and then gets lost in the seemingly endless field; the other goes right, and promises to take us straight up to the cabin on the hill.

"Hold on!" I yell, banking a hard right as the bike bounces onto the path. All of a sudden distance regains its perspective, and the hill gets closer relative to our speed. Soon the bike is going up, and I can slow us down. Even the rain spatters to a flutter and the thunder now seems distant, like an echo. I bring the bike to a standstill under the awning of the cabin. Light appears to emanate from inside, and I realize it's the only light currently in existence. The sky is so black like we're under the earth, and along the edges of the tree line from where we came fades into a black nothingness like a shadow painted on the wall.

I help Jesús off the bike. If he notices any of these idioms straight out the epics, he doesn't seem to care. He takes off his helmet, wiping back damp hair from his forehead and happy that we've arrived at a destination, no matter what or where. Jesús stretches out from our harsh ride. Where I would normally feel my heart pound out of my chest at the turn of day to night and thunder without lightning, I feel nothing at all. No thump, no beat, no heart. I turn away from Jesús and put two fingers to my neck. No sign of life. But I can hear a babbling stream. I look behind the corner of the cabin and see water pouring down the hill into the darkness. It's source, an open pipe sticking out of the cabin wall. There's an inscription just above the open pipe. I bend down to read the perfectly formed Greek letters while holding my nose from the stench of sewage; the words are clear to any speaker of the language, either ancient or modern, mythical or mortal. *The Acheron*, the words say above the open pipe. The first river the dead must cross on their journey into Hades, to be ferried across the river by Charon the ancient and decrepit boatman. But this stream of what smells like sewage hardly seems to be a river one needs to be ferried across.

"Why does that sign say The Styx?" Jesús asks, looking at a rusty metal plate swinging above the door and grating an awful sound one octave above the depths of thunder. "Isn't that like…the entrance to Hades or something?"

"Oh that," I jump up and hop back over to him and try to laugh, casually snatching his bike helmet holding them up like shields. "It's one of the rivers, yeah. Just a silly joke of Zotos," I lie, as I take a deep breath of hot, stale air and lead us toward the cabin door and its otherworldly light. How hasn't he noticed he has no heartbeat, or is it just me? Despite the rain falling across the darkened fields and the unending pounding of thunder, I'm sweating. I'm hot and afraid, just as every nightmare and every daydream and everything I thought was fiction comes suddenly, nauseatingly to life. I can only hope our bike crashed and Jesús and I are lying on a hospital gurney somewhere, attached to a breathing machine and kept in a medically induced coma. If that's the case, then why Jesús looks so anxious to get in and I'm far from it wouldn't really make sense in my subconscious. He's watching me, my back to the door while I hold both helmets, glaring at Jesús blankly as my mind flicks through thousands of pages of mythology to try and remember a path out of the Underworld.

"Well…we're here," I say, trying in vain to understand why *here* is the entrance to Hades.

Chapter 10
Disco the Styx

I don't know what I expect the entrance to the Underworld to look like. I've only ever pictured it when Mom read me stories of Odysseus descending into Hades' domain on his way back to Ithaca from Troy. In Odysseus' *katabasis*, or descent to the Underworld, he meets all manner of heroes after being ferried across by Charon, the grisly boatman who takes the souls of the dead across the river Styx.

In my mind, the entrance to the Underworld is something like Galveston Bay at night. The lights of the oil rigs flaring in the distance, the stench of sulfur and oil on the tail end of every breath and sniff, and just the suggestion of land somewhere beyond the dark horizon of impassive water.

The journey would be perilous, hence the need for a boatman to take across the souls. And much like the Gulf of Mexico, the waters were not at all something you wanted to get on your skin, dead or alive.

But I never expected the entrance to the Underworld to look like this: an empty bar. I'd never been inside a bar or Hades before, so I can't say for certain, but it seemed to have all the architectural prowess of a rural shack dressed up as a saloon. Jesús stares at me, open-mouthed. I can see from his face that he too is just starting to realize he has no pulse, otherwise it would be rapidly quickening.

To our right is a long, faded couch bolted into the windowless wall, with dirty tables placed along the way, and a few wooden tables and chairs strewn around it. At the far end of the bar is a Rubik's-cube dance floor, complete with flashing lights and a disco ball, but no music. In fact, we seemed to have entered a place of all flash but utter silence, like the TVs for sale in a department store. Along the far wall, between the empty tables and the empty dance floor, is a black curtain hiding an even blacker entrance. *Tartarus* is written on top in Greek, in the same hand as the sign for *The Acheron* river outside. Tartarus is the deepest abyss in the Underworld, used as a dungeon of torment and suffering for titans and giants and all the evil in the world.

Yet the silent dance floor, empty tables and entrance to the worst place ever conceived of behind a velvet curtain are not what I'm most struck by, or Jesús, for that matter. If I'd been asked to conjure up an image of a gay bar, this would be it. All along the walls, in every space available hanging on the fake wood paneling, are framed posters of the heroes. Depicted naked and in far more suggestive poses than any skin mag would dare show; the toned, tanned, and impossibly muscled bodies of Ajax, Jason, Odysseus, Achilles and his son Pyrrhus, Icarus, Ganymede, even the Trojans Hector and Paris, each with his own image and name written in Greek beneath. They watch us proudly, flexing biceps, turning their backs, raising their legs and winking at the empty bar for no one but us to gaze upon them.

And as if all the naked men on the walls isn't enough, rainbow flags, and Greek flags, and the Greek flag but its stripes displaying the colors of the pride flag, hang down from the ceiling like they've all been washed for the night before a parade.

"Aki…" Jesús says after taking it all in once and once again, "why is your uncle's cabin so—"

"Gay?" says a grave but excited voice. We both jump. We, or at least I, had been so taken in by the silent dance floor and posters on the wall I haven't even registered the bar itself in the back left of the shack. Half a dozen bar stools stand expectantly along a wood and brass-finished counter, behind which is the bar itself not just fully stocked but actually overflowing with multi-colored bottles of every conceivable alcohol humankind has ever distilled.

And on the second stool from the wall sits a single solitary figure, bulky and broad-shouldered enough to be a hero on the wall, but wearing a floor length gown that sparkles as they move. The figure turns on their stool slowly, as their face comes into full view. I've never seen a man in drag before, but like this bar, if I—in my stereotypical mind—had been asked to conjure up an image of a man in drag, this would be it.

Their jaw is square and with too much skin, their advanced age is apparent, even caked in make-up. The only thing out of place is their sodden red synthetic wig, which seems cheap compared to the obvious expense of the ball gown. The figure wears pearls, and I notice thick bejeweled rings twisting around every finger. Long false eyelashes flutter at the two of us, still standing by the entrance, flabbergasted beyond belief. I don't even realize I'm still grasping our two bike helmets as I step forward, instinctively shielding Jesús behind me.

"Excuse me, ma'am, Is this…Hades?"

"Honey," they say, holding up a martini glass of pure black liquid and taking a long sip before smacking their blood-red lips together. "You're in a gay bar in Bumblefuck, Texas. You really think this is the afterlife?" Legs crossed on the bar stool, they peer behind me to Jesús who, far from sprinting a mile, seems more intrigued than afraid. "Who's this little cream puff?" they ask with an unplaceable accent; like Greek lacquered with Cajun. The drawl of a southern dame with the inflection of a Puerto Rican grandmother and an unsettling, deep-throated, tobacco-scarred tone.

I push Jesús back with the bike helmet and take another step closer. Like in those precious few seconds of a wrestling match, I count out all the possible moves; from running to attacking, and sketch out the three most likely options in my mind. One; the bike crashed and we've been badly injured and this is some sort of coma or fever dream. Two; this is still reality and we have stumbled upon some gay bar inside a shack in the middle of the Sam Houston National Forest…although that wouldn't account for my lack of pulse or lightning-less thunder. Or three; this is in actual fact the entrance to Hades, which would mean option one is a lot more serious than just an injury. And we are actually dead. Man, if I still had a heartbeat, it would be pounding like mad right about now. But whatever the reality is, the best course of action I can see is to get more information.

"Are you Charon?" I ask, hoping that this really is just

a random gay bar in the middle of the forest and this drag queen will have no idea why I'm referring to the boatman who ferries souls to the Underworld.

"Ha," they laugh and snap their fingers. "Only on weekdays, darlin'. Because it's Saturday night and I'm in the mood to party."

Jesús gulps with laughter, and I push him back again.

"You're not helping," I whisper to him. "If you're Charon," I say loudly, maybe hoping to wake some sort of general manager. "Then why aren't you old and ugly…with a beard…and a dirty cloak." I try desperately to re-imagine any more details of Charon from the stories. "Or a hook nose."

"Aki…stop," Jesús pleads, pulling on my arm as their face turns hurt and insulted, then angry. I step back. Jesús does too.

"I should wash your mouth out with soap, young man." They flick back the permanent curls bouncing down from the too-shiny wig. "Just because that damn Odysseus caught me once on a bad hair day three thousand years ago means I gotta be as ugly as a Gorgon for all time?" They sniff away a tear, a real one, but the thick layers of mascara and eyeshadow swallow it up like it never existed. Charon, I'm still working on the basis that this is in fact Charon, turns away and snaps open a compact mirror. Suddenly Jesús rushes forward, and with both hands holding bike helmets I can't stop him.

"I think you're beautiful," he says, brazenly mounting the next stool as they fail to fix the loose curl in the wig. "And this dress is just stunning."

"Oh my," they say, smiling and fumbling around the bar for a fan. They flip it open to reveal a hundred peacock feathers, beautifully woven together and with eyes in each that I swear dart around the room independently of each other…while some stare at me. "Athena herself wove it for me."

I drop the bike helmets on the long couch and edge forward, ready to snap Jesús away at the silent sound of danger. But he reaches straight out and touches the sparkling gown which I can now see is not just silver but gold as well.

"But of course Hera had to peer down her nose and say I still looked like a bloke in a dress, so I stole her fan." Charon continues flapping themself and gently dabs at her wrinkled neck with a cocktail napkin. "Those Olympians, they get in one smart crack and everyone laughs because they're the gods and are always so damned pleased with themselves. So they found the obvious flaw and pointed it out. *Brava*. They've got one good read in them, and that's about it. Because, honey," Charon says, leaning closer to Jesús but also keeping an eye on me, just as the peacock feathers are too. "Down here in the Underworld, it's all about shade. Say it with me, sha-ayde. Shade."

"Shade," Jesús says, happier than perhaps I've ever seen him. And utterly untaken by the fact he's sitting on a bar stool with one of the most terrifying figures in all mythology patting down their dress and flinging out compliments. Charon now glares at me with a deep smile, and I feel more exposed than ever standing in the middle of the bar where anything could come up behind and grab me. I edge closer to the bar and take up a stool beside Jesús.

"Shade," Charon says, seemingly for my benefit because Jesús looks like he knows exactly what they are talking about, although looks perfectly happy to hear it explained again. "Shade is I don't tell you you're dead, but I don't have to tell you because you know you're dead, otherwise how else would you be in the Underworld?"

"Are we dead?" I say, again failing to feel the emotion of my own words without a heartbeat. Charon responds with a smokey laugh.

"See?" They nudge Jesús who laughs at my expense as well. "That's shade. And no honey, you're not dead. Hades just wants to see you."

"Oh…kay…"

"Let's have a drink," Charon says, snapping up the fan and smacking their palms on the bar. "We gotta have some soothing libations so we don't go upsetting the Furies. And by Zeus are they furious." The double palm-smacking has done whatever trick Charon needed it to do, because they lean over the bar and pull up two martini glasses filled to the brim with the same black liquid they're drinking. "It's called a Nyx, a Nyx in the Styx, how's that for a pun." They pass one up to me, and then to Jesús who looks just like Carla when Mom offered her an octopus tentacle. "Or would you prefer a pomegranate martini?" Charon asks Jesús.

"No," I answer for him, "No pomegranates."

"Ah ha," Charon says with a grin, raising their glass in congratulation. "Someone knows his stories."

"What story?" Jesús asks us both like a wide-eyed kid in the middle of a family dinner.

"Hades' lovely lady wife Persephone, the dumb bitch she is, ate six pomegranate seeds on her first trip down here. Now if you eat the food in the Underworld, you stay in the Underworld. Although she gets let out for six months of the year because they said she only ate six seeds. Eugh, what a cop out. Now she spends the summer months up top getting her face lifted and lipo sucked out her ass and injected into her lips. I said to Zeus they should keep that cow locked up down here like the rest of us. But who listens to little old me. Although I wouldn't bring it up when you see her. She's still a little sore about it," Charon mouths the last words silently, as if Persephone might jump out at us at any second. "Anyway, you're safe drinking these, you gotta cross the dancefloor to get to the Underworld."

I look out at the rainbow spotlights spinning over the flashing dance floor and lighting up the naked portraits. It's almost impossible to see, but there is a double-door fire escape on the other side. It's not far, but I get the feeling it's agonizingly difficult to cross.

Jesús, braver than I, takes a sip.

"Mmm," he says, faking it as his face turns sour. "Licorice flavor."

"I know, isn't it hideous?" Charon says with a delighted grin and takes a deep gulp from their own glass. I can't say mine tastes any better, but both of us drink long and hard given how much our host seems to like it.

"Um, Charon," I say, unsure how else to broach the subject. "Why exactly does Hades want to see me?"

"Up-bup-bup-bup, I told you, it's Charon only Monday through Friday. On the weekends it's ah-Disco…Styx." They say it with a two-handed flourish, snapping their fingers all around. Jesús takes another sip, he seems to have finished off half the glass and whatever alcohol is inside has given him the courage to say:

"Isn't that from a Lady Gaga song?"

"Why yes, banana muffin, thank you for noticing. I've also been known to moonlight as a muse from time to time. *The Fame* was my greatest achievement since Paula Abdul's *Spellbound*."

"You lie," Jesús says, almost slumped over the bar. The drinks are strong. Very strong. And my forehead almost misses my palm as I have to look away from the terrifying sight of Jesús arguing with the gatekeeper of the Underworld.

"I do no such thing. You think a mere mortal can write *Bad Romance* and *Shallow* all by herself? She had every muse in the damned pantheon working on those albums. I myself am responsible for the *ra la pa-pa-ra* part."

"Really?" Jesús asks, still seemingly unconvinced. "All of her albums were written by muses?"

"Inspired by, sweetheart, there's a difference. We don't get writing credits, or royalties. Although I do go to The Grammys every year. And also, no, not *all* her albums. You know *Joanne*?"

"Uh huh."

"She did that one herself."

I cough obviously, trying to steer the conversation away from drunk bar talk.

"So Disco Styx, Hades wants to see me, right? But I… we didn't die?"

"No, you didn't *die*. Hades just wants to have a little chat. And don't ask me about what, I have no idea. You think he comes down here talking to me? Not often. Not while Persephone's around, anyway. But what's your rush? Stay a while. Keep an old crone company. Here," Charon slaps their palms on the bar again, then leans over and lifts up two large golden eggs on stands and places one in front of each of us. I look at Jesús who looks at me. But I have no piece of wisdom to add.

"Go on," Charon says, "open the top." We do so, the egg easily cuts in half, and sweet-smelling steam pours out of gently bubbling, gold-colored liquid. "It's an ambrosia daiquiri, probably more to your taste."

I lift the half golden egg with both hands, as does Jesús, and we take a sip. It's an impossible flavor. Like the richest honey mixed with the sweetest mango but cut through with a sharp taste of berries. There's no question that this is the perfect drink. And even if this is a fever dream, I have no doubt that in it we're being served the ambrosia of the gods.

"I like that one," Jesús says, smacking his lips while Charon drains their black Nyx and slaps for another one. "What's over there by the curtain?"

"Oh, that's the darkroom," Charon says, immediately swapping the empty glass for the full.

"But it says Tartarus," I say, looking at the sign above the curtain again.

"That's right, it's the abyss where the Titans and other beastly sorts are kept."

"So, why do you call it a darkroom? Isn't that like…for developing photographs?"

Jesús snorts into his ambrosia, and I realize they are both in on a joke I am out of. What could possibly exist above or below the earth that Charon and Jesús know but I don't?

"This one knows what I'm talking about," Charon says, nudging him. "You cheeky little chimp."

I glance at Jesús smirking and remember how Carla called him the chimp. I guess he kinda does look like a chimp when he laughs. His cheeks fold inwards into the deepest dimples I've ever seen, and he giggles like a cute little six-year-old who's just learned a dirty joke.

"*If* you're going to have a gander," Charon continues, "you'll need this." He reaches over the bar again but instead of pulling out a drink, puts a small medicine bottle and places it in front of Jesús. It's got a red and gold label wrapped around it, and says *Golden Fleece*. "I assume you've never bottomed for a giant before?"

"Close enough," Jesús says, inspecting the bottle.

"What is that?" I demand to know. "What are you giving him?"

"Relax, it's freshly bottled from the Lethe River."

The name is familiar. Another river in Hades. This one is associated with forgetfulness and oblivion.

"I don't think you should drink that," I whisper to Jesús.

"'Course you don't drink it," he replies, still keeping me out of the inside joke. "It's for sniffing."

"The Lethe is all amyl nitrite," Charon says, snapping the cap off his own bottle and inhaling the vapors one nostril at a time. Even I can smell the pungent stench from six feet away. Added to the alcohol I have to turn away to keep from collapsing.

"God, that's strong," Jesús adds, but still puts the bottle Charon gave him in his pocket.

"One can always have a quick sniff of the river before venturing into Tartarus, and you'll forget your inhibitions on the shore," they say before cackling into their drink.

"Uhm," I clear my throat again and with one eye on the exit beyond the dance floor, "are you sure you can't tell me anything about why Hades wants to see me?"

"Says he has some kinda deal for you, I don't know."

"And…we'll both go back to being alive, you know, after? Jesús and I?"

"Your name is Jesús?" Charon gasps. Jesús nods with a drunken smile.

"Oh mercy, don't let Hades know. He *hates* anything connected to Jesus. Why do you think the Underworld is so empty? I think I'll call you…Mary. No, wait, Patroclus. Ahh, Achilles and Patroclus. Lovely name for a couple, don't you think?"

"We're uh, not a couple," I say. "I'm not gay."

"Sure, honey," Charon adds, smirking into his drink. I imagine without a heartbeat my face can't go red either. But at least we're one step closer to getting out of this nightmare.

"So, after Hades has offered this deal, how are we meant to get back out?"

"Oh just travel through the Underworld. There's an exit that'll leave you somewhere around Mongolia or LA, one of those barren wastelands. Although…if you do me a favor, I could let you back out this way." Charon nods to the door we came in which I realize has been subsumed into the wall. "It's not really allowed, but you see, Cerberus has been using my good wig as a chew toy."

"The…three-headed dog?" I ask.

"Aww, I like dogs," Jesús says, surely not listening properly as he tips the last drops of the ambrosia daiquiri into his mouth.

"If you can call that monster a dog. But yes. He's stolen my good wig and I'd very much like it back. If you'd be so kind as to get it for me." Charon swirls the Nyx, as dark as night and twisting like a collar around the neck of the glass.

"Fine," I say, getting off the stool. Only the real Achilles managed to subdue the terrifying creature once before, but I reckon I'll cross that bridge when I come to it. This shack doesn't look too difficult to barge through anyway. "Jesús," I say sharply as Charon glares at me. "I mean…Patroclus, are you ready to go?"

"Not so fast, darlings. It costs two coins to get across that dance floor."

"I…don't have any coins. Neither of us do." Jesús shakes his head in agreement.

"I know," Charon says with a sickly smile. "Lucky for you I accept payment in many other forms."

"What forms, exactly?"

"Your shirts. Both of your shirts."

That feels worse than the coins.

"I'm not taking my shirt off."

"Oh, so you'll wrestle the entire gym practically naked but won't take your shirt off for a little dance?"

"What dance? And how do you know about what happened at the gym?"

"Oh, honey, all of Olympus watched that one. And that shower scene after? My my." Charon whips out his fan again and I feel Jesús' eyes on me.

"Nothing. Happened."

"I know, but imagine if it did, oh my word."

"Okay," I say, practically lifting Jesús off his stool before he can ask me about the shower scene. "Can we go now?"

"Why sure thing, honey pie. Now, listen here, real good. Soon as I hit the music, we're gonna have all the worst parts of humanity descend on that dance floor. This is a gay bar after all. You're gonna have grief, and anxiety, and disease, and old age, and fear, and hunger, and agony, and death all dancing their cute little butts off."

"Is that all?"

"Not quite. Clinging under their tongues are the leaves of false dreams. Prepare yourself for all the worst parts of your deepest nightmares thrown at you on the dance floor. Don't get distracted, otherwise you'll be trapped there for the rest of eternity. And, boys, you don't even wanna know how many souls have got lost chasing a wild dream on a dance floor. Now, shirts off, boys."

Jesús lifts his T-shirt off first. His thin frame is still battered and bruised from the night before, and I can't help feel horrendous at the trouble I've caused him. His body looks so real; dusty skin clouded with the deep purples of a

Houston storm. If this is real, I've led us into an impossible reality. Making deals with Hades, fighting Cerberus or wandering through the entire Underworld as if we were heroes in an epic when we're just two kids from the suburbs. With a reluctant sigh, I take off my shirt too and instinctively try to suck in my stomach. But without breath in my lungs, it's impossible. In the meantime, Charon has helped themselves to another drink.

"All right, boys, it's party time." Charon snaps their fingers, and the world of the cabin explodes with a thunderous disco beat.

We stand at the edge of the dance floor, Jesús and I. The sight is unbelievable to say the least. But so is everything else. One step onto the flashing lights of the glass floor, and we'll be inside a twelve foot by twelve-foot cage stuffed with our greatest horrors disguised as our basest desires.

Endless ripped bodies heave with the pounding disco beat; an unknown singer belts out an unfamiliar song in an endless, pounding loop. It sucks me in even as I try to look away, to focus only on the exit beyond shrouded in smoke and sweat mist.

"You can do it, Aki," Jesús says. But it's fine for him. His slight frame can likely squeeze between the muscle gods or zip under their legs—bare legs, of course, because why would anyone be clothed—practically unnoticed. "See you on the other side." He steps in, through the invisible veil which divides mere purgatory from the afterlife.

"Jesús?" I can't see him. "Jesús?" I rush along the edges

of the dance floor, looking high and low, under strobe lights and between grinding bodies like rocks tumbling down an avalanche. I glance back at Charon who sits at the bar, legs crossed, casually folding up the two T-shirts we left behind. I have no choice. I must go in.

I'm struck by the immediacy of the situation. Like stepping off the plane in Greece in the height of summer. The heat, the smells, the taste, the sights, it all hits at once as if I'm pushing through a brick wall into another reality. The music is even louder inside, if that's possible, and I have less than no space to maneuver. My body is no longer my own, but the property of every other being on this dance floor. Hands, chests, abs and hips knock against me to the hellish beat and I'm pushed forward, no, not forward, inward, against my own will. I try to turn to see what's behind me, but the veil of purgatory has gone. There's nothing in existence beyond where I am right now, just endless bodies and endless dancing. And I still can't find Jesús.

I spin around as I'm not just grazed against, but touched and prodded. But I can't see from where. The hands of these nymphs, giants, titans, whatever they are, all seem to be lifting their arms toward the clashing, dazzling ceiling. But low down, unseen hands take liberties. One grabs a handful of fat from my hip. I flip to knock him away, but then one tweaks my nipple, and I spin to see nothing. I can't fight it. It will drive me insane. There's an exit, and I have to focus. But I've spun around so many times I don't have a clue which way is out. There's only deeper.

So deeper I go. The stench of men is not what I know

from juvie or the gym. It's not sweat, or not only. But the smell of…a rush. A thrilling undercurrent I know is wrong, is only a myth, a legend. Yet here I am. The grabbing and pinching relaxes; beings touch me, but their touch is soothing. Their touch is one I've been starved of for longer than I know. The touch of desire.

Just for a moment, just to get my bearings, I close my eyes and let the beat of the music carry me up off the floor. It infects my bloodstream like a drug. I just want to dance. To let go of everything, and spend five minutes, ten minutes, an hour, just dancing. What would be so wrong, after a lifetime of pain, a lifetime of suffering for crimes that were not mine. What would be so wrong just to dance?

I open my eyes, and I'm in the heat of the battle. The center of the floor, because it cannot get any deeper. A hundred or a million bodies all push into mine, twirling in beautiful chaos. But they are not just dancing. Not here, in the depths of this place where no one on the outside could possibly see so deep in.

Like a piece of Greek pottery one sees in a museum, then stops to give a second glance, these creatures are also…fucking. Sweat drips down their backs as one moves into another, and out, and to the next, and around. I can't look. I can't see this, not now. I'll never get out of here.

Suddenly someone takes my hand. For a flash of a second I wonder if it's Jesús, but then I can't really remember who Jesús even is anymore. It's a man, a demi-god, like one of the posters from the wall come to life. His body is a marble sculpture, but it moves like liquid gold. Sweat glistens from his chiseled jaw and neck as thick as a column. But his skin is not smooth like a Ganymede, but hairy and rough—like a Poseidon. His chest expands out with every snake-like move of his arms to the thundering beat, but I don't even dare to look any further down. Not when his eyes are boring into mine. Two brown whirlpools calling me in. I glance down, only to his mouth, which is open and cut with a half-smile. He draws me closer like a flock to a pole.

Now in the space he has created for us, there is only us. No other hands reach out to molest me. It's just the two of us. His body vibrating, pulsing, and mine, now only inches away, wanting nothing more than to feel his skin against mine. What harm could be caused by one touch, one kiss. He wants me too. His mouth flares open like a caged tiger. He licks his lips. Every part of my body, every ounce of my soul, wants, needs him. His touch, his taste. I've suffered enough. Let me have this.

I keep my eyes open, not wanting to miss a single moment. The heat from his skin radiates into mine. Our legs touch. Our hips, stomachs, chests. Thick arms wrap around me, pulling me, sliding down the small of my back. He smiles with all of his face as he sways with me to the beat of the music. I want to live forever in this moment; to be seen and desired and wanted and held. His mouth opens, sucks me toward the kiss. I've never wanted anything more, never needed anything. Close, close, closer. His tongue stretches out to meet mine in mid-air. There's a dot on it. A white dot fizzing on his blood-red tongue. A pill. Something he wants to give to me. I'll take it. I'll take whatever he wants to give me.

Chapter 11
The House of Hades

"Aki!" The scream is louder than the music, louder than thunder or an airplane taking off directly over my head. And it's accompanied by a yank. A hard, double-handed grab of my arm from just underneath the elbow, which jars my joints. But it works, it pulls me out. I stumble sideways, my lips just grazing the hot tongue of the man who wanted to kiss me as I fall out of the dance floor, into the subdued stillness of the other side.

Jesús pulls me out. He's standing, face aflame with anger, the double doors of the exit open and leading out of the bar into a hill of darkness. The memories flood back, the temptations dissipate, the inhibitions jut back into place. I turn back to see the crowded dance floor, and the creature who was about to kiss me. His face is not like it was inside. Like a poorly rendered video game, in the time it takes for his face to twist away from me, I see the creature for what it truly is.

A forked tongue as long as a serpent flaps between two sets of jagged needle teeth. And his face is not of a square-jawed god. He has the pointed features, scratchy hair, and beady black eyes of a demon. I scramble away, toward the cold breeze of the fire escape; I'm desperate to get away and suddenly so ashamed of what I nearly cost us.

"Come on," Jesús says, splashing a questioning eye over me. "Let's get going.

Outside the shack, the darkness returns. In fact, it's as if the shack never existed in the first place. The palette changes so suddenly from bright sparkling fabulousness to dark, foreboding black and pewter. We trudge up a steep sodden hill through a light mist which hangs heavier by the climb. And it's still hot; sticky and disgusting, with the grime of ten thousand years clinging to our bodies.

"Do you want to talk about it?" Jesús asks, "What happened?"

"No."

We continue the climb toward an unknown destination. But the only way is up, and I reckon in the Underworld, going up is the best direction to go.

"Do you have a heartbeat?" I ask after the silence grows too terrifying to bear.

"Nope." He doesn't need to ask me the same question. He knows I don't have one either. We share an odd look, as if we're both about to get detention yet still burst out laughing. "It's getting less and less likely we're in a coma."

"Yeah, that's what I feared."

"So how are we meant to get this wig back from the pup?"

"It's not quite a pup. More a three headed monster in the form of a dog. That's how Cerberus is described, anyway, although Charon wasn't exactly described as a drag queen, so who knows, it might be a ball of fluff."

"Something tells me it won't be."

"Something tells me you're right."

Without breath to run out of, our ascent isn't hard, but I worry it's going to be endless. The mist obscures any sense of upward or downward, like we're in a cut-scene of a game that's not been fully designed; just climbing in stasis. I wonder if Sisyphus is around, pushing his rock up this very mountainside.

Before I can start to worry though, the hill spreads out into a broad flatland of wild grass as dark as deep velvet. The mist clears just enough to bring the pinnacle of the hill into view. On it sits a house; an old rickety home that looks horrifyingly like the one from *Texas Chainsaw Massacre*, complete with a rickety picket fence sunk around its creaking wooden architecture, dark blue in the missing light. Off in the distance of a so-called garden is a chalk white cypress tree spindly against the darkness, like a silvery spider's web.

There's light emanating from inside the house, though, a fiery orange, flowing and flickering from boarded-up windows. Jesús stops in his tracks, staring at the foreboding building then looking around for any other escape route. But the mist obscures it all.

"So the devil lives there, then?" he says with a sense of resignation fully appropriate for the situation.

"He's not the devil," I say, as if it can offer reassurance. "Just king of the dead."

"Oh, that's all right then."

Although it's not, Jesús carries on forward, toward the

House of Hades. Without another choice on offer, I follow. As if on a dramatic cue, the wind picks up, carrying the scent of darkness, death, decay. Jesús hangs back and covers his nose with his bare arm, but I keep going. The stench is a reminder that wherever we are, it's real. This is the Underworld. There's no point in freaking out. Just keep walking, and we'll get the hell out of Hell.

"Can you hear that?" Jesús asks a dozen feet from the fence. I stop and listen beyond the whistling wind which rattles the house.

"Is that…snoring?" It is. The slow, drooling groan of a beast asleep. Not just one nose snoring, but three.

"Oh fuck," Jesús says, peering beyond the fence which has neither an opening to approach the house, nor any sort of protection from whatever beast lies asleep beyond. I silently step toward him, closer to that damn fence, and catch sight of what he sees. It's Cerberus all right. Bigger than the biggest Great Dane, basically the size of a warhorse, curled up in a sodden paddock, three heads attached to his muscled and short-haired body, each head asleep. But their ears point straight up, listening for anyone like us who might approach.

The cheek of the head closest to us is folded up against its whiskers. Skin, pink and frothy, exposes a yellowed fang as long as my hand. The other two heads rest against each other. As if out of a comic book, a black collar with silver studs wraps tightly around each of their atrociously thick necks.

"Look, there it is," Jesús whispers. In a moment I see it

too. It looks like a furball wrapped under two giant shovel-sized paws.

"How the fuck does Charon expect…Jesús, come back here." If he had a shirt on I'd have grabbed it, but without he slips from my grasp and darts under the fence. "What're you doing?"

He ignores me like he's done this a million times before. Creeping forward, he's in biting distance of Cerberus who, I suddenly realize, isn't even chained up. He must've lost his inhibitions, because going right up to the beast to simply grab its favorite chew toy from under it doesn't seem like the best plan of action.

"Jesús," I call again from the fence. But one decibel too loud. One ear of six, one on the head farthest from us, twists in our direction. His snoring ceases, and he snorts instead. Jesús freezes. One eye opens. A tarantula's web of bloodshot red against a filthy white eye that's black, open, and angry. A low growl starts to rumble from the head as his cheeks edge upward. Jesús has woken the beast. I freeze as well. If one head starts to growl, the others can't be far behind.

"Jesús!" He's not running, not like I'm preparing to. Does he think he can't die down here? He's doing the exact opposite, he's leaning down, moving closer to the head of the hellish dog. The growling remains low, but it's getting stronger, watching Jesús' hand, no more than a quick snack for this beast, edging closer.

The beast watches. Teeth bared. The growling is like an earthquake waiting to swallow us all whole. I want to close my eyes, to wait for the agony to happen. Maybe I can plead with Hades to fix him. I can swap my life for his. I can stay down here forever. But I can't look away. Jesús reaches out, almost touching its black soggy nose as thick as Velcro. Cerberus sniffs: thick black fur wrinkling up as he examines Jesús' hand. Or what's in his hand.

The bottle that Charon gave him — he's holding it out, cap off, letting one third of Cerberus snort in whatever's in that bottle. Amyl nitrite: the thing Charon and Jesús shared a giggle over. The dog's eyelids flutter and grow heavy, his breathing slows, and the growling regresses into a sullen, sleepy snore. Just to be sure, Jesús runs the bottle along the line of heads, pausing for a moment under each of the four remaining nostrils so Cerberus has no choice but to inhale the fumes from the bottle. Then, without a single protestation from the sleeping beast, Jesús pulls the drool-soaked wig from between his paws.

I hop over the fence, not taking my eyes off the hellhound, as Jesús snaps the cap back on the bottle and douses off the otherwise fine looking silky brunette wig.

"Well," I say as we head around the corner of the house toward its porch. I still have an eye on the sleeping dog, though. "Defeating Cerberus makes you the greatest hero since Heracles."

"And all it took was some extra-strength poppers."

"What the hell are they, anyway?"

"I'll tell you when you're older," Jesús says, ending the conversation with a wink.

"Who's there?" an angry voice calls out from behind the screen door. We're not even on the porch yet, but we both stop. "Huh? Someone out there?" the voice calls again. It's a man, at least I think it is. And old. Crotchety; with a hardcore Texas intonation like Yosemite Sam is sitting behind the screen door cradling a shotgun. Then I hear two cartridges be loaded in, and the barrel clicks. Jesús hears it too.

"Eh…it's Achilles." I call out from the steps, shrugging my shoulders at Jesús who suddenly seems more nervous than me.

"And Patroclus," Jesús yells up at the house.

"What are you doing?" I hiss.

"Maybe if he thinks we're a couple, he won't shoot us."

"What in tarnation do you two want?"

"Who is it?" another voice calls out from deeper inside the house, this one definitely female, but also old and crotchety and sounding exactly like Yosemite Sam's wife.

"It's Achilles and Patroclus," Mr. Sam replies.

"Tell them we ain't home," Mrs. Sam replies. "I'm not watching their damn Griffin again while they're off to Mykonos. Last time it shit all over the carpet."

"They can hear you, woman. Can't you ride and chew at the same time?" The floorboards creak from behind the screen door. Jesús slips behind me, but I stand firm on the precipice of this old decrepit porch, waiting to meet my destiny. "Did she learn to whisper in a sawmill?" he mutters to himself. The screen door flies open. He kicked it with his boot. A cowboy boot. Tucked into it are raggedy gray long johns which hang loose off the old man's frail body. He holds the shotgun, but it's pointed at my feet as his worn-out face and beady eyes look me up and down. Shirtless and shabby.

"Fuck me, Achilles, you've gotten as big as all Brewsters County."

We sit at a long, dimly-lit table in the heart of the house. Jesús and I wait anxiously beside each other, while Hades holds court at the head, swinging on a rocking chair and sucking down cans of Greek beer. Persephone is in the kitchen. We seem to be waiting for her to start this meeting. I take in all the objects on the table; a cornucopia of objects I once assumed were nothing but mythology. A literal giant spiral cornucopia spills fresh fruit out across the table; succulent grapes and Kalamata olives and perfectly formed, ruby-red pomegranate seeds. It all looks so inviting and I find it strange that even though I'm dead, or at least in the Underworld, this feast looks so inviting.

The food spreads out across the table, swirling around goblets and collections of cutlery and even arrows. But it stops in the center of the table, as if some invisible magnet repels anything coming close. I turn my head slightly, one way and then the other, and I realize there is an object sitting there. Light reflects casually off it, but it is something, nonetheless. I try to see it from as many angles as I can without gaining Hades' attention—he's working on yet another beer—and from the side I can just about make out the shape of the object through the ripples of light. It's a helmet. The Helm of Darkness, forged for Hades by the Cyclops which turns the wearer invisible. That must be it!

I bite my tongue, keeping myself from blurting to Jesús that we're sitting inches from an object straight out of the myths. Perhaps Charon's cocktails have worn off, because he sits quietly, smoothing the tangled hairs of the wig he took from Cerberus, letting the weight of the Underworld fall on his shoulders.

Hades burps, long and loud, and crushes the beer can with one hand, tossing it behind him. But it never hits the wooden floor. Instead, I hear something scurry along the floor, squeaking as the invisible creature carries the can out of the dining room. I lift my feet off the floor in fear, and nudge Jesús to do the same. Hades leans across the armrest of his chair—I think for a moment he's falling—then he picks up a spear from the ground. A strange looking spear, because it's sharp at both ends: Hades' Bident. He points it toward an unseen box on the floor, and stabs something, the sound of metal piercing metal. Then he lifts the bident high. Another beer can. And he's speared it on the top, making a hole big enough to drink from.

"Some refreshments for our weary travelers," Persephone says, coming in from the kitchen carrying a shield-shaped tray. Hades whacks her with the bident on her backside and she jumps and smirks, like this happens all the time. Persephone is still breathtakingly beautiful. She doesn't look a day older than thirty-five. Her long golden hair flows down her lean body, making her look like one of those distance runners, with curves in all the right places. It's only in her voice her ancientness comes through.

She makes space on the table by shifting away fruit and olives, and knocking the invisible helmet onto the floor with a clatter.

"Dammit woman, now I'll never find it," Hades yells,

starting to look on the floor but quickly giving up to suck down more beer. She ignores him as she places the tray—the silver shield—in front of us. On it is a golden apple the size of a watermelon and four martini glasses filled with ruby-red liquid and pomegranate seeds stuccoed around the rim.

"Pomegranate martini?" she asks Jesús as she places a glass in front of him. "Pomegranate martini?" She puts one in front of me as well. She then gives one to Hades who ignores both her and the drink, and takes the last for herself taking a seat at the opposite end of the table. I jab Jesús in the side and slowly shake my head, but he's got the picture. As rude as it might be, he knows not to drink.

Persephone watches us intently with her hypnotizing ocean-blue eyes, and sips on her cocktail while her husband slams a boot on the table in order to lean as far back as possible to get every last drop out of the beer can. He burps even louder than before, like a clap of thunder, and once again chucks the can behind him for a creature to snatch and steal away.

"You know what makes a hero?" Hades says to none of us in particular. "It's fightin' against an injustice what been done to somebody else." Hades pulls himself closer to the table and, without touching the glass with his hands, slurps loudly at the martini. "Achilles never cared for Helen of Sparta. Or Troy, for what it's worth. He was perfectly happy—"

"Eh," Persephone cuts in.

"Happy enough, on Skyros with his wife and his boy Pyrrhus. He didn't want to be in a war. What does Achilles care that Paris is in love with Helen?" Hades waits, staring at Jesús and I for an answer.

"I, uh…"

"But Achilles," Hades continues, not interested in one, "he still goes to war. He travels all the way to Troy, spills his blood and the blood of his men on the shore, loses the love of his life Patroclus at the hands of Hector—"

"Eh, Hades," Persephone cuts in again just as the King of the Dead works himself up into a lather, "we don't need an *Iliad* right now, thank you."

He flashes a look of disdain back at his wife. The sort of look my mom still gives my dad, even though they've been divorced for almost as long as I've been alive. When someone grinds on you that hard, it's impossible to let it go. I can't imagine doing it for eternity.

"My point is, a hero takes an injustice that don't belong to him, that he's got no right to feel unjust about, and is willing to lay down his life to see justice be done. I've been watching you, boy. Your mom's been telling us about you all your life."

"My mom?" I say, shocked and unsure what they mean. Suddenly I feel vulnerable, naked even. Although I still partially am.

"She's been sacrificing to all of us," Persephone adds with a kind smile. "Even more so since you were imprisoned by your father's betrayal. Your mother has been diligently beseeching every god on Olympus and under it, every hero, every woodland nymph and satyr and primordial deity to fight for you. She prostrated herself in front of the Oracle at Delphi, so racked with guilt she let your father send you to prison on his behalf, and entreated us to help you."

"Not many people sacrifice to us these days," Hades adds. "Especially not every day, morning and night, for two years straight."

My body wants to cry, my eyes want to tear up, but they don't. I can't. No pulse. My soul must still be waiting at the edge of the forest. But even though it is there, just outside the Underworld, I know it is scrunched up hard in a knot of emotion that Hades and Persephone's words have sliced right through. All this time, all this bitterness and resentment lingering against her, somewhere in the background of my mind, for her acquiescence, it seems to vanish. At least the rational knowledge of the feeling does. The emotion I will have to wait and see. But all I want is to get out of here, and hug my mom.

"Anyway," Hades continues. "I've had a gander into your soul, boy. And you have it in you to be a hero. Zeus and Poseidon both agree."

Persephone nods in agreement. "We believe in you, Achilles. We believe you can be an even greater hero than your namesake."

"I...I don't know what to say." I look across at Jesús, who is taking all this in with a supportive smile. He lays a soft hand on my thigh, and the touch is electric.

"That's why I want to offer you a deal," Hades says, reaching backward with the bident and piercing another can of beer and lifting it over his head and smacking it down onto the table. "I know the greatest desire in your soul is to see Marcus again." If I had a heartbeat, it would stop. Jesús' hand grows stiff on my leg, suddenly feeling out of place.

"And I know he was unjustly taken. So, if you complete the task which I will set for you, I, Hades, will free the soul of Marcus from the Underworld and restore him to the land of the living to lead a full and long life."

It can't be real. I know it can't. But the feelings are real. The emotions, even if they are only an echo of what they would be above ground, are real. Jesús' hand withdrawing from my leg is also real. I don't know what I can tell him, but I don't have an answer for him now. Hades is waiting.

"What is my task?"

"Hehe, I can't tell you that, my boy. First you must accept—"

"I accept!" I yell, bouncing out of my chair and shocking even the King and Queen of the Dead.

"Very well. If you, Achilles, defeat your demons, I will set Marcus free."

"I…" I sit back down on the chair. "I don't know if I've got any demons."

Both Hades and Persephone burst out laughing. They start banging the table, heaving over the side of the chair, out of breath type of laughing. Howling. Even Jesús chuckles.

"Boy," Hades says, wiping tears from his wrinkled eyes, "You got more demons than me and I'm fucking Hades."

Who are my demons? My mind races, trying to think through every piece of mythology I've ever heard or read for some kind of clue. Is it my parents? My school? Myself? What seemed so close now feels impossibly far away.

"And you," Hades says, pointing his bident at Jesús. "The fake Patroclus. You gotta help him."

"Me? I…uh…"

"It's okay, sugar plum," Persephone says, stretching her arm out towards Jesús, but he doesn't reach back, "You can stay here with us if you don't want to."

"I'll help," Jesús says, then wraps his arm around my shoulder as if to doubly emphasize the point. I can't blame him.

"Atta boy," Hades smacks the table. "Now, the best way outta is the Mongolian exit—"

"Wait," I say, it all feeling far too much for someone who is not even a hero to handle. I look around at the mythological objects on the table, even the Harpe I now notice on the wall; the half-sword, half-sickle Perseus used to slay Medusa, and that Cronus used to castrate his father Ouranos. And all I have in my arsenal is a former employee of Domino's Pizza with a strong bottle of poppers?

"Can't you give me, like, something to help? A tool or…or a spear?"

Hades and Persephone trade a look across the table, one Jesús and I watch with great interest. Suddenly this is not just my quest, or his. It is *ours*. And if Hades could bring us both down here that easy, there's no telling what else he can do. Although that's not true. There's an entire cannon explaining in great and deadly detail just what Hades is capable of.

"Oh, all right," he says finally, grabbing what he thought was the beer can but in actual fact is the pomegranate martini glass. He drains half the liquid while the rest stains the white whiskers, then hurls the empty glass behind him like he did with the cans. But this time it shatters on the floor and the scurrying creature squeals in pain like a branded pig. "*Alastor, aidos, deimos* and *pothos*. Those are your demons. Now get the hell off my property."

Jesús and I trudge down the wet hill, past the still-sleeping dog, and much more quickly toward the shack at the bottom than the time it took to get up. The silence between us, relative strangers who shared nothing more than a handful of interesting conversations, louder than the thunder that followed us on the way in.

The back door is still open, and fortunately the dance floor has returned to its silent lights and emptiness.

"My wig!" Charon exclaims, bouncing off the stool and rushing toward us as fast as their heels and the gown will let them. "Oh thank you, boys! Thank you." Charon rips off the polyester one and chucks it on the floor, and immediately pulls the Cerberus-chewed one over their bald, liver-spotted head.

"Our pleasure," I say darkly as the three of us head straight for the wall where we came in. Charon snaps their fingers and it turns back into a door and I am relieved to find the two bike helmets where I left them. I reach over to pick them up from the couch.

"Sure I can't tempt you to stay for another drink?" Charon asks again. "We can compare notes on Persephone's latest face lift?"

Jesús looks almost tempted, but I practically wind him by shoving the bike helmet into his stomach.

"I would rather be a paid servant in a poor man's house

and be above ground than king of kings among the dead," I say, surprising myself as the words spill out of my mouth. I don't know where they came from. I didn't even think about them. But the words I recognize, in the back of my mind, from a story long ago.

"That's the spirit," Charon says with a grin. And then I remember. They are said by the ghost of Achilles in *The Odyssey*. I spin around as if to catch the ghost of the great hero red-handed.

"Come on, Jesús, let's get out of here."

Jesús seems happy to follow. We step outside, back into the relative coolness, although still dark heat, of the field atop where The Styx sit. The Acheron trickles down the hill to the darkened treetops flowing in the distance. But it's different now, the sky is not as black as it once was. A break of light comes from just beyond the horizon. It's not dawn, though, it's the land of the living.

I jump straight on the bike, revving it up loudly. The storm is clearing now. The wind lowering itself to a gentle howl and I rev the bike louder again, making sure Jesús knows it's time to go.

"Thank you for everything, Disco Styx," he says with the helmet on but visor up, and they give him a tightly wrapped hug. "Is there anything else we can do for you?"

I stretch the bike's engine to the point of breaking to make it clear I don't approve of that statement. Charon is more interested, however, in the breaking storm and the streaks of light offering a promise of sun beyond the world of the dead. He pushes Jesús away with a bony hand, edging him toward the bike.

"Just stand a little out of my sun."

Chapter 12
Marcus of Troy

Miraculously, or not, I find my way to Zotos's cabin in the late afternoon light. It is exactly where I thought it would be, ten minutes along a clear-cut pathway just off the access road in the Sam Houston National Forest. I feel dumb as fuck that Hades and his minions must've led us off-route for quite a while before I admitted even to myself, I was lost. I stop the bike in the driveway of the cabin, more a log house than a shack like the Styx was, and Jesús unclips himself from me, although he was holding on far less tightly than before. We've got souls back in our bodies and breath back in our lungs. Our hearts thankfully beating once again, but mine is suddenly longing for those moments when it didn't pump at all, and Jesús saw me with different eyes. Now I fear whatever connection we had, or might have had, the spark that made me feel like I wanted to stay in his presence every time I'm around him, has been snuffed out in our descent to the Underworld and back. The Katabasis killed our vibe.

As we go inside, I collapse onto the plush leather couch, slide off my shoes and throw my feet up on the coffee table across from the fireplace. Jesús takes his time and looks around the immaculately-decorated and beautifully-kept cabin. I'm beyond the point of exhaustion. When the bike flew over the stream circling the field, The Styx, the emotional weight of being separated from the most innate part of my being slammed back into my body at a hundred miles an hour. The pain of losing Marcus welled up to the surface like blood from a bite; and the slow, eroding drips of betrayal. I wondered what it was like for Jesús.

"How're you feeling?" I ask while he pokes around the fully set up kitchen.

"Tired," he replies, opening empty cupboards.

"Well, we can stay here for the night if you want and head back tomorrow morning. My Mom is at my uncle's watching the boys, and there should be plenty of food…"

"This place…it's like a, I don't even know. Like a five-star resort."

"Yeah, well Zotos has a lot of money to hide, if you hadn't realized already. Just remind me to grab the ledgers from his office before we—"

"Fuck me!" Jesús has discovered a money launderers' drinks cabinet. I hear bottles clattering. I peer up from the couch, too tired to stand up. He turns to me, a broad grin on his face and holding two bottles up high like an Olympic trophy. One is a sixty-year-old bottle of single-malt whisky, and the other a fresh bottle of soda. "Let's get drunk."

Like two soldiers after the heat of a battle, we needed these drinks. The sun has just set behind the trees, and the fire crackles in the fireplace as we warm ourselves. Jesús is stretching out on a genuine bear-skin rug and I am sitting on the floor with my back against the sofa, letting the flames warm my feet as I drain another scotch-and-soda.

"Be honest," he says, rolling over and turning his back to the flames to stare at me. "You were more frightened of the drag queen than the King of the Dead."

I smile and look away. It's not true. The only person I was truly afraid of down there was myself. But I'll humor him.

"I'm used to hearing about Hades. I've been told about him all my life. Drag queens are a bit newer for me."

"Maybe we should have Greek myth drag queen story time, get you Greek boys used to what Charon really looks like these days."

"Maybe we should," I say with a soft smile, pouring another glug of golden whiskey into my glass. Jesús offers me the soda bottle, but I shake my head. I think I prefer it without. "Have you ever done it? Drag, I mean."

"I would, but I haven't. The suburbs aren't exactly overflowing with drag clubs. I'm kind of afraid all the drag shows will be banned by the time I'm old enough to really go."

"But there is in Houston, no?"

"Yeah, tons. But…you know. I can't really turn up to clubs by myself and watch them."

"Why not?"

"Um, I'm still seventeen?"

"Oh, right! Sorry I feel like that journey aged us by like ten years."

"Plus, I've got no one to sneak in with," Jesús adds, watching me.

"When's your birthday?"

"June."

"Mine is May, so perfect. We'll go for your birthday, and to celebrate finishing with these fucking parole conditions."

"You and I will go?" he asks with great expectation.

"Sure, why not? Disco Styx I'm sure is hilarious when they're not guarding the entrance to the Underworld."

"Those are the kind of queens I like," Jesús says, with a deep satisfying smile. "The haggard ones. The ones who are tired of shit. Those are the ones who kicked off the Stonewall Revolution. Big, nasty queens who'd smack a police officer in the face with rocks in their handbags."

"Stonewall?" I feel stupid for asking, but Jesús smiles at me kindly.

"It's this bar in New York, still there, by the way, I *so* want to go. But in the sixties or whatever, the cops would come around and beat us up all the time. But then we said: 'no, honey, not today,' and we fought back, and we won."

"That's…fucking incredible." And I mean it. Suddenly, I'm imaging myself at the forefront of that revolution, climbing the barricades of burning cop cars, shielding Jesús as we fight for each other. My skin prickles with goosebumps despite the heat of the fire. "If I had to pick a queen," I say, "it would be the Stonewall, bricks-in-the-purse kind too. Hey," I nudge him in the side with my bare foot, "what would your drag name be?"

"Christ Almighty."

I spit out my drink all over the carpet, and myself, as Jesús cackles with laughter.

"That's a good name," I say, trying to get my breath back. It does feel nice to have breath again, even if my throat is burning from the whiskey shooting up my nose.

"What would yours be?"

"Oh, I dunno… What about Linda Lesbos?"

"That's the worst drag name I've ever heard in my life," Jesús says with a straight face. I give him a friendly nudge in the side again. It only strikes me now we're still half-naked. And we went to all the trouble of lighting a fire instead of finding a couple of sweatshirts.

"So, you think of one for me."

"Well, I need to know more about you for that."

"Like…what?"

"I don't know, like, what kind of queen are you going to be? Sassy? Funny? Are you going to sing, tell jokes, do impressions, physical comedy? Are you going to be about the clothes, the make-up, the attitude?"

"Okay, okay, I think I'll pass. That all sounds like way too much effort for me."

Jesús nods, and I go back to sipping whiskey from the glass as the fire crackles. I know I've cut the conversation short, and maybe I shouldn't have, because now the silence seeps back in. Jesús plays with the fur on the rug and I can't help my eyes from roaming across his body. The bruises seem less than before. Still there, subtly, but healed much quicker than if he hadn't been into Hades, I don't doubt that. And, secretly, I'm glad he doesn't have the muscled body of the demon from the dance floor. I think if I ever see another six-pack again, I'll turn and flee as fast as my legs can carry me.

I know there are words on Jesús' lips just waiting to spill out. And there is much I know we have to talk about. How I'm—we're—going to defeat these demons: *alastor, aidos, deimos* and *pothos.* They're personified concepts; spirits really, that embody a form of the human condition. How they'll be defeated I haven't the slightest clue. But I don't want to say that now. The least we can do is enjoy the crackling fire and the peace that comes from being comfortable in the silence with someone.

"I guess…" Jesús offers, staring at the fibers of the rug he's twisting around his fingers, "you should tell me about Marcus."

It's not what I thought he would say. Not "what about these mythological Greek words you and I are supposed to overcome together," not "what even are they," but Marcus. The name that stole his hand from my leg. And, I suppose, the reason we've been set on this fucking quest in the first place. I rub my temples, looking down at my legs and the glass I've placed between them, for no other reason than the bright, snapping fire suddenly hurts my eyes, and the story of Marcus and I is best told in darkness.

"I'd just turned sixteen. I remember because Mom came to see me on my birthday. And it was the saddest moment of my life. Worse than getting dragged out of the school by the cops. Worse than getting sentenced. Being taken back to my cell on my sixteenth birthday. A cell. You can't imagine what that's like for a kid. I was still a kid…am still, but at sixteen, the thought of being taken back to those four walls was more than I could handle. Minutes after Mom left, I started banging my head on the brick wall. Whack, whack, whack.

"The Beasts just laughed, at first. But then their supervisor saw I wasn't stopping. And I wasn't gonna. I'd have kept banging till I either broke free or died. That's when they decided to give me a cellmate. I hadn't had one before. Because I was big and Greek and scary, they hadn't put me with anyone. It's like wrestling; they try make it a fair fight.

"Anyway, after a detour to the nurse, when they finally took me back to my cell, there was someone inside. The only kid in there that was bigger than me. A six-foot-something giant. He was sitting on the bottom bunk when I came in, and then he stood up and I was like 'holy shit,' this massive Black guy is going to kill me the second they lock the cell doors. But, the Beasts said, 'make sure he doesn't kill himself,' to Marcus as they left. He was there to look after me.

"There was no one like Marcus. No one. It's like…like he wasn't in prison, if that makes any sense? Like, he was there, obviously, but almost because he wanted to be, or didn't care. It wasn't painful for him, being locked up. I guess it's because of his childhood. He'd been shuttled around through every abusive foster parent in the county, and to be honest I think he was just happy to be somewhere safe. It's funny, isn't it. The idea of prison being the safest place for some kids. How awful their life must be for that to be true.

"And I know for him, it felt like he'd finally found a

friend in me. He always said he'd never been allowed friends. At school the other kids would either be afraid of him, or he was afraid of them. But there was no reason to be. He just loved…people. I dunno. He loved knowing about who you were. It wasn't just about Greek stuff or my life or shit like that, he wanted to know me. What I liked, why, what I wanted, why, who I wanted to be on the outside, why. I've…I've never had the kind of conversations with anyone else that I had with Marcus. I don't even think I could with anyone else. I don't think it exists. I've never seen it, not on TV or in any books, the way Marcus and I talked to each other…what we talked about, you know?"

"After a while, it just became easier to talk in the same bed. I'd climb into his bottom bunk and paint this imaginary picture of the constellations or the islands in the Aegean onto the mattress above us. Whatever we were talking about. Then…I just started to fall asleep beside him. And him me. Maybe prison changes you, I dunno. I never thought of myself as, you know, feeling that way about guys. And when you're stuck with someone in the same cell, it's a bit of a risk to try anything, even if we both wanted to. And I know we did. I wanted to kiss him, I'm not ashamed to say it. Not to you, Jesús, not to anyone. I wanted to, and I would've done it. If things…you know, had been different. If our lives had been our own. I would have kissed Marcus, because I know Marcus wanted to kiss me.

"We were just unlucky to never get the chance."

I sit on the rug, staring into the flames, sipping another glass of whiskey. The bottle is nearly empty now, but I don't care. We'll fill it up with one of the cheap ones before we go. I'm sure Zotos, of all people, will never be able to tell the difference. Jesús has been in the bathroom for a while, although I know he's just giving me some time. And for that at least, I'm thankful.

"Hey," he says from the doorway, holding two gray sweatshirts. "I found these."

"Thanks," I say, taking one but putting it behind me to lay back on. Jesús joins me on the rug, sitting cross-legged and flicking balls of dust into the flames.

"Have you thought about these demons? What or who they could be?"

"I know what they mean, if that helps."

"Maybe?"

I suck in a deep, sullen sigh.

"*Alastor* is the spirit of blood feuds and vengeance."

"Oh. All right. Anyone at school…or from juvie you've got beef with?"

"I thought about that, but I'm pretty sure it's about Hector, the other top wrestler at the gym. I know Zotos is going to make me fight him in the competition I have to qualify for. Like it makes sense; we're both in the same weight class and we can't both go to nationals. Plus, in case you didn't know, Achilles and Hector are the ultimate blood feud."

"Worse than Taylor and Kanye?"

"Almost as bad as that. *Aidos* is the spirit of reverence and respect. So I'm clueless as to how to defeat that demon."

"Maybe Mrs. McKenna? Or your parents?"

"Yeah, or like, respect for the system or something? Like maybe to defeat that demon I have to ace the GED or something? Or get a job? Fuck, I've no idea. Marcus will never get out at this rate."

"Hey," Jesús leans across and touches my shoulder. Holds it. How different than the hand he pulled away the last time Marcus' name got mentioned. "We're going to figure this out. Let's come back to that one. What was next, *deimos*, right?"

"Yeah. That's the spirit of fear and dread and terror."

"What's your biggest fear?"

I stare at Jesús as he waits for an answer, the flames brighten his skin. His cuts are almost all gone. The sight of him lying on the ground, bloody, bruised, beaten screams blue murder in my mind.

"Going back inside," I say quickly, hoping the image will fade. "Wasting my life because I never stood up to my dad. Or the judge. Or that Dad will rope me into something else, will make me take the blame for his crimes again and I'll throw away my future because I never just fucking fought for myself. That's my biggest fear."

Jesús listens, quietly. "I think that answers the previous question," he says. I stare blankly at him, then the fire, trying to see the connection.

"How do you work that one out?"

"Well, if failing to stand up to your dad causes you to go back inside, then maybe you need to defeat this reverence or respect you have for him. Because to be pretty honest, Aki, it doesn't sound like he deserves it. Not even Hades thinks so."

"Yeah, maybe you're right."

"And what's the last one, *pothos*, what's that?"

I don't want to say. I keep staring at the flames, almost wishing Hades had never given me these clues. Then I could pretend it was something else, or didn't exist. It would be better than this, better than to say what I had to say now.

"Sexual longing."

"You have to defeat being horny?"

"I don't think that's what it means."

"So what do you think it means?" Jesús creeps closer on the rug, switching the hand he uses to lean on the rug so our bare shoulders are practically touching. I wish he'd done it deliberately, but I don't think he did. I wish he would just say if he wants me or not. Make all of this so much easier. The game, the indecision is making my heart pound hard, and my stomach flip, so much that not even chucking back the rest of the whiskey from the glass can calm it. What does he want from me? But I snort with laughter from my own thoughts. The question I should be asking is what do I want from him.

"What's so funny?" he asks. I draw my knees up and wrap my arms around them, sealing myself off from his touch. Closing myself off to the world.

"Ever since I got out of prison, I haven't been able to… get hard."

"At all?" he asks.

I nod. "I thought it was just with Carla. She came over the first night and tried to, you know, but it didn't work. And we tried a few times after that and still nothing. And then I tried on my own because I was freaking out about it. Like, I tried a lot, and it still hasn't worked."

I don't know whether to mention this morning. God it's been a long day, and waking up with it happening in my sleep. Who knows if I'd been hard, though. Maybe it just happened. I decide it's not worth mentioning. The truth still is, something is broken down there, and Hades, for some twisted reason, wants me to overcome it.

"Last night…" Jesús says, like he's making his own confession, "you were hard as a rock."

"What?" I spin and study his face. He's deadly serious.

"Yeah, you were like, grinding into my back. I mean you were asleep, but you had your arm wrapped around me, holding my stomach," Jesús puts a hand on his, "and like, thrusting your hips into me."

"I would say I'm embarrassed but…I think I'm a bit relieved."

"Definitely getting hard isn't your problem."

"Yeah," I say with a chuckle and stare back into the fire, "I guess not."

"Maybe it's more about…who you get hard with."

I feel Jesús even closer, even though I don't notice him move. His bare shoulder brushes against mine, and I glance over at him on the rug. He's looking at me, up at me, like I'm some great big giant. His face is open, soft, not sad, but with enough sadness to show me he's honest. With all the realness of a guy who came down to the world of the dead with me and back.

With only his look, he makes my body unclench. My shoulders relax, arms fall to the floor. I turn slowly, heavily, to rest on one elbow. My toes touch the edge of the fireplace, and now we're on a more equal level, almost nose to nose. Alone in the cabin, alone in these woods. But he's not looking at my face, not as I stare at his. He's looking down. Down at the stomach I don't care hangs out, although a little less than two weeks ago, it's still a far cry from the bodies of the heroes Zotos expects me to be. Maybe Jesús doesn't care.

He reaches a hand out, and I watch it sail toward my chest like a missile. I let it land among the hair, then slide down the path of my stomach. The friction itself, the spark of an unfamiliar touch is causing a chemical reaction. I can feel it, and now Jesús can see it. His eyes flick up to my face, but I'm locked on the sight below. Yes, things are happening. Absent of words or actions from me, he keeps sliding down, stroking my skin, edging toward the waistband, the proof of his theory about how to defeat *pothos*.

"Stop," I say. And he freezes. His hand, his face. It all ceases to move. Just like when he approached Cerberus and its eye flicked open. Now he's woken the beast, it's time to worry about what's going to happen.

"Aki," he whispers, moving his body closer to mine, "it's okay. No one will have to know."

I know what he wants. I know what he's trying to do. To offer me a transaction, like Hector and Giorgos in the showers or so many boys in juvie. One hand helping another. One willing body offering a favor to another, like a pick-up game in purgatory where the only choice is to play ball with someone else or shoot hoops alone.

"No," I say again, and I wrap my hand tightly around his wrist. "I don't want this." I pull his wrist off my stomach, but not away from me, toward me. Back onto my chest where he first touched me, right next to my heart. Holding it tight against my skin I roll onto my back and practically hoist his slight frame on top of my body. He looks shocked, unsure of what to say or to do with his face so close to mine. "I don't want that," I say again, even though he's pressed tightly against my hard-on. The first conscious one in the land of the living, land of the free. "I want you," I whisper. *Pothos* be damned.

Jesús smiles—grins—right above me. His brown eyes come alive with the reflected flame from mine. The fire crackles in the silence of our aloneness. Let the storms rage outside, let the Underworld rise up and swallow us whole, just let me feel the heat from Jesús' body weigh down on me. With a suddenness that made me wonder why we'd not been doing this our whole lives, my lips meet his and we are lost in a kiss I wish would stretch from here to eternity.

Chapter 13
Carla the Betrayed

I didn't see Jesús for a week after the kiss. On that Sunday morning, I'd woken up beside the embers of the fire, while he'd found a bed. We didn't talk so much on the drive back; after a day in the Underworld, it takes more than a night to recover. Well, from that and the whiskey. And the kiss. It's not like he called or messaged. He couldn't, I don't have a phone. But I checked up on him through Zotos, who told me that he was coming to his office and getting started poring through the handwritten ledgers we'd taken from the cabin, and doing a great job, too. My excuse, not that anyone asked, but for myself, was that he needed some time to settle in at his new job, and I was doing fine enough on my own preparing for the GED. I knew we would have to talk at some point. I knew there were demons to defeat. I just didn't want to yet.

I don't know what he expected after the kiss. I don't know what I did, either. Did this count as overcoming *pothos*? I didn't think so. In fact, probably the opposite. Kissing Jesús, as incredible as it was, hardly solved my sexual problems with Carla. But the business of the days spent in the gym and in study books merged into the weekend. Jesús had no Domino's to spend his nights in, so what was he doing now? The thought haunted me all Friday night. I tossed and turned in my bed, utterly unable to fall asleep. The darkness and silence felt oppressive. What was Jesús doing? Had he gone off into Houston, roaming through those drag bars he mentioned? Or was he at home in his empty house, with his aunt in Vegas, inviting all sorts of men better looking than me to be with him instead.

That thought frightened the sleep right out of me, and by Saturday morning, I feigned illness so as not to have to face Hector at the gym once again...or Jesús in the office. Mom hated having me mope around all Saturday though. She was preparing for a Greek girl's night at her friends' house, so the kitchen was ablaze from six in the morning with pots, pans, and more cigarette smoke than a bar in Hades.

I just got in the way, but even sitting in my room in the dark bothered her.

"Go run," she yells at me when I venture out for food in shorts and a tank top.

"I don't wanna run."

"Then why are you dressed like that? Go clean up the pyre in the back garden then."

"I don't feel like it," I say, staring out the screen door at the burned-out logs heaved in the fire pit. But it makes me smile, knowing that it's all for something. Every sacrifice, every prayer goes somewhere. I know I can't tell her; I can't say a word. But even if I did, I don't think it would matter to her. She'd just say, "Of course the gods appreciate the sacrifice, that's why we do it." And it's not like there's any priests around. Hellenistic religion doesn't really have a clergy, at least not in Southeast Texas.

Zotos would maybe hear me out, but his initial reaction would probably be along the same lines as Mom's. Then he'd threaten to break my legs if I ever breathed a word of that to another soul. A rumor flying around the Greek community that mighty Zotos' nephew and his mother were devil worshipers would destroy his reputation, and ours. Not that I cared, but I couldn't do that to Mom, not after what she'd done for me.

I have to laugh at the absurdity of having seen evidence of the gods, yet not being able to tell a soul. I guess that's what it's like for most—

"Ouch!" Mom has smacked my bare shoulder with a hot metal spatula. I practically spin on the spot trying to see the entirety of the big red mark she's left on my skin.

"Don't stand there laughing at the mess outside, go clean it up." And she whacks me again.

At least clearing the garden passes the time. And I can take all the time I want to think about Jesús. At last I'd tasted real lips, not those smothered in flavored lip gloss. The light stubble under his chin left a satisfying red mark against mine, instead of being left dusted in foundation. Jesús didn't care when I grabbed a fistful of hair. He didn't complain that it had just been colored or straightened. I could roll him onto his back, hair first, then immediately climb on top of him without having to pause everything to find a scrunchy.

The fire pit was clear, and the garden trimmed and tidied without me spending an ounce of cognitive power actually thinking about what I was doing. Sweat dripped down my body and my skin sizzled in the late afternoon sun, but all I was imagining was sliding on top of Jesús; our stomachs pressed together, our mouths open and tongues dancing like Dionysus.

"Aki!" Mom shouts from inside the house. "Your father is here." Those words bring my fantasy to a screeching halt. I've almost forgotten about the fight I got into defending Jesús, but the memory—and fear—of being thrown back in jail steps in with my father. I wander inside the shady house, pulling the garden gloves off and using them to dab the dirt and sweat from my forehead, but not because of the heat from the outside. He's here indeed, leaning against the wall, chewing, smirking, his shirt buttoned low, chest hair spilling out and almost obscuring the gold crucifix buried inside.

"Do you have to dress like such a stereotype?" I say it low, quiet, almost without him hearing. Mom won't hear, she's in the kitchen. Dad comes forward, his face confused, angry. It doesn't matter; they are the same emotion in my dad.

"What did you say?"

I smirk. He's heard me.

"Here you are, Aki," Mom says, rushing out of the kitchen with a goblet of Coke and ice. "Oh, the garden looks lovely, well done!"

"Eugh, Mom. I asked you to get Coke Zero."

"I'm not buying two types of Coke. If you want to go to the store, you're more than welcome." And with that, she's back in the kitchen and I'm stuck drinking fully sugared Coke.

"What're you doing here, Dad?"

"I know this is your mom's girl's night, so I thought I'd come by and take you out. Spend some father-son time together." The words don't sit with him well.

"Uh-huh," I take a seat at the table, watching him start to pace. "What are you doing here, Dad?"

"Son," he grins through gritted teeth. "I came to Take. You. Out."

"To another whorehouse?"

"No," he says, staying calm is consuming all his strength. "We'll go get a bite to eat."

I smack the glass down on the table. Something about dying then coming back to life really helps you see behind people's bullshit.

"And what else?"

"I've gotta stop by a friend after, but that's—"

"No thanks," I say, getting up from the table. I know exactly what "stopping by a friend" means. Yeah, we'll eat, but he'll be on the phone the whole time, calling this guy and that, getting things ready for the pickup, the drop off, whatever that night's business is. I've already put myself at risk defending Jesús—and I'd do it again in a second—but I won't be going back inside for my dad.

"Son." He kicks the chair out of his way and comes within an inch of my nose. "I've come here to do something nice for you." The unshaved hair on his face froths with anger and spittle. Even the demon on the dance floor was more inviting than this. *Aidos*, I think. How pointless it is to have respect for someone who doesn't deserve it.

"I'll pass." And I head straight to the kitchen as he scrambles over the chair, half a second from a rampage. I put the empty glass on the counter as Mom scoops crispy chicken thighs into a large serving dish, expertly avoiding a single drop of ash falling into them from the cigarette between her lips. I snatch a thigh from the dish as Dad fumbles his way inside the narrow kitchen. Even he knows this is no place to get angry.

"Saphie, tell your son it's rude to disrespect his father."

I take a bite from the steaming chicken, chewing loudly, skin and all. What an idiot he is, thinking he has any power in this place.

"Leave the boy alone, Christos. He's had a hard week."

"A hard week jerking off, most likely. And why wasn't he at the gym last weekend? Or today?" Dad looks me over, his eyes threatening, like he's found out some big secret but not quite smart enough to use it to his advantage.

"That's Zotos' business, not yours or mine."

"I'm sure the judge wouldn't be too happy to know Achilles is skipping practice."

Mom slams the oven door shut, and finally pulls the cigarette from her mouth, dabbing an entire length of ash into the front pocket of her apron. She has my father in her sights, a feud as old as Achilles and Hector. I just lean back on the counter, picking through the chicken. It's almost a pity to watch a measly goat wander into the lair of the minotaur.

"Try it, Christos. Because I'll turn state's witness like

that." She snaps her fingers and my Dad jumps at the threat. But he knows when he's beat. He slinks back, out of the kitchen, heavy crucifix smacking against his chest. And he knows better than to say another word, to either of us. It takes him another long minute, of staring at us both, playing with his buttons and scowling like a good fight was just snatched out his hands. But he goes. Smacking the table as he snatches his keys and slamming the front door shut.

"I left a tray of wings in the oven for you, and there's salad and tzatziki in the fridge. Will that be enough?"

"Eh, I think so, Mom."

"Good then," she says, hanging up her apron and beginning the arduous exercise of gathering up all the trays wrapped in aluminum foil and bowls in saran wrap. It takes two trips to the garage, from both of us, to get everything into the back of the car. Mom waves from the window as she reverses the station wagon down the driveway, then drives off down the street, the car practically heaving under the weight of provisions for an army.

Inside, the promise of a silent house washes over me and sends a tingle down my spine. I lift up the receiver of the house phone and dial the number I know by heart.

"Hey. She's gone."

Carla arrives an hour later. I'm showered and ready, but anxious and confused all the same. About Jesús, my dad, the fight, prison, sex. So, it took me an hour. Most confusing of all is that fact I could stand in front of the bathroom mirror and suddenly get hard in an instant just by thinking back to last week. His touch. That kiss. What does it matter *how* I conquer *pothos*? Hades didn't say *eros,* did he? This doesn't need to be about love. Hades also didn't say *anteros* either, the spirit of requited love. What does it matter if I have feelings for Carla? If she wants to have sex with me, then so be it. I've got a magic trick to conquer this particular demon. I put prison and Marcus and the gods out of my mind. I just need to remember his touch while lying next to her body. Then I'll be fine.

Carla brings a cheeky smile and every single thing possible one needs to defeat the demon *pothos*. Her bag of leather tricks makes me think she's going to torture this demon out of me.

"Mom took me shopping," she says, blowing a bubble with her gum and laying out the things she brought on my bed.

"The woman at the store said these are a great natural substitute for Viagra," she hands me a pack of off-colored powder.

"I'm not snorting this."

"It's ginseng. You put it in tea or something. Read the label."

I read over the minuscule instructions on the back like I'm some sort of dad at the supermarket while Carla keeps unpacking her never-ending bag of horrors.

"I bought this," she says, holding up a black leather lingerie set complete with stockings and studs. It reminds me of Cerberus' collar.

"Carla, this was three hundred dollars." The label is still on the hanger.

"Mom bought it."

"I don't care if you won it at a rodeo, you're taking that thing straight back to the store for a refund. Three hundred dollars just to have sex. That's insane."

I realize I've left myself wide, wide open. But she doesn't take the bait.

"And there's this." She hands me a thick rubber ring which, even though I can stretch it between my fingers, looks far too tight and far too painful to put anywhere near my body.

"And there's these which are for me if you want to do…you know, that other thing."

I recognize the small brown bottle immediately. The same as the one Charon gave Jesús, just with a different label wrapped around it.

"Carla, no. I'm not taking drugs." I throw the pack of natural Viagra onto the bed. "And neither are you."

"It's not drugs, it's poppers. They're harmless, as long as you don't drink them."

"I know what poppers are."

"Oh yeah? How do you know?"

"I…never mind." I take them out of her hand and move her away from the bed full of terrifying sex gear. I hold her in my arms, between my arms, and look at her soft, pretty features. I feel it in my bones, she deserves to be loved the way she wants. And I know, deep down, it's my job as a man to do that for her. My Dad taught me one thing, at least. Zeus liked to kiss Ganymede, but that didn't stop him fathering an entire generation of Olympians. Just because

Jesús is stuck in my mind, doesn't mean I can't give Carla what she wants too.

"Look, we've got the house to ourselves now. I've been home a month and I'm feeling way more relaxed than before, okay?" I say it with such a fidgeting nervousness I wonder if she believes a word I'm saying. I can't tell her that I fear the cops bursting through the door because I saved another boy from a homophobic attack. The very same boy I kissed after descending to the Underworld with him to be given a challenge from Hades to rescue another boy who I…I can't breathe. "The GED stuff is going fine! The gym is…well, it is what it is but I'm not the ball of anxious fear I was when I got out!" I shout the words, but it triggers something in me. I wonder if that's *deimos* as well. Hector and the wrestling competition coming up is causing me dread and terror. I wonder if I can knock out *deimos*, *aidos*, and *pothos* all in one day. Maybe I can fight Hector at the gym tomorrow and be done with all of these damn demons. That just leaves *alastor*. But Hector could be a blood feud too. Suddenly I have such a massive urge to get it all over with. I'm already imagining getting lost in the forest tomorrow night to make it back down to Hades and tell him I've finished my tasks.

"All I'm saying is," I say, hugging her close and calming down. She smells like a Macy's display. "We're going to be okay. I promise. So why don't we sit down, eat something, and then—"

Carla has been watching too much wrestling. Because in a split second I'm thrown onto the bed. She swept her leg behind mine and knocked me in the back of the knee. I land

and the rubber ring and poppers bounce off the bed, but she ignores them and dives on top of me. I'm being attacked by cherry lips at one end and acrylic nails at the other. She tears into me like a boar gouging its prey. But I go with it. I have no choice.

It didn't work in here before. It didn't work in the car. But now there should be no excuse. I've not drunk, we're alone. Carla is beautiful. No one can deny that. She nibbles and bites at my lips, tempting me, teasing me. Forcing me to chase her all around the bed. I'm going to make this happen. I can feel it. Jesús, well, he can stay right there beside me in my mind's eye. I don't care. But as our clothes come off and the memory of Jesús' kiss fades. What do I need him for, I've got the most beautiful woman in the world, and she wants me.

An hour and a half later, we've tried everything to make it work. I even rubbed some of that ginseng powder on my gums. Probably mixed with tea would be better, but I saw plenty of kids in juvie rub stuff on their gums and it always hit their bloodstream quickly. We can forget the main event. That was a non-starter. And the poppers made Carla feel dizzy so that other thing was quickly binned as well. We've tried everything else, but the only thing that seems to work is me flat on my back on the bed, Carla sitting with her back to me, acrylic nails peeled off and my junk covered in half a bottle of the tingly lube she brought.

"Oh, Jesus," I say, throwing my head back on the pillow. As long as I keep my eyes sealed shut, as long as she doesn't speak or move or get her hair in my face. We're fine. "Jesus…that's it. Christ Almighty." I say it without thinking. It's just another phrase. Like damn or shit or hell or fuck. But all I can think about now is Jesús telling me that would be his drag name, and then I laughed, and then he laughed, and then we laid next to each other by the fire, and then we kissed. Oh man, that kiss. How we tumbled around the fireplace, wrapped up in each other's bodies. How quickly the *rest* of our clothes came off, and how right everything felt.

"For fuck's sake, Aki." Carla stands up in a huff, wiping lube off her hands with my T-shirt. I look down. We're not finished. Not in the slightest. In fact, we're back to square one. "What the fuck are you doing, jerking off five times a day?"

She starts to get dressed, angrily pulling on all of her clothes that are scattered around the room. I lay still on the bed and watch her do it, because I really didn't like the fact she'd thrown everything around. It was kind of a distraction.

"Carla, I'm sorry. I don't know what you want me to say."

"You know I'm fucking Adam, right?" she says with a furious face as she pulls her sweater back on. "Because it's important to me that you know that. I want that information to hurt you."

I wish I could be hurt by it. For her sake, at least. But I can't even work up the energy to shrug.

"Well, good for you. Are you two a thing?"

"Oh, we're so much more than a thing, Achilles Konstantinos." I smirk as she calls out my name like Mrs.

McKenna, and then quickly wipe the smirk off my face as she turns back around having gathered up the sex instruments from the floor. Just like I would if Mrs. McKenna was turning around to accuse me of making a fool of her behind her back. "And for your information, he's not dumb."

"I…never said he was?"

"And fine, maybe his cock isn't as big as yours, but at least it works!"

"All right, all right. Do you want to cut out the screaming?"

"It's not normal!"

"Carla." I sit up in the bed, holding onto myself to stop the lube going all over the bedspread. "You're not exactly being very supportive here. And what the hell do you want me for anyway if you've got Adam?"

"Now I have him, only because he thinks you fucked me in the parking lot last week."

"Is that what all that was about? You making him jealous?"

"I just wanted you both to fight over me," she says softer now, almost sobbing. I get up off the bed, holding everything in with both hands like an exposed soccer player. I give her a friendly nudge with my shoulder.

"Maybe it's for the best, you know? You guys can be together. I don't need to be in the picture."

"So what, you're not attracted to me?"

"I…" I stare at her. Clothes shoved back on but looking like she'd never taken them off in the first place. Her hair is a little bit ruffled, but not much. She could walk out of here and straight to Adam's or her grandma's and no one would know the difference. Maybe this *pothos* thing is not as easy as I think. There's more to our sexual selves than just shoving one thing into another. There's more than just…friction. I look at her, but I see Marcus. His life is on the line. More than that, his life is waiting for me to get things right, to do the right thing. Make the decisions that'll defeat these demons.

"Are you attracted to me?" she asks again, and this time, I have to answer.

"I'm…no. I'm sorry, Carla. I'm not."

"So you're gay."

"W-what? How the fuck do you work that one out?"

"It doesn't make any sense, Achilles!" she yells at me like I'm a bad puppy. "Two years ago you couldn't keep your hands off me. Every other day you want sex. You want blow jobs in the bathroom at school. You want me to jerk you off in the back of the movie theater. You want—"

"Fine, I get the picture."

"And two years later…what? You just changed your mind? There were *so* many beautiful women in prison that plain old Carla Gonzales just doesn't do it for you anymore?"

"Carla, it's not like that. I was fifteen then, what do you want?"

"I want the truth, Achilles."

"I don't know what to tell you."

"Tell me the truth."

"There's no truth!" The whole scene is utterly ridiculous. She's got her bag of tricks on her shoulder and

I'm still dancing around my room naked and sticky from the waist down.

"Who are you attracted to if not me?"

"No one!"

"Tell me!"

"There's no one! I'm not attracted to you, I'm not attracted to anyone." I know it's a lie. Maybe she knows it's a lie, too. But what good will the truth do? "Jesús!"

"What did you say?" she asks quietly.

Fuck. I said Jesús. But I meant to say Jesus. There was a subtle *hey-zeus* tucked away in there.

"Nothing."

"What did you say, Achilles?" she says, pushing me in the shoulder.

"I said nothing!"

"Huh," she snarls like a demon from the Underworld. Maybe this isn't about *pothos* after all, maybe this is *deimos* and I just don't know it yet. "*Hey-zeus* Alvarez. I hear you, Achilles. I hear you loud and fucking queer."

"Excuse *me?*" Now it's my turn to be indignant.

"I said I hear you loud and *clear*, Aki. You're gay for Jesús."

"I am not…" I start to yell, but my voice trickles away like a dammed river. Why fight it? Why try? If that's what she wants to think, so be it. "Fine," I say, throwing up my hands and letting everything flap out. She takes that as her cue to storm out of my room and I follow her out. "Fine, Carla. I'm gay. Sorry, I guess it happened in prison. That's how it works, right? 'Cause I missed that part of social ed since I was in fucking *jail* for a crime I didn't commit, trying to survive between fucking gangs and murderers." She grabs her car keys from the kitchen table, and her purse, and marches straight for the front door. "But, yeah, Carla, that's exactly what happened." She pulls open the front door and I go right to the threshold, one foot on the porch as she marches down the driveway into the soft peaceful evening. And I'm just a crazy person yelling naked into the street. "I guess I went in straight, Carla, and came out gay."

She flips me off as she gets into her car, and I slam my front door before I get a chance to hear her slam hers. But suddenly the house is peaceful again. And I feel like I can let my shoulders, my forehead, my tense cheeks, all relax. If that's what it took to let her go, and make it stick this time, then maybe it was worth "coming out", if she really took my sarcasm seriously. But you know what, I couldn't give a fuck. I pad into the kitchen, crank up the oven to warm up the tray of chicken wings I can eat all by myself now, and head straight into the shower to wash all this tingly pink jelly off my body. And maybe even think about Jesús.

Chapter 14
Hector the Trojan

"All right, boys," Zotos says, "fight!"

Like two raging bulls smacking into each other on the wild, tomato-soaked streets of Pamplona, they smash into each other with an almighty crash. Except these aren't bulls. They're barely calves. Two kids, one in a red leotard and one in blue, helmets and gum guards secured on tight, battle it out. Even the knee pads and elbow pads are coded with the color of their team; Trojan or Greek.

Hector and I watch our two proteges from opposite sides of the mat, as Zotos would have it, as they trip over themselves more times than they score a point on the other one.

"That's it, Alex!" I shout, clapping loudly as my other young Greeks follow suit. "Go for a far-drag. Remember it's all about those points. Show technique."

"Get off your fat ass," Hector screams at his kid from the other side. "Get up! Attack now, don't wait. Attack!"

The Trojans yell and bay like locked up cattle from their side, while my Greeks applaud and cheer on their comrade. I make sure every single one of them does. Zotos blows his whistle, and the boys separate. It was inconclusive, it could have gone either way.

"Greeks, twelve points," Zotos says, and my boys all cheer. Not a great score, but not bad.

"Trojans…eleven points."

I whip my head around and stare down every single one of my boys to get clapping and cheering, just as loud and long as they did for their teammate, Alex. Meanwhile on the Trojan side, Hector is leading the vicious criticism. Their fighter limps back to embarrassed shrugs and cold-shoulders. Alex rejoins our side to pats on the back and cries of "good match" and "well done." It would have been the same even if he had lost.

"Great job, Alex," I say, messing up his already messed up hair from the rubber helmet. "Nice move on the gut wrench, I think that's what got you over the line. Wait a moment…did you shake his hand?"

"Ehm…" Alex says, too worn out to remember.

"Back in the ring," I order him, pointing. Reluctantly, he trudges back onto the mat.

"Strategos!" I shout at Zotos, "the competitors did not shake hands after the match."

Zotos takes my word for it, and gestures to the Trojan side for their fighter to return to the ring as he totals up the points each side has gathered from the morning bouts. But Alex remains alone on the mat. He's hot and tired, it's been a long Sunday morning for all of us. He starts to unpeel his singlet; all the boys are ready to rush into the showers.

"Keep it on, buddy. In a real competition you can't lower your shoulder straps while you're in the hall. And you've got to shake your opponent's hand before you leave the mat…Hector! Where's your kid? He has to shake Alex's hand."

But Hector is too busy lecturing the defeated boy without even giving him a chance to take off his helmet and pads. The young Trojan just stands there sweating, depressed, disappointed, his hands on his hips while phrases like "piece of shit" and "waste of space" drift over from Hector's side of the gym.

"Okay, final scores," Zotos shouts, and we all quiet down. "One hundred and eighty-one points for the Greeks." My side cheers and claps, even poor Alex still standing alone in the ring. "But one hundred and ninety points for—" He doesn't need to say anymore. The Trojan side erupts in a horrendous display of showboating, led of course by Hector. They don't congratulate themselves on their victory, but attack us for our loss. I see more than a few middle fingers crop up from middle school boys. My Greeks are crestfallen. Not so much from the loss, but the ripping they'll get in the locker room. But it's Zotos' fault for creating such an unhealthy competitive atmosphere inside his own gym.

"Um, *strategos*, I say, pointing to Alex who has still not left the mat where I told him to wait for his opponent for a final shake.

"Hector, where's your boy?" He's busy flipping off our team, that's where he is. Zotos, with all the fury of an Olympian scorned, marches across the mat right up to the smirking Hector and blows his whistle full blast in his face. Then he grabs Alex's arm and raises it into the air.

"Disqualified! Trojans, you've lost those eleven points.

One hundred and seventy-nine. Greeks win this week's bout. Trojans, go collect the mops and buckets. It'll be cold showers for your lot today."

My Greeks fall over themselves in shock. They've snatched victory from the disappointment of defeat, and Alex is hailed as a conquering hero. Now it's the turn of the Trojan boys to be dejected, as they shuffle over to the janitorial closet to complete the losers' humiliation of wiping the sweat of the victorious team from the mat. My boys don't flip off the Trojans though, they offer their hands to shake.

"Bullshit!" Hector cries out as my Greeks head into the locker room to get first shot at the limited hot water. He storms across the mat and shoves me hard in the chest.

"Hey, what are you doing?"

"Strategos," Hector says, coaxed in anger. "This is nonsense. Philip tried to shake his hand, but Achilles pulled Alex away before he had a chance."

"So why did Achilles send Alex *back* onto the mat, then?" Zotos says, not buying a word of Hector's protestations.

"Trojans!" Hector calls out across the gym. "Put down the mops. This is a total set up by Achilles."

"Oh, come on, Hector. Just follow the rules next time."

"Trojans! Put down the mops. Giorgos, get them to stop." Hector's furious face spins back to me, a sword-like finger threatening my throat. "You fucking set me up."

"You lost, Hector. Deal with it." I glance behind him as the rest of his team aren't bothering with this recount request. They know the quicker they finish cleaning, the more likely there is to be at least warm water left in the showers. He looks behind and sees his team's betrayal, and knows perfectly well there's nothing he can do about it. Even Zotos has lost interest and shuffles back to his desk by the entrance.

I gaze beyond him, out of the gym and toward the tinted window of the accountancy firm next door. I wonder If Jesús is there now, pouring through ledgers, or making coffee, or watching me through his window. Watching me watching him. But suddenly I'm falling, like Hades has reached up from the Underworld and is trying to pull me back down.

I fall hard on my shoulder, and spin onto my back as Hector lunges toward me with a furious fist. I roll to avoid him, and manage to lock my feet around his legs and bring him crashing down as well.

"Oy!" Zotos yells. "Enough fucking around, both of you." We stare up at him from the shame of the floor. Even the Trojan boys shrug away our feud, preferring to stick with cleaning. I realize we both look like fools. At least my Greeks are happily in their hot showers, though.

"Strategos," I complain, "*he* came at *me*." But immediately I regret saying a word. Zotos is not the type to care about excuses.

"Ten miles, outside, both of you." We remain on the floor, not moving. Maybe if I pretend I'm hurt? "Now!" Zotos screams.

I avoided running past the accountants' window, but that

meant the only other Hector-free route was on the Domino's side. I know I shouldn't be returning to the scene of the crime, but I did anyway. I stood over the sight of Jesús' attack behind the dumpster, and glanced around the brick wall and concrete ground in the breezy spring light. The ground had a little bit of discoloration, like there had been an oil spill or something. But of course it was blood from those two guys who'd attacked Jesús.

No one had been here, at least not to clean it. I followed the memory of the attack, and caught a glimpse of a loose tooth lying on the concrete; blood encrusted on its ripped-out root. Looking around to check I was alone, I picked it up, slipped past the dumpster, and kept on jogging around the wide, Houston block. At the farthest point of my run, I bent down to untie and then re-tie my shoelace, and dropped the tooth down the drain.

Back at the gym, the boys had already been picked up by their parents, and since it's Sunday, the Brazilian Capoeira guy is setting up for his soon-to-arrive class. Hector's already sitting at Zotos' desk, sucking down a sports drink as Zotos steadfastly ignores him, making notes in a printed spreadsheet through half-rimmed glasses with all the grace and airs of a Nevada boxing coach. He notices me come in, but doesn't look up. But he does fling me a bottle of sports drink which I catch, open with my teeth, and I pull the chair a decent distance away from Hector before sitting down.

"Listen up, knuckleheads," Zotos growls, flinging his pen down on the crowded desk and whipping off his half-moon glasses. "You're going up against each other at Regionals in Houston next month."

"But, strategos," Hector complains, "I'm in the two hundred-and fourteen-pound class. The competition is a few weeks away, how is Achilles meant to lose all that weight before—"

"Shut up, Hector," Zotos snarls. "The coach from Team USA will be watching, and I do his taxes. You understand what I'm saying?"

"Yes, strategos," we both say, although I answer a bit quicker.

"You two cause a scene like that out there at Regionals, then neither of you will be going to Nationals and I'll have bribed an Olympic coach for nothing, you hear?"

Hector and I swap an uncomfortable look. Zotos was nothing if not a Greek. Rooting around in the mud and dirt to get one of us a straight shot to the Olympics, then holding it over us like Damocles' sword.

"Now, Achilles, can you handle this and your GED?"

"I can, yes."

"Cause if not, you can wait and qualify for a competition in the fall."

"And keep me on parole till then? No way. I'll be fine. Jesús is helping me study."

"He's a good kid," Zotos cracks a smile. "He's waiting for you over in the office, says he hasn't seen you all week?"

"Oh, I, uh—"

"Cause if you're not keeping up with your studies—"

"No, I am. I'm going there right now to study with him."

"Good," Zotos says, standing up. "Now, fuck off, the pair of you."

Our chairs clatter and scrape loudly across the linoleum floor as we trudge to the locker room, two big lions in the one small cage.

"Fight with your boyfriend?"

"Fuck off, Hector." We step into the locker room, empty except for the remnants of fifty teenagers having showered and changed half an hour ago. Although Giorgos is sitting on a bench, a towel wrapped around his waist. He stands up quickly, looking shocked at seeing us both, as if he was only waiting for Hector. I smirk, finally feeling like I've got one thing over him. "Huh, seems like your boyf—"

The punch comes hard and heavy from behind. Hector strikes me on my left jaw line. The punch vibrates around my skull, ringing in my ears. I turn, angrily, lumbering, ready to thump him hard. But he dodges the attack, and suddenly the world goes black and tight around my eyes. Giorgos has whipped a towel over my head and pulls it back, hard, so I stumble backward.

"Fucking faggot," Hector says, grabbing the skin of my singlet and ripping it in two. Now I'm blind and naked. My arms flap around without cause, trying in vain to catch Giorgos behind me or Hector in front. "Look at that fat belly." Hector laughs, slapping my stomach hard from both sides as Giorgos laughs behind me.

I suck in a tricky breath through the wet towel and try to regain some balance. Giorgos keeps pulling me backward, but the hard edge of the towel chokes me and makes it near impossible to not stagger around. But I strike out with my right foot, where I think Hector is, and my heel hits his thigh. He grunts and I hear him stumble into the lockers. Progress. I then whack an elbow backward and sideways, and strike Giorgos in the ribs. I can hear him fall back, but I'm not quick enough to get my hands up and remove the towel before Hector slams me into the wall, and the side of my face ricochets against the concrete. Couldn't he have thrown me into a locker?

I stumble worse this time, the dark world dizzying around me. I hear them both laughing. Giorgos' laugh is strained though, I've winded him. Fuck the towel, I can sense where they are. I lunge forward, arms outstretched ready to grab whatever I can by the throat, but then I smack straight into a wall of ice.

The coldness burns from head to foot, and I feel like I'm drowning as the soaking towel sticks to my mouth and nose. Hector and Giorgos shriek with laughter in a crescendo. Only after a few throbbing beats do I feel the sharp cuts inflicted by the chunks of ice in the bucket of freezing water they hurled at my body.

Finally, I whip off the towel and suck in a desperate breath. Giorgos is dancing around in nothing but a jockstrap, his eyes wild like fire as he films the entirety of this encounter on his phone. He's still filming; moving the phone in and out and side to side to capture every inch of this carefully planned humiliation. Hector is a more sensible few steps back. I'll need to go through Giorgos to get to him. But that I have no problem with.

"Ha, ha!" Giorgos cries like a harpie, "TokTok is loving this. Hey…wait a minute, isn't that his girlfriend?"

I stop dead. Giorgos leans over to show Hector the screen. Hector burrows his face, and then it starts to split into vicious laughter like an earthquake.

"'Two years in jail,'" he reads, "'and he still can't get it up. Guess I've turned another one.'"

Giorgos turns the phone around to show me, but from a safe distance. It's a selfie of Carla in the car with the same clothes she was wearing last night, the words in gray across the screen. In fact, it's a picture from her car in my driveway.

"Hey, don't worry, Achilles," Hector says with a fake concern, "if you can't drill that *chica*, I'll *happily* do it for you."

Giorgos can wait. In fact, he can keep filming for all I care. I leap forward in my torn singlet, but I don't give a shit. Hector is within striking distance and I take the shot. My shoulder slams into his chest, but I don't stop. I keep going. We both careen into the wall, him first. Hector's body crunches against an immovable force. One foot to the right and I would have got him on the corner entrance to the showers. I curse myself that I missed. But I whack him against the wall again, give him one punch in the stomach, and then raise my fist to smack him right in the face.

"Stop!" he pleads, coughing and clasping his belly. I don't know why I would. I thump him hard in the face. Not too hard, but enough that he'll know not to do this to me again. But in the corner of my eye, I can see Giorgos dancing around like an evil fawn, still filming. Hector notices him too, and starts to groan and gargle as if I've slashed his belly open.

And then I realize what they've done.

Hector throws a bloody grin my way, his teeth stained red and he laughs. Slowly, I back away.

"You're fucking going away for this, Achilles. Fucking assault."

"Unprovoked assault," Giorgos throws in, getting a close-up of Hector dramatically sliding down the wall and leaning over to spit out blood, then panning to me standing over his battered body, my skin soaking, flaming red in anger.

Suddenly Giorgos starts to pant, kneeling down while filming with the phone as Hector pretends to drift in and out of consciousness.

"Oh my God..." Giorgos shrieks, "look what he's done. Look at what this animal's done to Hector."

I suck in a deep breath and calm myself. I want this to come from a place of serenity. I approach the two of them as Giorgos nips backward, out of my way, but the camera still trained on me. I kneel down and help Hector sit up. He spits out blood again. But it's really only red tinged saliva.

"Hector," I say, with one hand on his shoulder. "If I'm going away again," I whack my other hand on his other shoulder too, and gently move my hands to meet in the middle. "I'm going to make it worth my fucking while."

He starts to choke. Genuinely. His hands grab onto my wrists but he's in the wrong position to get out of a stranglehold. I squeeze hard, holding his windpipe closed. Giorgos is filming, but suddenly stops.

"Hector?" he says. This is clearly not how it was meant to go. "Hector!"

Hector meanwhile is turning a funny shade of blue. His

eyes are starting to engorge, almost pop out of their sockets while he desperately tries to scratch at my arms. But they won't budge. I've got them locked hard, kneeling over him with his legs trapped under mine.

"Hector!" Giorgos cries out again. He lunges for me, but with his precious phone in hand there's little he can do but scratch at my back like a fly on a horse. His Hector is now a lovely purple. Just like the color of the bruises he's left me with.

"What the fuck's going on here?" Zotos calls out. Immediately, I let Hector go and jump back. He sucks in a raspy, ravenous breath. Coughing and spluttering on the floor. Giorgos, still in just his jockstrap and holding the phone, bounces to attention, but Zotos' fury is trained on me. Partially naked and red and angry and caught red-handed choking his other star pupil. Zotos emerges forward like a leviathan moving to the sounds of Hector's hoarse coughs. But he swishes past me and straight to Giorgos. Zotos lays his palm out, expecting the phone. Giorgos can only comply.

With more strength than I've ever seen on a man, Zotos crushes the phone inside one hand. Giorgos, me, even Hector stop and stare as the glass and plastic crinkles and shatters as he closes his hand into a complete fist, eyes never leaving Giorgos. Then he flings the mangled device into the shower room and it scatters useless and lifeless across the damp tiles. Zotos turns away from Giorgos in disgust.

"Next time," Zotos says to Hector while stepping over his still-recovering body. "I'll let him kill you."

Chapter 15
Phobos and Deimos in Southeast Texas

Jesús pours me a large soda from the mini fridge in the back of the office as I recount the story from that morning. I swivel on the chair at the desk next to his, my feet on top of the table because why not? It's Sunday and no one else is here.

"So they set you up?"

"Yeah," I say, gratefully taking the large cup from him and drinking deeply. "That fucking Hector. He's desperate to get me out of the competition. Even if that means putting me back in juvie."

"Why?"

"Because he's a dick. He knows I can beat him, and whoever wins at Regionals will qualify for Nationals and is pretty much guaranteed a place in the Olympics. Zotos made sure of that. "

"I hate that these dickheads can keep hanging this prison thing over you all the time. It's like you're free but not really."

"The sword of Damocles," I say, re-crossing my legs on the table as Jesús sits back on his chair to listen. "That's the allusion you're looking for. Damocles was a brown-noser at the court of the king of Syracuse, Dionysius, and always talking about what an easy job the king had. So one day Dionysius offers to switch places with Damocles. Suddenly Damocles finds himself on the throne, surrounded by all the luxuries any ancient king could want. But above the throne hangs a sword held up by a single hair from a horse's tail. If he makes one wrong move. Bangs the table too hard or even a gust of wind from an open window could bring the sword crashing down on Damocles and split him in two."

"Sounds like the American justice system," Jesús says. "My Mom went to get gas one night. She only went at night, somehow she thought it was safer than going in the day. Someone rear-ended her at the gas station. And a police car just happened to be driving by. They stopped to make sure everyone was all right and...and then she was gone. Stolen away by ICE." Jesús smacks the ledgers closed and rubs his forehead.

"They're monsters. Fascists," I say, but it doesn't help. None of it can. To live inside the racial dystopia where most people don't care because it doesn't affect them is the hardest thing of all. It's like being dead, but everyone sees you as awake. Or sitting on a throne, but no one can see the sword hanging above your head.

"No, the real monster is Hector, who wanted to entrap you into being sucked back into prison. It's those guys who beat me up then threatened to turn you in."

"You don't think the State...ICE, the police, they're not at fault? You don't blame Hitler for giving the orders?"

"And the Nazis for carrying them out, yes," Jesús says. "But it was ordinary people who made that happen.

Ordinary Germans who either agreed, or didn't care, or couldn't be bothered to disagree."

I think carefully about his point. I can't say I disagree.

"Mind if I use that in my social studies essay?"

"By all means. You're going to ace it anyway. You should apply to college."

"One step at a time, Jesús buddy."

He smiles and it lights up his face, and mine. It's the first time I've sat with him properly, as friends, since coming out of the Underworld. But it hasn't broken our connection, it only made it stronger. The longer I sit here watching him, the less I ever want to leave.

"I ran past the dumpster this morning. I found one of their teeth. And there's still blood residue on the ground."

"What did you do?"

"Dropped the tooth down the drain, but I don't know…if they go and bring forensics or something. I guess there's not so many places to hide. They've got every piece of DNA on me, and forever."

"Just say Zotos made you and Hector take your fight outside, and that's how your DNA got there," Jesús says with a knowing smirk.

"How would you know we were fighting if you weren't there?"

"I could say I saw on the cameras."

"Zotos has cameras here?"

"Everywhere."

"What?" I stand up, looking around to see that I'm not also being watched right now.

"Calm down! Zotos has the gym covered by security

cameras set up in here." I follow him into the back of the small office unit, into Zotos's private room, although it's hardly private. The door is wide open and the desk, the bookcase and the floor, is overflowing with box files. So it's basically the store room for the firm.

"Look," Jesús says, tapping on the keyboard to wake up the screen. And there it is; the entirety of the gym, and the back entrance, covered by six security cameras. We stand for a moment, watching the Capoeira class move with far more grace than us wrestlers. "Best thing about it is you can zoom in," Jesús says, scrolling with the mouse to hone in on the tall, muscled instructor.

"Is that what you do all day? Sit and perv on us in the gym?"

"Maybe," Jesús replies with a smirk. "But, hey, you're welcome to watch me write numbers into a spreadsheet for five hours a day."

Suddenly, I feel bad for the week of silence I've imposed on him. It feels selfish of me. Unfair. Like I was punishing him for…being himself. I don't like how that feels.

"Look, Jesús, I'm really sorry about how I acted this week. It was super unfair of me to—"

"Hey," he puts his finger over his mouth and shakes his head. "Don't. No apologies needed. I'm sure after Odysseus got out of Hades he needed a bit of a breather, too."

"You read it!"

"I read the Wikipedia page, Achilles, let's not get carried away." He pulls his phone out of his pocket and starts flipping through apps to find the place where he was reading about *The Odyssey.* But as he flicks through recent apps, I spot a familiar picture.

"Isn't that Carla's TikTok?" I say.

He looks sheepish, like he's been caught.

"Um, yeah. Sorry. I screenshotted it. Kind of felt like a big deal, you know. I guess I should say congratulations on coming out." But he can't say it with a straight face, and a split second later we're in fits of laughter inside Zotos' office, as the computer screen cycles through six different angles of Brazilian Capoeira.

"I guess she's not *pothos*, then."

"Nope," I say with a firm nod. "And if it turns out she is then I quit. I'd rather go back to the Styx than try that again…yeesh."

"So we're still zero for four?"

"Well," I say, hopping onto Zotos's desk and nudging Jesús with my swinging leg. "I think I've made some progress. I pissed off my Dad yesterday."

"That's *aidos*, right?"

"Yeah. At least I assume so. He wanted me to come and be an alibi or a lookout or do some illegal shit with him. I told him where to go."

"Wow, that's…amazing. Well done!" Jesús taps my leg in a "good for you" gesture, but leaves his hand there on my swinging kneecap.

"It just didn't *feel* like defeating something, you know? Like, how do I know if I've done one of them or not?"

"Well, maybe you don't do them one at a time. Maybe it's cumulative, you know. Do one, and then next one and the next and the next, and then at some point Hades will just pop out of the ground and be like 'hey, Achilles, good job.'"

"Yeah, maybe." Although I had the strongest sense it would not be that easy. In fact, it sort of felt like I was going backward. Rising to the bait with Hector, pushing Carla out instead of talking with her, and then basically telling Dad just fuck off instead of actually confronting him about his behavior.

"At least you know what to do with one of them, though," Jesús says with a grin trying to cheer me up. "The blood feud is with Hector. And you guys are going to be fighting each other. That must be it. Unless you've got some other mortal enemy waiting around."

"No, he's the main one."

I guess Jesús is right. Hector is the very definition of blood feud. *Alastor.* It's not that we just have the names of two diametrically opposed heroes, as people, we're the exact opposite. How I treat the kids in my team versus how he yells at his. We both want victory, but at very different costs.

"First weekend in June in Houston," I say, for no other reason than to put a finality to the date of this quarter of the deal with Hades. "Do you want to…you know, come and watch?"

Jesús looks stunned. He has to find his own corner of the desk to lean on, like I've tumbled the ground beneath him and he can't trust his legs anymore.

"I'd love to come. Yeah."

"Good chance for you to watch wrestling in real life instead of through Zotos' security cameras."

Jesús blushes, but I'm only teasing.

"Hey, that's the day after your GED!"

"Yeah, I know. Thank fuck. I can get both parole conditions over with, in one weekend. Then I'm free to go murder Hector in his sleep."

"Shh, don't say that." Jesús gives me a playful slap on my arm.

"Since we're going to be in Houston that weekend…" I edge closer to him on the desk and give him a nudge in the shoulder. "How about we hit those drag bars on Saturday night? Celebrate all that freedom."

Jesús looks beside himself. But then a flash of reality whacks him in the back of the head and he deflates.

"Senior prom is that Saturday night." I also deflate. "Before you say anything, I already asked Mrs. McKenna if you can go and she said of course you can come."

I snort out a laugh. Of all the things on my mind these last few years, I can't say senior prom was ever one of them.

"Think Carla will still want a gay guy as her date?" I say with a broad grin. Jesús looks bashful, and I can't understand why. We sit quietly for moments that stretch into minutes. Watching the floor, then the computer screen, then the names on the folders on the boxes, anything to avoid looking at each other. The weight of being alone together is pressing down on both of us, I can feel it.

It's Jesús who breaks the silence threatening to evolve into something awkward. "Shall we get to studying? I'm pretty much done with work stuff for today." He makes to move out of Zotos' office, into the rows of empty desks which feel far less private, less intimate. Like nothing at all could happen out there. Not like in here. I grab his arm as he seeks to get past me.

"Jesús, I am sorry about what happened this week. About how I behaved by ignoring you. It wasn't fair. It's not okay."

"Aki…honestly, it's fine." He wriggles out of my grasp. "The cabin was…well, you know. We'd both had a lot to drink. We'd just survived the fucking weirdest experience of our lives…and well, you're hot. So with all that going on, no wonder you felt a bit confused and stuff. It's totally fine, and it's totally normal. It can just be what it was. A fun kiss, I don't expect anything more, okay? I…just don't want you to feel uncomfortable around me, you know? 'Cause I really love being friends with you." He gives me a light, bro-style punch in the arm. "And I really wanna watch you mop the floor with Hector's ass at Regionals."

"Jesús," I stare into his big brown eyes. The slim, strong-willed face that I'm sure has broken the hearts of a thousand guys. But every time he looks at me this way—no, every time he looks at me ever—it's with this chained longing. Like he's some poor broke homeless kid staring through an ice cream store's window. I seize his wrist, just like I did in the cabin last week. My fingers encircle it completely, cuffing him. He can't run. He can't sit outside and gape and watch any more. I can't stand it.

"I'm not confused," I say, holding his gaze with mine. Holding his wrist, nudging him closer to me. He's reluctant, he doesn't want to come, to break the spell. But I must. I can't bear who I am without him. If there's an invisible sword hanging above my head which could go snap at any point, I can't live without having his lips on mine one more time.

"I'm not confused at all," I say again. "In fact, I don't think I've ever been thinking clearer."

I pull him toward me, and it's like raising an anchor from the deep. Everything inside him says this can't be true. And I know what he feels, it's written all over his face. In what world does the geek fall for the jock? Or the Greek for the Mexican? But I don't care, and finally, neither does Jesús. With my fingers still closed around his wrist, now he follows my lead and swerves into me, like a magnet finding its other half.

Once again, our lips meet and tongues merge in a circle of memory of the things we've done and the things we might. The places we've been, the places we haven't. The promise of a lifetime wrapped up in a pair of soft lips as my hand slips down the small of this back.

From the edges of the office door, I hear the groan and tinkle of the bell announcing someone has arrived. But I don't care if Zotos wanders all the way into his office and sees us here together. He can stand at the doorway all he likes, watching my fingers run through Jesús' soft brown hair, gently tugging at the roots as my tongue swerves inside his mouth, as his stomach rubs against mine, as my hand falls further down the line of beauty that is his back. Zotos got me into all this mess with Hector; so I'll kiss whoever I want in his office.

"Well, well, well..." a dark-lit voice, caustic and

spiteful, calls out. It isn't Zotos. It isn't even Hector. "If it isn't Achilles Konstantinos." It's the voice of a Beast.

I know this Beast. Anderson. That he's a dick is a given. Casually cruel, nonsensically nasty; mean because he thinks that's the job description of a guy working at a juvenile penitentiary. As far as I know, he wasn't one of the worst ones. The guys who kept a whiteboard of who they were going to fuck with that week. The ones who took bets on which kid would attempt suicide, then do everything in and out of their power to win that t+en-buck stake.

He wasn't the worst, no, but he certainly was one of the ordinary ones. The "only following orders" type. The Nazi guards who live till ninety before being sentenced to community service. What he's doing here in Zotos's office though, him and an older Black guy with a bushy gray mustache who couldn't look more like a TV detective if he tried. It's only then I realize Anderson is in a police costume. That's odd, I think, why would a Beast pretend to be a police officer?

"Jesús Iguardo Alvarez?" the Black man asks. Jesús nods, and I hold him into me. They're not taking him anywhere. "I'm Detective Jones and this is Deputy Anderson. Mind if we ask you a few questions?"

"And the other one," Anderson adds, as if he's afraid the detective will forget about me.

"Of course. If you two wouldn't mind," Detective Jones says, stepping out of Zotos' personal office followed by Anderson who throws an evil smirk my way.

For a brief moment, we're alone, Jesús and I, and the fear overcomes me. I'm frozen to the desk, which is unfortunate because I need to vomit. But I swallow it down, I don't want Jesús to think it was because I kissed him. It scalds my throat.

"It'll be fine," Jesús whispers, squeezing my thigh and staring deep with his big brown eyes. Oh, how easier life would be if I could only trust those eyes. "It's going to be okay. It's probably nothing."

"Jesús, that guy worked at juvie. He knows me."

"So what? You haven't done anything wrong," he says it, but we both know it's not strictly true.

And tell that to *deimos*. Abject terror does not respond to logic. In fact, reasoning tends to make terror worse, because the deepest fears, like the greatest myths, always contain a grain of truth. We are afraid to die because we know death is inevitable. We fear pain because pain is always just one trip away. And I fear Anderson, because I know the promise the Beasts made as I left. I'll be back. Now two men with guns and handcuffs have come to make that happen.

Only because there's no back exit from Zotos' office, I follow Jesús out into the main room where the two officers have already pulled up two chairs to a desk. My heart thwacks like a pneumatic drill, banging so hard they must be able to hear it. Sweat drips down the crack in my spine, a steady stream polling around my ass which Jesús nudges into a chair so we are sitting opposite the two officers, only six feet of carpet between us, no space to run.

"How do you know Zotos Kalanasis?" Detective Jones

asks Jesús, hands sunk into the pockets of his tan suit. He's wearing a holster across his chest, a leather hide which likely contains a six-shooter. This is Texas after all. It takes a moment longer for me to understand what he's asking. It's not about me. But Zotos.

"I, uh, work for him," Jesús says with a straight face that makes me think dealing with the police is something he's well versed in. I feel one ounce more relaxed. Like I'm in the hands of a professional.

"Doing what, exactly?" Detective Jones asks, his face still as cool as all get up. Anderson is the dogsbody scribbling notes down with a stubby pencil. I like this change of scenery for him. He must've thought torturing kids in juvie was small potatoes compared to his potential on the force. And now he's got the badge and the gun, he's stuck taking notes. It makes me smile.

"Odd jobs around the office," Jesús continues. "Cleaning and tidying, double checking figures sometimes. I'm going to CalTech in the fall. Numbers are kind of my thing."

"Oh yeah?" Detective Jones says with a kind smile I can't see as being anything but genuine. "Well, good for you, son. That's really great." Anderson coughs loudly, as if pushing Jones to the point. "Are you aware of Mr. Kalanasis' whereabouts last Friday night?"

"Last Friday? Uh, no. I don't think so. I wasn't working here then, actually. I was working over at the Domino's across the parking lot."

Detective Jones and Officer Anderson share a telling glance, and Jesús and I share a worried one. Jones winds his hand in front of Anderson. Anderson sighs as he flicks back through his notebook.

"'We're going to kill that fucking fag,'" Anderson says, causing both Jesús and I to sit back in our chairs. "'He's a dead man walking. We're gonna cut him into little faggot pieces and put him through a meat grinder.'"

Anderson finishes his quotes and looks back at us, slightly bored, but Detective Jones is wide awake.

"Do these quotes sound familiar to you, Jesús? Or to you, Achilles?" We both shake our heads. But I feel there's far more to it than that. "This is what multiple witnesses who were in the vicinity of the parking lot last Friday night heard two young men say as in regards to a young Hispanic man who worked at the Domino's. Those two men were later found badly injured after their friends in the parking lot reported what they'd said to us, fearing something awful had happened to the Domino's employee. Said employee could not be located or identified. He didn't appear in any hospital records in the entire county. Not even in the immigrant-friendly ones. We were starting to think some kind of Batman was responsible for saving this kid and laying out justice on those two attackers." Detective Jones gave a half grin, which Anderson only politely returns when he sees his boss looking right at him. "Jesús, are you that victim?"

Detective Jones sits forward on the chair, suit jacket closing around him, and he even reaches back to tap the notebook in Anderson's hand. Tellingly, Anderson puts it away in his pocket. "I want you to trust me, Jesús. We're not working with ICE out here. No one's reporting you to anyone."

"He's an American," I say loudly, angry that an authority would even make the suggestion that reporting a crime would endanger one's life and liberty. Furious at the fact they even have to say so. Jesús pats my leg softly.

"They jumped on me, yes. I was taking the garbage out the back down to the dumpster, and when I turned around, they were standing there."

"And they attacked you?"

"Yeah." Jesús responds quietly. I can almost hear each of our heart beats in this silence of the room still with tension. A hurricane warning system would be sounding a full-on alarm at this drastic drop in atmospheric pressure.

"And now you work for Mr. Kalanasis."

Jesús nods.

"Son, we've got multiple witnesses saying they saw a large man carrying someone out of the alley where the two attackers were found, and then into a car. And now you work for Mr. Kalanasis. Jesús, did Zotos Kalanasis rescue you and attack those two boys who beat you up?"

Now I fear for Zotos. It was my actions. My decision to beat them within an inch of their sorry lives instead of just helping Jesús.

"I—" I start to say, but Jesús cuts me off. The cops eye me up.

"No, it wasn't Zotos."

"Son," Detective Jones says again, leaning so close he might slip off the chair. "You can tell us the truth. Nothing is going to happen to him if he did help you. The DA is not going to charge the man who saved a young kid from a hate crime in progress. And no jury or judge in this state is going to let a man stand trial for defending a child from assault. He could've shot them both in the face and he'd most likely be rewarded by the governor."

"Nothing?" I snap. "Nothing will happen?" I say it with indignant anger, but I genuinely want to know.

"Well, not ultimately, no. There might be a spot of legal bother first of all. We might have to take a statement, or those boys could sue him in civil court, although I highly doubt they'd win a cent."

"So, not nothing," I reply.

"Nothing to someone who's done nothing wrong," Anderson snaps back. I shift uncomfortably on the uncomfortable chair. Not nothing to someone out on parole, is what I hear.

"Son," Jones starts up again. "If Zotos helped you, you need to tell us."

"Yeah," Anderson adds with a snarl. "So who carried you out of the alley if not him, then? Must've been someone who knows how to put two kids in hospital. Possibly someone who owns a wrestling gym? Or someone who's a wrestler. Hey, Achilles, isn't one of your parole conditions to return to the wrestling team?" Anderson asks, but he already knows it's true.

He stares at me, smirking the way Beasts do. When they're proud of themselves for banning a kid's book, or tricking a kid into losing his visiting privileges when their dying mother is waiting to see them. The usual trickstery shit. I know I'm going back inside. I can feel it. I can feel all the things they're not saying. The video footage from some forgotten camera, a sliver of DNA, a confession from one of Jesús' attackers. I know how Beasts talk. Change the uniform, but you can't change the man. A thug's a thug, even if he's got a badge and a gun. I suck in a deep, shivering breath. I can't keep this tension. I feel like I'm drowning. Hector and Giorgos have thrown a wet towel around my face and are hosing freezing water straight into my mouth. I can't breathe.

"It was m—"

"His dad," Jesús cuts right in, surprising the two officers who've been watching me sweat profusely as I prepare for my confession. I whip round to stare at Jesús, but he's not looking at me. I could've not existed for all the attention he pays me. "Aki doesn't want to say, of course, he doesn't want to get his dad in trouble. His dad's a bit of a gangster, you know."

"Yes," Detective Jones agrees, "we're familiar with Christos Konstantinos. But don't worry, son," he says to both of us, "this will never get back to your dad. I promise."

I know what the promise of a police officer is worth. About the same as the compassion of a Beast, but Jesús is playing the game like a grandmaster.

"Oh, thank you, Detective. I was just so afraid, you know?" Jesús crosses his legs like he's wearing a tight skirt and lightly fans himself; playing up to every stereotype these two officers can imagine. His accent even seems to have taken on a deeper southern twinge like he's a Carolina dame.

"Those brutes heaved upon me. Young Achilles was

sitting in the Domino's the whole time. He'd come to take me home, him and his dad, that is. I'm tutoring him for his GED and these streets are just so dangerous for a boy like me. Anyway, Achilles was watching the store for me while I took the trash down—remind me to get that camera footage for you—and his Dad was waiting down there in the car. He must've seen those two guys come after me, because in a flash he was there, rescuing me."

"And why didn't you go to the hospital?" Jones asks.

"Well, Mr. Konstantinos took me back to Achilles' house and his mom patched me up. She didn't think I needed it. And then his dad, his wonderful, selfless dad, asked his brother Zotos to take me on as a junior, so I can save for college."

"Well," Detective Jones stands up, placing his hands back in his pockets and nodding at us both. "That clears things up. At least your father was there to look out for you and your friend. Thank you, son," he says to Jesús, "for telling us the truth. I know it can't be easy for you, being the way you are and all."

Jesús nods like it's his cross to bear. I can see the lines on his lips threatening to burst into laughter, but he plays the part of the damsel in distress like a movie star.

"And Achilles, I'm sorry for…what happened to you, too. Our department should have done better. We let a DA get carried away in an election year. Unfortunately, jailing thugs is a vote winner."

"Usually a vote winner," I respond. The DA that prosecuted me lost his election.

"Usually, yes. But we should have seen through that

flimsy evidence. I hope you know though we've sent all the case files to New York. There's a team at Columbia working on taking your appeal to federal court."

"So I hear."

"Well, anyway. Leave the rest to us. *This* DA will be charging your attackers with a hate crime, that's for sure." Jones shakes my hand, and then Jesús', who clasps it lightly and nods quietly like he's Mother Theresa. "Anderson?"

The Beast stands up, glaring daggers at me. He leans into Jones' ear and says:

"Sir, it's him. He did this, I know. He probably even beat up the poor gay kid then turned on the other two. He's an animal."

Jones nods, but the smirk on his face tells us both he doesn't care for a word of it.

"Enjoy your Sunday, gentlemen."

"Wait," I say, standing up and taking a step closer to Anderson. "Am I free to go?"

"Free to go?" Jones doesn't understand. "Son, you're not under arrest. We just came to ask you a few questions."

"Sir," Anderson is pleading. "Please, we should take him in for questioning. I know this kid, I'm telling you."

With a look of abject resignation, I lift up my hands like I'm waiting to be cuffed. I even lower my head for dramatic effect.

"Anderson!" Jones snaps, visibly shocked by my meekness. "These are victims, not suspects."

"But, sir," I address him directly, lifting my sad puppy eyes to his baffled face. "I'm sorry I ain't been doing my exercises like you taught me. Do you need to inspect me again, like you used to in prison?" I lower my hands down to my pants and start to edge down the waistband. I can hear Jesús' shock out loud. Jones is astonished, but Anderson… Well, his face is worth a thousand words.

"Keep your pants on, son," Jones demands, shaking his head and turning for the door. Anderson glares at me, terrified, before rushing to catch up with his detective.

"Sir, I don't know what he's talking about—"

"I always knew you were a sick fuck, Anderson."

The door twinkles open, and the officers leave, far more disturbed than when they came in. I turn to Jesús, a gigantic grin across my face as he is still in shock.

"Achilles…is that true?"

"As true as my dad rescuing you. What, you think a Greek doesn't know how to act in a tragedy?"

Jesús can't quite compute it all, but he doesn't need to. We've defeated a demon, I'm sure of that. *Deimos* can go fuck itself, I think, as Jesús launches off the chair and flies into my arms.

Chapter 16
Uninvited Guests

What do you call the bit when you're falling in love? It's not the actual being in love, or maybe it is, I don't know because I've never felt love. Well, obviously love from my mom and stuff, but this is totally different. Love mixed with desire. With longing. With…whatever it is that pumps through our heart each and every time we lay eyes on the person whom we're falling for.

From the gym to studying together in the office…to making out in the office when no one else is around…to the pair of us keeping Lynette company in exchange for a free pizza…to getting lost in studying as the hours tick into night and then making out on the floor of Zotos' office with the door closed.

Halcyon days drifted into Elysium weeks. And as spring yawned into summer, I began to feel what it was to be happy. Not just to survive, not just to move through the motions like I'd done with Carla and our *friends* back in the days before I went away, but to have a genuine smile split across my face as I fall asleep at night. My tired mind no longer had to be filled with the epic fantasies of glorious revolutions because I had something else to hold onto at nights: the first springs of love. And sometimes, but only on the weekends, sometimes Mom would see us in my room, with the books stacked high on the desk, and do the dutiful Mom duty of asking Jesús if he'd like to stay for dinner, and to stay over, as if she didn't also know he had nowhere better to be.

I knew our time was limited. I knew things would end, like all things do. But like death, it felt so far away as to not be worth bothering about. What's the fall to someone so infatuated with the first shoots of summer love?

The GED was creeping closer, but Jesús and I both knew I was more prepared than I needed to be. "You're not dumb, Achilles," he always said, "but you're exceedingly handsome." Then, his hand would slide up my shirt and grip all the bits of me I used to hate, and he'd kiss me through a smile and make me love myself that little bit more because he loved me. And I wanted to love everything he did. If that meant watching his favorite episodes of *Drag Race* on my laptop in my bed in the middle of the night, one air pod each, and chewing our lips so we didn't laugh out loud, then so be it.

And if for him it meant watching YouTube videos of wrestling moves, freezing frames so I could analyze and scribble down each movement of a winning combination, then for Jesús, so be it. In fact, watching wrestling videos, he did not mind at all.

"Can I watch you try your singlet on again?" Jesús asks from the desk. I'm lying on the bed, finishing another round of equations, but willing to be distracted.

"You already saw me with my singlet on," I say, stretching out on the bed in only my shorts and a vest. He swings around on the desk chair, unsatisfied with my answer.

"I know I saw you with it *on,* I want to see you *try* it on. Regionals are in a week, you don't want to make sure it fits?" His grin tells me everything I need to know about what's going through his mind. I sigh and slap the book shut. I know what he's after. I know what he wants. And I want it too, but there's a fear bubbling underneath. The fear of the first time. What will happen? How will it change us? With so much already weighing on my mind, the thought of sex is one more distraction I don't think I can handle, even though it's all I can think about. I stretch my upper body off the bed as if I'm doing pushups again, as Jesús leans toward me and our lips meet in midair. I nuzzle my face in the softness of his shoulder, his skin as delicate as crushed velvet. He smells like a river, and I want to bathe in it forever.

"You ever think about what's going to happen?" Jesús asks, kissing my cheek as I groan like a bear reaching for a honeypot.

"You mean with the GED next Friday?"

"No, silly." He kisses my cheek again. I know what he's talking about. But the further I get away from the insanity of Hades, the less real it feels.

"Honestly Jesús, I don't even believe it's going to happen. Or happened. Or I don't know…maybe it did happen, but how is Hades going to bring someone back from the dead? And then what, put him back in prison? I don't understand. I can't even think it's real. And anyway…" I kiss his lips and bite the bottom one and don't let go.

"Why are you so worried about me? Aren't all your other boyfriends getting jealous with all the time we're spending together?"

"Other boyfriends! I wish."

"You wish?"

"No, I didn't mean…" Jesús starts to flush red again and it makes me giggle. I pull him forward on my chair, pull up his T-shirt and blow the biggest raspberry ever on his stomach. "Stop!" He cries through tears and pushes me off and I roll back on the bed, running my hand up my own shirt, edging it away from my body, but it doesn't distract him from his phone. "See?"

"See what? The folder is empty."

"All the apps are gone. And all the boyfriends with it."

"When did you do that?"

"When we drove back home from your uncle's cabin. That's when I realized I can't imagine myself with anyone else. Now, I've been to Dallas with a guy before, but I've never been to literal Hell and back."

I fall back on the bed, hand draped over my head and sigh out all the weight on my shoulders, but it only makes me feel heavier.

"If it was just these fucking parole conditions," I say to the ceiling, "but it's Hades. And not just Hades but the police, and my dad, and Carla, and Hector, and…" My heart starts to pound, thick and fast. I can't catch my breath. It's short, shallow, I can't suck in any air.

"Hey," Jesús says, moving across to the bed. He reaches down and starts to rub my feet. "It's going to be okay. I promise you."

"I just don't know what will happen if I fail. I don't even know how to succeed."

"I guess you'll know when Marcus arrives." Jesús says it with sadness. His face is pointed at my toes, but I can feel the drop in pressure. The fall in excitement. The realization that what we're fighting for is the return of a man I already admitted to loving. Where is that going to leave Jesús?

Mom knocks on the door and Jesús drops my foot mid-rub and grabs the book I was looking at before. He's holding it upside down. She only gives us a second before coming in.

"Dinner will be ready soon," she says, going straight for the laundry basket. "Are you staying tonight, *hey-zeus*?"

"I told you he is, Mom. The GED is next Friday we've got tons to do."

"All right, I'm only asking. But sort this room out in the morning because the twins are coming tomorrow and it's impossible to keep them out of here."

"Fine, Mom," I tell her as she heads back out, closing the door behind her.

"You really don't need to do that much more studying, Aki," Jesús says.

"I know," I grab his chest and pull him on top of me as he starts to shriek, until I cover his mouth to keep him quiet while kissing his neck. "But I don't want you going anywhere."

"Mom, why are there four place settings?" But she's busy

slicing off ribbons of meat from her kebab cooker with an electric saw and doesn't hear. "I don't want to eat with Dad."

Suddenly the doorbell rings. Jesús is in the bathroom, and I drag myself reluctantly to the door, stealing myself for the face of my father.

"Mrs. McKenna," I say with shock, not just because it's her, but because of how she's dressed. Her braids, normally tied back and out of her face, have been undone and fall down over a colorful blouse, one I could never imagine her wearing to school.

"Oh, Achilles," she says, as if she wasn't expecting to see me, either. She comes in just as Jesús comes out of the bathroom. "And Mr. Alvarez, what a surprise!" She drops her bag on the table, and also glances twice at the four place settings on the table. "Saphie?" she calls out over the grating electric knife, then wanders into the kitchen.

She's here for dinner? Jesús mouths, as I catch the terrifying sight of my Mom and my principal greeting each other warmly in the kitchen. She seems to be asking the same thing of my Mom.

"We need to eat, the boys need to eat, what's the problem?" I hear my Mom say over the grating electric knife.

Despite our collective surprise, we're all hungry enough to happily eat the kebab meat and hand-baked pita Mom has piled the table along with four different salads, dips, sauces and olives.

"Saphie, this is wonderful," Mrs. McKenna says, helping herself to more shredded meat from the platter. Mom blushes at the compliment. I've never seen my Mom blush in all my life. Jesús sees it as well, and we share a look. "I have to say," she continues while stuffing meat into the pita, "how proud I am of you both. Achilles you've really applied yourself these past few months. I'll be writing to the judge next week to let him know that you've more than fulfilled the educational side of your parole conditions. And Jesús, you've gone above and beyond with your tutoring. I spoke to the admissions people at CalTech a few days ago to tell them how much of an impact you've made on Achilles here. You're a shoo-in for that scholarship."

The thing that I'd put off like death, Jesús moving to LA, is suddenly present. The fifth guest at the dinner table. This one uninvited.

"Thanks," he says quietly, looking down at his plate still full of meat. He's barely eaten. In fact, he's barely said a word all dinner. Mom seems to have noticed too.

"I hope this—not eating—isn't you getting ready for LA? You'll waste away." Mom leans across the table and piles more meat onto his plate to emphasize the point.

"And what about you, Achilles? What's your plans for after the summer?" Mrs. McKenna asks. Her question strikes me hard, because I think it's the first time, possibly in my life, or at the very least since they put me inside, anyone asked me about my future, or even considered that I could have a future.

"I'm going to be an actor," I say, without missing a beat. And because it is the first thing I think of when anyone says LA. Mom stares at me, open-mouthed. Jesús is still playing with his food, so I say the next sentence louder. "As soon as my parole is up, I'm moving to Hollywood…in California,"

I add decisively. Now Jesús takes notice. He's stunned. Speechless. The entire table is. But it all feels perfectly right to me. I can't let him go, not when the idea of the future is full of him. His smell, his smile, the taste of his skin. I can't let it slip away. Not when there's a reason I could move to LA. "Us Greeks invented drama, you know. And someone's going to have to make sure this one eats," I say, nudging Jesús who looks close to tears. Mom, however, already is.

"Oh, Aki!" she cries. I'm unsure with what emotion, but there's a lot of it spilling out. She throws herself from the chair and wraps me up in a suffocating Greek hug. "How wonderful!" Mom is sobbing and sniffing and wiping her nose with her sleeve, while simultaneously pulling me into her bosom. "Oh I can't believe it. I prayed to Thamyris all your life that you'll follow his path, and by Zeus it worked."

Mrs. McKenna clears her throat, singularly unmoved by the show of emotion.

"Of course you'll need something to fall back on," she says sternly, but with half a smile. "Acting is a tough business to get into."

"I'll have my GED, and I can coach wrestling or teach Greek or work in a restaurant, every actor has other jobs. But as long as they have a reason to be in Hollywood…" I say it all directly to Jesús, my hand reaching for his above the table, not hidden under it. He reaches out too and clasps mine, as Mom returns to wailing.

"Saphie, it's okay," Mrs. McKenna says, getting up and leading Mom back to her chair. "Here, have a drink." She pours her a large licorice-flavor ouzo drink and Mom knocks it back in one go.

"Oh, thank you, dear, that's so much better," she says, patting her thumping chest. "Oh my, oh dear." She wipes tears away from her eyes then clasps her hands together and looks up to the ceiling. "Thank you, Thamyris, *Efharistó pára polí*," she repeats the thanks in Greek.

"Who is Thamyris?" Mrs. McKenna asks me quietly.

"He's my personal god…like my guardian angel, I suppose."

"Uh huh," Mrs. McKenna says, turning her attention back to Mom, who is still babbling thank yous in Greek.

"Is this real?" Jesús whispers to me.

"You came down to the Underworld with me. You crossed The Styx and left your soul on the shore of the living. You rescued us both from Cerberus, you sat beside me in the dining room of the King and Queen of the Dead. You gave me life, when I thought I had none. You gave me hope, when I didn't think I deserved hope. You showed me how much I know, when I thought I knew nothing. I'm falling in love with you, Jesús. That's what I know, and that's all I want to know."

I lean over to him, my mom and my principal watching, and I kiss him long and deep. The sweet softness of his lips swirls into the saltiness of mine, stained by the meat and bread. No, not from the meat, I realize as I pull away and see his soft brown cheeks dripping with the tracks of tears.

"Now eat your dinner," I tell him, wiping away his tears with my thumb. I return to my plate too, and to the vacant stare of Mrs. McKenna. My mom, however, is now silently praising Thamyris, again, with a renewed outburst of vigorous emotion. Mrs. McKenna pours her another drink which she also knocks back, and that seems to help her regain composure.

"Oh Thamyris," she says again, "you have truly blessed me." Then, Mom notices Mrs. McKenna's shocked face. "Thamyris is Achilles' personal god. Like a guardian angel, almost."

"Yes I understood that. But did you know about these two?"

"I always prayed for it."

"Prayed?"

"Yes, I couldn't stand a *daughter*-in-law." She shivers. "I don't want any woman to love Achilles more than me."

"Well that sounds healthy," says Mrs. McKenna, but Mom ignores her.

"Now, Achilles, you must give proper thanks to Thamyris for bringing you Jesús."

"I will, Mom."

"I'm serious. And make libations to Apollo, so he doesn't send a temptation to steal Jesús away. You know what happened to Apollo and Hyakinthos."

"Yes, Mom."

Both Jesús and Mrs. McKenna look at each other across the table, and then at me for an explanation, as Mom has returned to eating.

"I think you're going to have to do a bit more explaining, Achilles," Mrs. McKenna says sharply.

"Well, this actor-slash-poet-slash-musician Thamyris could out-sing all the muses," I explain, "and he competed with the goddesses in singing and poetry and in playing the lyre."

"That's not what I'm referring to!" Mom barks, her mouth full of food.

"Fine!" I say with a harsh eye roll. "Thamyris was in love with this handsome boy Hyakinthos." I lean back on my chair like Zotos and wrap my arm around Jesús' shoulders like my uncle used to do to mine, when recanting a Greek story. "But Hyakinthos was so hot that he also caught the attention of Apollo who flirted with him, like, *way* hard. Thamyris was gutted because he couldn't stop Hyakinthos from doing it with Apollo. But Apollo got jealous because Hyakinthos was also doing it with another god...um, Mom, what was his name?"

"Zephyrus."

"Oh yeah, Zephyrus. God of the west wind. Then, Apollo decides to get rid of Thamyris, so he can have Hyakinthos all to himself. So he throws this, like, massive banquet for Thamyris, and invites all the muses to come and sing and dance, but Apollo tells the muses Thamyris thinks he's better than them. Apollo basically tricks him into a contest with the muses, where the winner gets to choose a punishment for the loser. The muses win of course and blind and maim Thamyris so he can never play or sing again. Thamyris is out of the picture, but Zephyrus is way jealous that Apollo won Hyakinthos' heart. So, one day Zephyrus sees the two of them playing catch with a discus in the field. He asks to play too, but Apollo tells him to get lost. Zephyrus is really pissed at all this and he blows a gust of wind which sends the discus straight into Hyakinthos' head and he dies. Apollo is, like, devastated, but he creates the hyacinth flower from a pool of his dead lover's blood to you know, remember him and stuff."

The table falls into silence, well, Jesús and Mrs. McKenna are in quiet shock anyway. I look over at Mom to check I've told the story right, but she's busy eating which means I must've remembered the details correctly.

"Well then," Mrs. McKenna says, utterly unsure how else to react. "Jesús, I suppose you'd better be on the lookout for Apollo coming to steal your heart away."

"I guess I should," he says, albeit darky, and immediately I think of Marcus. I suddenly wonder if Hades has pulled us both into a trick. Will he restore Marcus to life, only to tempt Jesús away? Or me? I shiver at the thought of how fragile love is.

"Anyway, Saphie, are you nearly ready to go?"

"Oh yes, of course," she says, wiping her mouth with a napkin, then taking off her apron, which she normally wears while eating. It's only then, I realize she also has rather nice clothes under her apron. A long summer dress as opposed to her usual tracksuits. "Achilles, clear the table, will you?"

"Where are you off to?" I ask in surprise, and for some reason a little hurt that Mom's Friday night is far more interesting than mine. Although I have just kissed my boyfriend in front of her and my principal, so it strikes me that perhaps they might want to leave us alone.

"Girls' night out in Houston."

"Since when do you go out in Houston?" Girls' night meant only one thing; Mom and all the women of the clan eating, smoking, drinking and shitting on every man in their life; sons, husbands and fathers included. "And since when is Mrs. McKenna one of the girls?"

"Never you mind about your mother's business, Achilles," Mrs. McKenna says sternly, leaving no space to argue. Mom looks flushed and swerves out of the conversation and into the bathroom. "I hope you boys will be studying tonight?" Mrs. McKenna says. The way she asks it, it's like shooting an arrow of shame, disdain, or something akin to it. If Carla had been sitting here in the same situation, I doubt Mrs. McKenna would have had that tone. I leave Jesús to field the question though, as I take the mounds dishes into the kitchen, stacking them up on the counter already crowded with used pots and pans. Mom has never believed in a tidy kitchen.

She comes out of the bathroom, make-up on, and Mrs. McKenna helps her on with her coat. The familiarity between the two of them, the strangest part of the night by far.

"Car's here," Mrs. McKenna says with a burst of excitement as her phone buzzes.

"Bye, boys. And remember and have your room tidy for the morning, Aki!" are Mom's parting words, as Mrs. McKenna practically shoves her out of the door. Her version of "don't wait up." I return to clearing the table, but Jesús rushes to the window.

"Um, I don't want to alarm you," he says, "but it looks like they're holding hands, and she's holding the Uber door open for your mom."

"Uber? That's weird. How would Mom know what an Uber is? Wait…what was the thing you said before that?"

"They're holding hands?"

"Yeah. What do you mean, like…she was helping Mom into the car?"

"No, not really. Aki…Aki…Achilles!"

"What?"

"You're dropping meat all over the table."

"Oh fuck, sorry." Distracted doesn't even cover it. I don't understand, yet it all makes perfect sense. The principal is having an affair with my Mom. That's one I didn't see coming. "Wait, isn't Mrs. McKenna like… married?"

"I think her husband died a long time ago. And she just kept the name. Didn't your Mom and Dad divorce like five minutes after you were born?"

"Yeah," I say quietly, with the whole world crashing down like meaningless rain. Why does it matter to me? "Mom signed the paperwork in the hospital."

"And she did pick a gay god for you."

"Huh."

Jesús comes over to me and wraps his arms around my waist, taking the silver platter from my hands and planting three soft kisses on my neck. "Who would've thought your coming out would've been overshadowed by your Mom's?"

"So it's official now?" I ask Jesús with a smile and a kiss back. "I'm out of the closet?"

"And into the streets!"

"The streets?"

"For a protest. Or for Pride. Don't worry, we'll get there."

"Oh, okay," I say, suddenly not wanting to waste my

mouth on words, when I could be kissing him instead. "Man, I wish I could remember my Facebook password, so I can tell everyone. My first post in two years would be quite a comeback, huh?"

"I don't want to burst your bubble," Jesús replies, wrapping himself in my arms, "but I think Carla stole your thunder with that one on TikTok."

"I couldn't give a literal fuck," I say, and I mean it. I lift Jesús' chin with the tips of my fingers. When we're standing on the same level, he needs to lean up to kiss me, and I lean down to kiss him. "So, when does the good part start?"

"How about right now?" Jesús whispers breathlessly as his warm hands slide straight under my T-shirt, rubbing my stomach and then edging downward.

Someone knocks on the door. No, bangs. We freeze. Mom must have forgotten something. But why would she knock? Why would she bang? Then the doorbell rings. Jesús looks frightened, and to be honest, so am I. Even though I have no idea why as I edge toward the door and the person on the other side clearly so desperate to get in.

"Carla!" I almost choke at the sight of her. It's been weeks, if not a month or more since I've seen her, since I've thought about her. She takes one quick glance at me, before peering over my shoulder at who's inside.

"Hey, Jesús," she calls out emphatically while chewing gum.

"Hey…Carla." He edges to the door like the other woman. I feel embarrassed, but then shake it out. Why should I?

"Come in," I say, opening the door wider.

"I can't stay, I just came to invite you to the after-prom party that Adam and I are throwing at my house."

"You and *Adam*, huh?"

"You and *Jesús* are both welcome," she says, hitting my point straight back. Her smile says "we were both right" and I'm fine to share the hollow victory. "And…I wanted to apologize to you as well. Since you still won't get a phone, here I am. Apologizing."

"For what?"

"Outing you."

"Oh."

"Yeah," she chews with a loudness, barely concealing how awkward she feels. Saying sorry isn't in her DNA. "Although, it seems I was half right."

"So, I'll half forgive you."

"Deal," she says, and we shake on it. "Bye, then." And she turns away from the door with a wide grin, back to her car parked on the street. "Oh," she says, calling back, "you two make a cute couple. See you at prom."

I close the door and breathe an epic sigh of relief. I can literally feel the weight off my shoulders that I didn't even know was there.

"You look better," Jesús remarks.

"Yeah. God, you've no idea."

"So, I guess Adam finally gave in."

"What do you mean?"

"She's been after him for years…" Jesús slows and reevaluates like he's just realized who he's talking to. "After you went away, obviously."

"He didn't want her, right?"

"Yeah. Adam always thought she was trashy. But, hey, I guess trash finds trash."

"Hey," I say with a stitch of seriousness. "She's not—"

Another whack on the door stops me mid-sentence. And I'm standing right by it so I jump. We both do. Now the fear cracks through me like thunder. Through both of us. It's not Mom, it's not Carla, so who? I reach behind me and grasp the door handle, shrugging at Jesús since it's my only answer. He edges behind me as I turn, take a deep breath, and open the door.

"Dad."

"Hi, son. I'm gonna fucking kill you."

Dad forced his way inside, and brought us both to the table with the sharp edge of a knife. He twisted the point into the wood of the table like a screwdriver, scarring it forever like it would make his point. Spilled food and our glasses from the meal are laid out like trenches on the battlefield between us. Jesús, once again, is an innocent victim of male aggression. He must be terrified, although he doesn't look it. I just feel sick; sick that men give themselves license to burst into houses with knives. And what's worse, I get the strongest impression that he's only sitting at the table playing with the knife — instead of doing something worse — because he isn't convinced he can take me in a fight. Even with a weapon.

"I had to get a fucking lawyer 'cause of you." He drags the knife sharp across the table, making the dark wood bleed light dust. "I have to give a deposition!" He says it with such fury and indignation, like it's the worst fate which can befall a man.

"Don't worry, Dad, I'm sure they'll throw the case out when they hear how heroic you were."

"They said I defended some faggoty-ass prick who worked at Domino's." Dad says it without even looking at Jesús. I wonder if he even knows he's sitting here? "Channel Two news even called me, wanting an interview with the guy who saved some queer from having his guts grinded. I said what the fuck do I know about rescuing queers? What am I? Some goddamn rainbow Batman?"

"That's a great idea for a TV show," Jesús says. I mutter under my breath for him to keep quiet. Now Dad turns the point of his knife to Jesús.

"Are you the fag?"

"The very same, Christos," Jesús says with a drag-queen smirk. "And word of advice, when the news comes calling or the judge asks you what you did, try to avoid the phrase 'faggoty-ass' or such variations thereof."

"What am I, a filthy Turk? I'll say whatever the fuck I want. But you," Dad slices the knife through the air and aims it back at me; one stab away from my throat, "you keep your fucking mouth shut, son, you hear me? 'Cause if you ever speak to the cops again, I'll gut you like—"

"Like Poseidon and a mermaid," Jesús says with a callous disregard for the knife or the crazed Greek holding onto it. "Or like a tasty lobster blessed by the virgin waters of blah blah blah? We get the picture, Christos." Dad's face melts in shock. I kinda want to laugh. Jesús is already grinning. "And it was me who told the police you saved me, not Achilles."

"You?" The question asked, but Dad is not the one to wait for an answer. He jumps up from the chair, smashing away the table with a furious hand. It just moves, not flips. But I've anticipated all of this, every motion he's going through. Ever since he sat down, I knew where this conversation was going. I dive up at the same time, blocking his knife hand with the back of my arm. It clatters to the floor, I kick it away and it slides under the couch. Now, there's just one angry man, and I'm the only thing holding him back. I'm a wall he cannot get through. I'm taller, I'm bulkier, I'm stronger, and with just one arm holding him back like a crossing guard, he knows he's beat.

Jesús remains perfectly still on the chair, the table now tossed away, so he looks like he's sitting on a throne. Unperturbed by any of this, Jesús crosses his leg, mini-skirt style.

"Yes, Christos, it was me. I did it because you're a piece of scum. You're worse than scum. You're frothy residue, so limp and impotent you don't even stick to the side of the ship. You just float on the waves, like a poorly cleaned up oil spill."

"What the fuck is he saying?" Dad demands of me.

"He's speaking English. You can understand."

"You know, Christos," Jesús continues, re-crossing his legs. "There's a special place in Hades for men like you. Ones who betray their children. Tartarus, I've seen it. It's a massive darkroom full of giants and Titans and monsters, ready to slam their column-sized dicks into every pathetic hole in your body, for eternity." Dad lunges forward, but he can budge past my arm. I push him in response, and he stumbles back. I keep pushing him, right toward the door.

"Word of advice, Christos," Jesús continues, yelling over his shoulder, as I edge the angry Greek closer to the permanent exit, "Ask Charon for a bottle of poppers to sniff. It will relax your sphincter muscles and makes getting fucked in the ass way easier. Believe me."

With one last roar of fury from Dad, I push him out the door, slam it and lock it as I hear him storm away down the path and slam his car door shut.

I exhale and look at the courageous guy still sitting in the chair, with a satisfied smile plastered across his face, "Jesús…you're insane."

He gets up and wraps his arms around my neck, as I survey the damage to the room. Nothing bad, but with the table pushed to the side everything feels out of place. Almost in a good way, though. Like the satisfaction that comes from moving furniture for a thorough, deep clean.

"Shall we tidy up?" Jesús asks, more concerned with the piling of dishes in the kitchen.

"Sure. And…thank you." Jesús tries to wave it away, but I pull his body close into mine. "No, seriously, thank you. I didn't know what poppers were for, and all this time I was too afraid to ask."

Chapter 17
The Highway to Troy

We hit the road to Houston early, six in the morning early, the high clouds of a steamy day crinkling across a pink sky. But the car is in darkness. Mrs. McKenna drives while Mom sits in the passenger seat, counting her cigarettes to know if she'll need to buy another pack to get through the day. And Jesús, beautiful, tantalizing Jesús is in the back beside me, his face smashed against the window, sleeping soundly.

I sit with the memory of last night, happy to be lost in the sky the color of a healing bruise. So much is behind me; the last GED exam yesterday is done. Passed, I hope. When Jesús came round last night, and quizzed me about every answer I'd given in the test, I could barely remember any of it. The hours under exam conditions ran through like the streetlamps on the highway, the minutes flicking by. Afterward, the last thing I wanted was to talk about school work, when it's the one subject I should never have to speak of again.

I wanted to show him the headshots Mom had got me as a present. During the week she sprung a surprise visit to a photographer to kick-start my acting career.

"*Achilles,*" she'd said as I tried to keep a straight face

under the flamboyant lights of Ricardo's studio. His other work was hung on the walls and seemed to consist mainly of toddler beauty pageants and poodle dogs dyed horrendous colors. "Take off your shirt. You're not fat anymore! Ricardo, my son is going to be the next big thing in Hollywood!"

"Saphie, darling," he drawled, as I did what my mom told me and took off my shirt, "you are not wrong." As Jesús and I looked through the prints last night, I couldn't quite believe it was me. They were right. Months in the gym had shed what I'd been so self-conscious about since getting out of juvie. And there I was, in black and white, smiling and shirtless. A thick leg up on the chair and glancing back at the camera. On my side, head resting on my hand as Ricardo had somehow managed to use the lighting to magnificent effect to show off every muscle I never realized I'd had.

Why had Hades not made *that* one of my demons? Self-consciousness. The spirit of feeling good about yourself; of working hard to change the things you don't like about yourself that can be changed, and learning to love the things that can't change. It's not about the external. Jesús always said he didn't care one way or the other. In fact, he preferred to rest his head on my water-bed stomach rather than the taut muscles which had taken over.

But like painting a house, working on my external self had impacted how I felt about my internal self. And even if I wasn't perfectly proportioned like a sculpted statue, hard work and sweat had brought me something not Mom, not Zotos, and not even Hector could take away. The knowledge that the outside doesn't matter. It's how you feel inside that counts. And hard work, no matter what for, made me feel good.

And inside, I felt farther from the boy who'd kicked around twigs on the street outside juvie while waiting for my mom, than Houston from our house. This concrete highway I'd traveled down was real. I'd changed, I knew it. And I had the boy sleeping next to me in the back of the car to thank.

I sink back in the seat, far enough down that the tops of the street lamps are like bugs flicking by. I want to lose myself forever in the memory of last night. Stifling laughs and giggles and freezing still every time the bed creaked. Me diving onto the blanket on the floor when we heard Mom get up to the kitchen for an after-midnight snack. Then Jesús "testing" my *pothos* when he informed me that Mrs. McKenna had in fact not gone home after dinner. While I had been packing up my bag for the wrestling competition, she'd retired to the back garden with Mom, and stayed the night.

Even that had not stopped me. Nor the sinking realization that in order to determine if I had indeed defeated each of my demons, someone, be they god or hero or even Charon in drag, would be watching. Well, we gave them quite a show.

But then came the sour note. The one string played out of turn. Every victory brought me closer to the end; yesterday the GED, today Regionals, and some day very soon, I hoped, the completion of the task Hades had set for me. Then what? That's what I couldn't answer, and I was afraid to ask. Would Marcus come waltzing back into my life? Were Jesús and I destined to live as Achilles and Patroclus, in the version where they didn't go to war, or succumb to the terror of temptation like Thamyris, Apollo, and Hyakinthos? What myth were we in? That I could not answer. And what if Marcus had been in my bed last night, instead of Jesús? That, I could not ask.

We pull up to the Toyota Center in downtown Houston, imposing like a Colosseum, and are directed to park at the Hilton across the street. Senior competitors had been given a room for the day to change and shower between bouts. Team USA was here to scout, as Zotos had so often said. My ground crew came up to the room with me, marveling at the view of the stadium and the stillness of the surrounding city at eight AM, on a Saturday morning. But we had little time to chill. Mom gives me a hug, Mrs. McKenna a handshake, and Jesús a kiss, as they wave goodbye, and head for their seats in the audience.

Alone in the room, I have nothing to do but shower and change. But, the only thing on my mind is Marcus. Standing at the window of the hotel room, staring down into the streets below, while I watch the lines of spectators snake into the arena, he is all I see. And I feel guilty. My mind is cheating on Jesús by imagining Marcus. If Hades had never said a word, if he'd never offered me that deal, this would not be happening. I could be happy. But, no, Greek stories never end in a happily ever after. Death or

Glory are the only tropes on offer, and usually those endings are one and the same, the Greek Tragedy.

Is Marcus hiding somewhere in the city? Have Hades and Persephone bundled his lifeless corpse in the back of their pickup truck, ready to return his soul to the land of the living as soon as I slay this one final demon?

Because *alastor* is the last one. I can feel it. A dramatic end to a twisted story. One final day, where I must defeat my nemesis and then take my boyfriend out to prom on the same night. This must be it, I've decided. *Aidos* was slayed with shoving my father out of the house last week and slamming the door in his face. *Deimos* was done the moment I started to pull my dick out in front of Anderson and Detective Jones, and showed the Beast that here on the outside, in the land of the living, I have power over him he cannot comprehend. And *pothos*. If last night did not satisfy the conditions of claiming victory over sexual longing, then I don't know what could.

And now I'm left with *alastor*. The blood feud. The final demon to slay. Hector and I, in direct competition for the one place at nationals, and a ticket to the next Olympics. But as I stare out the window, forehead pressed against the cold glass, I ask myself, why do I care? I don't need to win to be free. I've qualified. I am already free.

The door to the room opens and my stomach drops twenty floors. I half expect Marcus to walk in, or Hector come to slash my ankles before the fight. But it's only Zotos in his coaching outfit, basically the same outfit he always wears, the gray tracksuit and half-moon glasses, but now his jacket has *Team USA* emblazoned on it.

"How are you feeling, son?"

"Did you tell the judge I qualified?"

"Huh?"

"The judge. My parole. Mrs. McKenna sent a letter last week saying I was taking my GED tests yesterday, and then confirmed I'd done it by phone," I step closer, only the corner of the bed no one will sleep in between us. "My parole condition was to qualify. And here I am, qualified."

Zotos sighs and unzips his pocket to pull out his phone. He moves it closer, then farther from his face like he's adjusting a camera lens, and bashes the screen with his index finger like an old fashioned calculator as I wait in anxious silence.

"'Hello Mr. Kalanasis,'" Zotos reads from the screen. I peer over and see the words from an email in large font upside down. "'Thank you for the update about Achilles Konstantinos. I am glad to hear he has qualified for the competition. Alongside the glowing report from Principal McKenna at Jefferson High, I am now satisfied Achilles has completed his probation conditions, and therefore I am attaching a signed Certificate of Early Termination, which I have also sent to the Texas Juvenile Justice Department. Thank you for looking out for the best interests of this young man, and I wish him all the best in his forthcoming competition. Regards, Judge Minos.'"

Thank the gods the bed is there, because I collapse onto it. It's done. With a bit of Greek cursing, Zotos manages to open the attachment and I stare at it, zooming in across every bit of the page. Staring at the signature of the Judge. Suddenly I start to laugh. Loud, hard, free.

"He's Greek!" I say, reading the name on the email again.

"Of course he's fucking Greek!" Zotos snatches the phone away. "So, there, now you're done. You can fuck off and let Hector qualify, even though he doesn't deserve it and you're ten times the wrestler he'll ever be."

I can't stop laughing. Or crying. Or laughing, I don't know. I don't care. Zotos is angry, but I don't care either.

"I didn't tell you before, Aki," he says, already more than pissed off at me, "because I wanted you to fight. Heroes fight. Even if they fall, they're remembered because they stood on that battlefield and fought. Not because they ran away the second they got their ticket home."

I spread out on the hotel-sized bed, running my hands over the starchy sheets and letting the laughter die down. Zotos is muttering. He hates it when people aren't moved by his little speeches. That's why he gives them to kids at his gym.

I jump right off the bed and land on both feet like my batteries have been replaced with a bolt from Zeus. It shocks Zotos who steps back. I swing my arms, feeling so light I wonder if I'll still qualify for my weight class.

"Oh I'm not quitting," I say emphatically. "I'm gonna wipe the fucking floor with Hector's ass."

"Ha ha!" Zotos shouts back, "That's my boy!"

I follow Zotos into the arena like a soldier after his commander. The battlefield already rages with the morning's lighter weight categories. Groans and slams and the screech of rubber fill the void of the arena, where basketball games or concerts are usually held. Five competition-level wrestling mats are spread out across the wide floor, as more than a dozen teams from all across the Southwest huddle by the sidelines. The judges sit on high, although their table is floor level, like the three judges of the Underworld who decide the fates of souls. I forget their names.

I scan the audience looking out for Hades. Perhaps he can tell me their names. The bleachers are not full, but not empty. Greco-Roman wrestling still manages to draw a crowd beyond the immediate families of the participants. Behind the judges' table is a television camera from the local news and a peroxide-blonde sports reporter standing in front of it.

Returning to the competition after a lifetime away, I can see it like non-wrestlers do. Hundreds of young men wrapped in spandex singlets, grouped by weight, or more accurately muscle mass. It smells not like a battlefield, but a locker room. Zotos used to tell us Greco-Roman wrestling is the closest sport we have to ancient battles. Like on the fields of Troy or in the valley of Thermopylae, pinning one's opponent to the ground long enough for him to be stabbed with a sword or have his head crushed by an ax will result in an immediate victory. But that's a rare feat unless an experienced hoplite is facing off against an untamed barbarian.

More often, a win comes after two grueling three-minute periods of intense competition. A victory is eked out through technical superiority, by default, or by judgment—

based on points. Like Olympians staring out over an endless battlefield, the gods add points based on skill and risk, and declare which hero has won their favor.

Walking through the arena with my junk on horrendous display underneath the spandex, I just feel stupid. But I can see why Jesús likes watching the videos with me. I catch him up on the stand, sitting rather awkwardly between Mom and Mrs. McKenna. He waves down from on high, and I wave back and smile. I want to run to him, to leap over the barriers and hop across the seats, wrap him up in one great big hug and tell him I'm free. But I'll have to wait. Hector must be defeated first.

He's waiting at Zotos' section of the side court. Six folding chairs to carry the weight of all of our water and sports drinks and energy bars. Alongside a couple of the younger kids good enough to qualify in their age brackets, I see Giorgos prance through the doorway holding a tub of Vaseline; the useless Paris has come to add absolutely nothing to the battlefield.

"Aren't you a bit old for the kids' competition?" I ask Giorgos, as I stretch out my thighs on the chair. He doesn't answer me, though. He's got a job to do, smearing petroleum jelly across Hector's arms and chest. Freshly waxed, and his red hair gelled up for the camera, even though his helmet will destroy it in a second.

"Suck my dick and I might let you win," Hector says to me while Giorgos is on his knees, rubbing Vaseline along the inside of Hector's thighs. Giorgos stops for one beat, perhaps assessing the seriousness with which his man, if that's even their thing, is inviting me to suck his dick.

Hector clearly couldn't care if Giorgos lives or dies, his only reason to breathe is to see me humiliated, one way or the other.

"Thanks for the invitation," I reply, "but I've seen what you've got on offer and it's hardly something to bargain with."

I turn away from them both, letting the comment hang in the air. As I stretch, I see something odd in the stand just above me. Way closer than where Jesús or Mom are, across the other side of the arena. A broad-shouldered man in a Cher-style wig and a pure white dress, complete with golden broach and floaty train, glides down the bleacher stairs, like Athena herself. Beside him is a younger guy, (what Jesús would describe as a "twink") wearing expensive sneakers, a backpack and baseball cap, clutching a phone with one hand and the hem of the Athena-figure's dress with the other.

I glance around the arena to see if anyone else has spotted this bizarre apparition, or if I whacked my head on the way in. But, no, two boys from the next team along have also spotted this queerest of couples. They point and smirk before their coach smacks their hands for making a scene, probably fearing the kids could be disqualified for making fun of audience members. But not even a scolding from the coach can close their gawking mouths as the Athenian figure takes a seat right at the front like an Empress, and waves right at me.

"Coo-ee!"

It's Charon. The recognition smacks me like a

backhand punch. I slink up to the low barrier separating the audience from the competition floor.

"What're you doing here?" I hiss, looking this way and that. But the competition is in full swing, and it seems like no one else in the immediate vicinity cares about me whispering with a broad-shouldered individual and what, from a distance, would appear to be her teenage son.

"Well, there's the cutest little drag club on the corner here, and since it's Saturday Disco Styx is here to snap a little tail." Charon adds a wiggle of amplified breast, while their companion busies himself on his phone. It starts to ting and whiz with the sound of a hundred messages being received all at once.

"Fuck me," he says, tapping away at literally lighting speed with one painfully expensive sneaker up on the railing. "Scruff and Grindr are lighting up in this bitch."

"Hermes," Charon scolds and slaps his rapidly typing hand, "put that away." The name of Charon's companion rings in my head like another sucker-punch. Hermes: the quick-footed messenger of the gods. And also the one Olympian tasked with guiding freed souls from the Underworld. Charon leans across the barrier towards me while Hermes continues to send and receive a hundred messages a minute.

"Can you believe he's not said a *word* about my dress?"

"I already told you it's gauche as hell."

"Oh, what do you know," Charon spits with fury. "You people wouldn't know taste if it smacked you in the backside."

Hermes looks up from his phone and lifts his cap. His

beardless face tightly wound like it's trembling faster than the eye can see. "*Me* people?"

"Yes, you Olympians."

Hermes' messages continue thick and fast, while Charon settles themself with all the poise they can muster on a plastic chair. I stare at them both though, wondering exactly when to start yelling. I guess now is fine.

"Well?" I screech. Charon jumps and clutches their pearl-less chest, while Hermes grins privately at the messages he's receiving, turning the phone sideways and gawking. "Why are you here?"

"All right, keep your singlet on," Charon says, picking up Hermes' backpack from the floor and rummaging inside. Hermes, meanwhile, takes a quick break from his phone screen to look me up and down and smirk, like a god flirting.

"Or don't," he says with a sly wink.

"Well then, let's see." Charon pulls out a literal stone slate from the backpack and I bend over the barrier to see what's on it. As if I didn't already know. Four words written in Greek, evenly spaced out on the gray slate: *alastor*, *aidos*, *deimos*, and *pothos*. But what sends my heart soaring is the fact the middle two, *aidos* and *deimos*, the spirits of reverence and terror, are crossed out. The happiness is cut short when I realize I'm only half way.

"Only two?" I complain. "What more do I have to do for *pothos?*"

"Oh right!" Charon says, "Last night. I forgot. Mazal tov to you both." I feel my cheeks flush bright red. In fact, I can see the blood rush to my skin all down my arms, made far worse by Hermes' smirking at the comment. "Hermes, if you could be a dear."

He drags a finger along the bottom of the slate to the sound of nails on a blackboard that somehow reverberates across the entire arena. But I don't care, because one more demon has been solidly defeated. It's written in stone.

"It's so exciting!" Charon says, sliding the slate back into Hermes fabric satchel and pulling out a martini glass instead, miraculously filled with the same black alcohol from our time together at the bar, with not a drop spilled. They sip the licorice cocktail and scan the arena floor, clearly enjoying the spectacle on display. I'm still hanging onto the railing, waiting for another word or a clue as to how I'll defeat this one last demon.

"If you do win," Hermes says, snapping a picture of himself with his tongue stuck out as the phone crackles under the weight of dozens of sent message sounds, "what does this Marcus look like?"

"Are you serious?" I ask, my heart suddenly pounding at this last-minute trick. "Charon, don't you know?" Sweat pricks my forehead, and spills down the crack of my back. I feel faint, ready to collapse, another victim of the gods' nasty tricks.

"Shh!" Charon responds. "It's Disco Styx up here."

"Achilles Konstantinos to mat three," the announcer calls out. *"Achilles Konstantinos to mat three."*

At least that makes Hermes look up from his phone and he sees the look on my face.

"I'm just messin' with ya! Don't worry, I know who Marcus is."

I try to ingest the words, to breathe, to relax, but I'm shakier than an earthquake. I have no choice but to trust the trickster, Hermes. He smiles at me, almost genuine, as I jump back down and trudge to the mat, following the call of my name. Blood and fear prick my skin; and suddenly the spirits of reverence and fear, and even the longing for Marcus, crash over me like an overdose. The slate might show I've defeated these three, but a crass comment from an Olympian god has sent me into a spiral of terror, inviting not just these four demons into my mind, but every single negative personified trait in the Greek pantheon.

"Hey, Achilles," Hermes calls out, as I'm walking away. I spin around, hoping to hear the words that will wipe away this walk to hell. "Marcus is the Black guy, right?"

Chapter 18
Achilles vs. Hector

My first victory comes by fall. In about twenty seconds. The referee's whistle shrieks out after two seconds of me pinning my opponent's shoulders to the mat. And that's it, the match is over. The kid from Dallas drags his sorry ass away as I take the bottle from Zotos with one hand and shake the kid's hand with the other.

I haven't broken a sweat, but I'm still tingling all over. I can't keep my eyes off Hermes and Charon in the audience. From the other side of the arena, I know Jesús is watching closely, and he's seen them both as well. He wants to communicate with me, but I've got another match to fight.

I hand back the bottle to Zotos as I reach out and shake the hand of the new guy. He's short but bulky; black hair, black eyes and a pock-marked face. The singlet strains to keep his body inside it. He might be better as a sumo wrestler than a Greco-Roman one. But he won't be so easy to defeat by fall.

We size each other up from opposite sides of the mat, waiting for the whistle to start. Yet my attention is squarely on Charon and Hermes. Is Charon watching? Is Hermes? Is Jesús? I try to mouth "over there" to Jesús, maybe he can get across and talk to them, but I have no idea if he understands. He shrugs from the seats, unsure of what I'm saying. I try again but I'm distracted by whistles blowing in the background. Where my new opponent was standing he's not anymore. He's hurtling straight toward me. I'm not ready, so I spin out of the way and he fails to stop his own trajectory.

The referee's whistle blows once, twice, three points.

"Penalty," the ref shouts, "out-of-bounds."

My opponent roars in frustrated anger. He was so set on smacking straight into me that he found himself penalized for fleeing the mat. It's a dick move on my part, but an easy three points.

We start again, and this time he doesn't need to chase me around the mat. I've already anticipated exactly what he wants to do. The kid's next mistake is he's trying to go too big too soon. On a battlefield, only a suicidal commander will order a full-on infantry charge on untouched walls. Not even an arrow volley to soften up the defense. On the battlefield, this charge would constitute a criminal waste of life.

On the wrestling mat however, it's just a pointless throwaway of a perfectly good opportunity. I swivel into a near-drag, spinning the guy's bulk against him, so he has no choice but to tumble onto the mat. And he falls on his back. Unfortunately for him, he's built like a turtle. I barely have to apply an ounce of pressure to keep him on the floor for the required two seconds to scratch down another victory by fall.

I help the guy up, we shake, he nods and turns away. It

was an unfair fight, but he knows he didn't stand a chance. Everyone else in this round is barely halfway through the first half of their first match, and I'm done.

I want to take the opportunity to clamber through the audience to grab Jesús. We have a good half hour to sit and talk to Hermes and Charon. But Hermes is gone. Charon is still there, drinking and watching the action through a pair of opera binoculars attached to a hand-held pole.

"Hey, Achilles?" I turn around and face a tall guy in a short-sleeved shirt and tie. "John Dunn, head wrestling coach at UCLA." He thrusts out a vigorous hand which I have to shake and splashes a wide grin across his face like he's meeting his hero.

"Oh, hi, Mr. Dunn." I try to search the bleachers inconspicuously, looking for Hermes or Jesús.

"Fantastic work out there. You just floored the number one kid in the state."

"Him? Really?"

"Oh yeah, Danny has been on our Talent ID scheme since middle school, and you wiped the floor with him." Mr. Dunn talks about the defeat of a child with more enthusiasm than I feel is appropriate, but it's also hard for me to care because I'm trying to figure out if I can see Hermes' backpack under Charon's dress or not. I think I can. "What are your plans for after the summer, son?"

"Oh, I'm moving to LA."

"Really?" Dunn says. I thought it would destroy his interest, but it seems to have ignited it. "Because we've got a training facility at UCLA, and we'd love to bring you on as a coach, if you're not too busy training for the Olympics, that is."

"A job?" Suddenly I'm panting. My heart's thumping, but not from the two matches or the missing Hermes. This is a chance to make a real life in LA, not just some mythological dream.

"Sure, as long as Frank over there doesn't steal you for Team USA first." I follow Dunn's nod toward two men in Team USA jackets, Zotos and Frank. They both look up as if they can hear my thoughts. Dunn, visibly nervous at their attention, hands me his card, "Well, here's my card," quickly shaking my hand again. He glances back at Zotos, and his face pales a little, like he might get jumped for trying to steal away their chance at a gold medalist. Patting me on the shoulder, he says, "Come and see me when you get out to LA," before walking away.

I wander back to our team's area, thinking about it all. The idea of moving to LA. It's real, not just a dream. I don't have to pretend to want to act. I feel like I'm walking into my future; an air-conditioned arena swirling in spandex and sweat, with Jesús waiting on the competition floor.

"Hey!" he says, rushing forward and hugging me tight. I kiss him quickly on the lips. Funny how it's that which draws the stares. "You were fantastic."

"Thanks," I say with a shrug, like it was nothing, because it wasn't. "Hey, have you seen Hermes?"

"Like…the god, Hermes?"

"Yeah," I say, ignoring the surge of the crowd coming toward us, and staring up into the bleachers to see if I can spot him. At least I can see his bag still beside Charon. I'm just fearing that he's dipped down into the Underworld to bring Marcus straight into the crowd.

"You mean the kid who was sitting with Disco Styx?"

"Yeah, I can't find him anywhere. Although, good news, they said I've only got one last demon to slay. Hector, of course. Not a clue what they want me to do."

"He was in the bathroom," Jesús says with a look I don't quite understand.

"Oh? You saw him?"

"Yes. Busy with, um, someone."

"Ah…I get you. Oh, there he is."

I relax as I see Hermes hop down the steps two at a time, a great big smile on his cheeky face and squeezing back in beside Charon.

"Satisfied?" Charon asks.

Hermes shrugs, but I don't catch what else he says, because Jesús has turned me around to face the coming onslaught of the last thing I expected, a TV camera crew and the blonde reporter. The lights from the camera blind me and Jesús.

"We're live with Achilles Konstantinos, formerly ranked first—"

"Fourth," I correct her.

"In the state and who has just returned to competition after serving two years in juvenile detention. Achilles," she says, thrusting the microphone into my face, "do you think prisoners should be allowed to compete in competitive sports?"

"I'm not a prisoner," I say straight into the camera.

"I'm sorry," she says, but she's not, "prisoners out on parole?"

"I'm not on parole either." Now she looks confused, as if she's mentally fact-checking her information.

"You're not?" Jesús asks me quietly, while the camera creeps closer.

"I'm not," I say with the biggest grin I've ever felt. "I'm free."

"Oh, Aki!" Jesús is on the verge of fainting with tears, but I catch him. Easier than wrestling one of the pre-teens still grappling out on the mat. I lift Jesús up and he wraps his legs and arms around me, and we kiss like no one in the world is watching.

I can hear my name being shouted and yelled. I can hear whistles and boos and cheers. I can hear the whole confluence of a battlefield as we kiss, but I don't care.

"*Achilles Konstantinos to mat one.*" The announcer says. "*Hector Dardanus to mat one.*"

That's the only person I care about calling my name. I put Jesús down, his mouth rubbed red from kissing mine. We've gathered a crowd who stand a safe distance behind the cameraman and TV reporter. She looks like she's got tears in her eyes. I glance up to the audience where Charon and Hermes are both standing, and applauding, although Charon is lightly tapping one hand onto the other, which holds the glass.

As I jog across the floor to the main mat right in front of the judges, I look up into the crowd where Mom and Mrs. McKenna were sitting before. It's far busier now, as if all these people have swarmed in for the main event, and some, no, a lot, are standing up, cheering and clapping even though a single point has yet to be won.

I get to my side of the mat, and I can see nothing but the bright spotlight shining down on me. The cheers of the audience rattle my ears, like the cries of the men who followed Achilles to the shores of Troy. But best of all I can still taste Jesús on my lips. His touch is real, even if nothing else is. His love is real. That's all I need to face my mortal enemy, like Achilles has fought Hector since the dawn of time.

A thousand campfires gleamed upon the plain,

Like a herd of cows maddened with fright, when attacked by a lion,

Like some fierce tempest has swooped upon them from the sea,

A hound from the mountains gives chase to the fawn, thirsty for blood,

And even if he finds shelter in a valley glade, and cowers in a thicket,

The hound tracks it down for the hound does always win against even the noblest fawn.

So Achilles chased Hector around the walls of Troy,

Brandishing the mighty Pelian spear in his right hand,

Bronze armor blazing like fire over the rising sun that blinds all the watchers on the field,

Achilles pursues Hector like a hawk, the swiftest of birds, in terror below the Trojan walls.

All the while the gods look down at these two warriors,

Three times they swiftly circling the mighty walls of Troy,

Mighty Zeus looks down upon their sight,

And calls to his brethren from an Olympian might:

'Oh well now, what shall we do? Hector is a man so dear to me, chased around these walls times three, my heart is in sorrow for thee. Now noble Achilles, the great runner, hunts him around Priam's city. Take counsel, immortals, and decide the fate of these warriors, what will it be?'

The two men run as in an open dream, one cannot escape, the other cannot catch,

And as they reach their fourth full sprint around Priam's fair city,

Zeus, the father, raises up the golden scales and sets upon them the death of Achilles, and the life of Hector,

Down sinks Hector's lot towards Hades, as bright Athena, the wisest of women, sinks to the mortal earth and whispers in the hero's ear:

'Glorious Achilles, so beloved of Zeus, you and I will vanquish Hector together, and bring glory to the Greeks. Stop now and catch your breath, I will go forth and bring this prince of Troy to fight you, face to face.'

So Athena appears to Hector, and steels his heart for the final fight,

'I will not run from you,' Hector calls out after three times around the city they ran,

'My heart tells me to stand and face you, to kill or be killed.'

But Hector did not know it was not his heart that incited him so,

But the whispers of fair Athena, who played an act of trickery on the heart of her hated hero of Troy,

'*Come, Achilles, let us swear an oath before the gods. If mighty Zeus allows me victory I shall not mistreat your corpse. I will return your body to the people, if you will do the same for mine.*'

'*Curse you, Hector,*' came Achilles' reply. '*Do not talk of oaths to me. Lions and men make no pacts, nor can wolves and lambs find themselves in sympathy. They are opposed, like us, to the very end. There is no escape from me. Now pay the price for all my grief, and give yourself for all my friends you've slaughtered with your blade.*'

Hector dodges the mighty spear from Achilles hand, and the point buries itself in the ground.

'*It seems you missed, oh god-like Achilles. Despite your certainty. It was a mere figure of speech that you could slay me. You'll get no chance to pierce my back as I flee.*'

So Hector raises his long-shafted spear and hurls it forward, striking the great shield of Achilles square in the circle as it bounces back off and clatters in the sand.

The mighty Athena, on the side of Achilles, returns the spear of Peleus to the right hand of Achilles, but no god is there to give Hector a second missile.

'*Aha!*' cries Hector, his eyes now open. '*I see the gods have lured me to my death. Athena fooled me, and death is no longer far away. Where the gods were once so keen to defend me, now they allow destiny to overtake me. Alas, let me not die without a fight, without the true glory of a deed that will echo in the ears of all unborn men.*'

And so Hector brandishes his sword, and runs forward to meet mighty Achilles, as Achilles does the same, covering his chest with the great shield, the tip of his spear gleaming brighter than the evening star.

The bronze armor Hector had stripped from the corpse of Patroclus covered all Hector's flesh save for the opening at the throat, where collarbone knits with neck and shoulders.

Noble Achilles, enraged at Hector so callously trampling upon the memory of his fallen love Patroclus,

Brandishes his might ash spear and lunges forward,

Drives the heavy bronze blade clean through the tender neck.

Although the blade does not rob Hector of the power of speech,

Hector falls to his knees as Achilles stands champion over the man and shouts:

'While you were despoiling Patroclus, no doubt, you thought yourself quite safe, Hector, and forgot about me. I should have been his helper, but I stayed behind. And now it is I, Achilles, who have brought you low. The dogs and vultures will tear your flesh apart, but the Greeks will triumph.'

Then Hector, in a feeble voice, replies: 'At your feet I beg you, do not let the dogs devour my flesh. Accept the ransom my royal father will offer so the Trojans may grant me death through fire.'

'I wish I could carve and eat you raw for what you did,' comes Achilles' reply, 'no man living will stop the dogs from gnawing at your skull, not even if I am offered twenty, thirty times your worth in gold, or even more. Let the dogs and vultures devour you utterly.'

As death enfolds the once mighty Hector, one final line comes to him at the point of death: 'I know you truly now, Achilles, and

I see your fate. It was not mine to sway your iron heart. But as the gods have turned on me, so they will turn on you, and as brave as you are, Paris will slay you, with Apollo's help.'

And as Hector's soul descends to Hades leaving behind a youthful corpse, a corpse it was that Achilles addressed:

'Lie there in death, then, and I will face my own whenever Zeus and the gods will decide it should be so.'

A hundred people all come to me at once, shaking my sweaty hand. Zotos throws a towel over my shoulders as, exhausted, I can barely keep standing. But I have others to lean on, Dunn and Jesús. Zotos sprints across the mat to help Hector. He throws a towel around his glistening body and gives him a drink, before pouncing off to gab with Frank from Team USA.

We can only wait in sheltered silence, the echoes of the battlefield falling away. I pull off my helmet and see Hector do the same. It was a closely fought match, and I know we have spent too great a fortune of ourselves on this bout, when we both have an entire afternoon of fights to go. But in my exhaustion, I forget the one thing I can never do. I push away those around me and run back onto the mat.

"Hector," I cry, "Hector, come back. Shake my hand."

I look over in fear as the judges count the scores, comparing notes and deciding our fates. And while we both have matches still to go, and this one battle shall not decide our war, it is the only clash we face together.

"Hector!" I shout again, now the judges' attention has been caught, as has Zotos'.

"Hector!" he shouts at his retreating hero, with more fear in his voice than I've ever known, "come right back here and shake his hand."

But the judges will not be moved, not by this. One looks at his watch, the other at me, and the third at Hector, inexplicably standing not thirty feet away. But he is deep in conversation with Giorgos, who is surely singing all sorts of tales into his ear about why Hector will win. I can see him counting the points off on his hands while Hector drinks deeply, sweat still pouring down his body like a waterfall.

But time is running out. Zotos shakes his head as the great judge raises his hand. If I had not dived onto the mat and caused such a fuss, it could have been sorted out afterward. We both could have taken the breather, or feigned a moment for injury. But, no, I've played an awful trick on him, so it will seem to Hector, so it will be written in the ages.

The judge lifts his hand.

"Disqualified!" he shouts, banging his palm flat on the table. The judgment of Hector has been delivered.

Five minutes later, all three of us are at the judges table, pleading the case.

"A flagrant breach of the rules means disqualification from the competition, not just this match," the steely-faced judge with the dreaded watch says. "Hector had over a minute to return to the mat for the handshake which was offered by his opponent and refused after repeatedly being called to do so. He is disqualified from the rest of the day. Hector, please leave the competition area."

Hector's face drops in shock. I can feel his blame fall on me. A trick of Athena, I have the judges on my side.

"Well, hold on a minute," the second judge says, "why can't they just replay the bout?"

"Why would Achilles agree to that?" the third judge asks. "He was going to win anyway, look, eighteen points to twelve."

That, I didn't know. Nor did Hector. Nor Zotos. I won. Not only did I win, but Hector cannot compete for the rest of the day. And likely will not qualify for Nationals. I have only two more kids to knock back, and I'll have a Team USA jacket with my name on it. I glance over at Jesús, standing confused with John Dunn. I look up and see Charon and Hermes both standing, trying, like the rest of the crowd, to understand what happened, and what's happening. And beyond, in the middle distance, is Mom and Mrs. McKenna, sitting close together, possibly holding hands, as their anxious faces watch the proceedings at the judges table on the big screen.

"*Well, folks,*" the announcer says. "*Looks like we've got a bit of a ruckus here. Achilles has won on points, but Hector is facing disqualification from the rest of the competition for violating the handshake rule, and refusing to return to the mat when his name was called several times. This means Achilles will be going straight to nationals.*"

"No," I say, shaking my head at the three judges. Like a revolutionary standing before an oppressor's court, I reject their judgment. "It wasn't Hector's fault. Let's have a rematch."

"But, son," the third judge says, clutching his score sheet, "you've won."

"No," I say again, this time staring at Hector who looks on in quiet shock. "I'll win in a fair fight."

We've been moved to mat two because the first mat is still drenched in sweat from the earth-shattering battle we've already fought. Hector stares at me from across the mat. I stare back. It is not an ideal situation for either of us. We're both exhausted, and spending another bout of energy now will harm both of us in the afternoon rounds, although hopefully not by much since we're still a head and shoulder above the rest of our weight class.

The bigger problem is psychological. The match is lost and won in the first few moments of eye contact before the whistle blows, and I've given away every psychological advantage I could possibly have had. Since the judge decided to shout out my previous score, now spinning around the jumbotron, anything less will be a failure. But anything more is probably far more than I can give. Because already my mind is not on this afternoon, it's on tonight. It's on Jesús, and LA, and the rest of our lives.

Mighty Hector is now the underdog facing a reluctant Achilles. The tables are not where they should be. I've used up all my moves, spent all the coins I've saved through months of quiet research. Every secret I left out on the battlefield; Hector knows them all. Technique and skill and stamina can take a back seat in this rematch, it's simply a case of who wants it more.

The whistle blows and the mat calls us together. We swerve and swoop in the first dance, knocking swords and clashing spears, both of us with more missteps than the other. I'm distracted by the totality of the crowd, by the TV camera, but most of all by Charon and Hermes. Charon is on their tip toes watching the bout. Hermes doesn't even have his phone out. I nearly get floored by Hector. I'm so distracted by what they are doing. Charon holds the slate tablet in their hands. Hermes points and says things. Charon nods. The slate is there. The ending is closer than I know. I just wish I can read to the next page, to know how this ends, to know what I have to do.

And then my eyes fall on Jesús. Beautiful, tender Jesús. He is standing courtside next to Mom and Mrs. McKenna, who have come down from the bleachers, breaking protocol in this dramatic scene. And Zotos, and John Dunn and Frank from Team USA. Which one of them asked me what I want my future to be? Which one of them cares?

Hector makes a leap for a take down. It's early, but he's trying to add up points. That's his strategy. Forget the victory by fall that a more naive wrestler might go for, parrying back the attacks and waiting for a mis-step or an anticipated move. Hector is playing his own game, racking up the moves like I'm nothing but a punchbag. It's a good strategy, but one that tells me everything I need to know about what's important to Hector. Not saving his strength to clean sweep his next matches and perhaps beat me out on points. No, he wants the points for bravery, for risk-taking. He wants to be remembered as the man who was given a second chance at Achilles and proved himself the victor in the second round of the greatest battle in history.

But what do I want? I ask myself as I whip away his obvious move. It's not the same as what Hector wants. We're not fighting over one prize, one ticket to Nationals. No, we want the opposite. From the side of the mat I've ended up on, I have a perfect line of sight of Jesús, and behind him Charon and Hermes. Not perfect, though, drenched in sweat that stings my eyes like sand. I watch all three at once, and I know exactly what needs to happen.

An exhausted Hector spins on his heel, and lunges back at me with every sinew of strength he can pull, but it's like he's fighting against the gods, because I know everything he is about to do. I have two choices, to swerve and let him fall, probably converting his failed attempt to score a brave point into a potential victory by fall, or let him cut me down where I stand.

I realize then what the *Iliad* tells us about heroes. They are only remembered in their fall. Odysseus made it home, eventually, so he needed another book to have his name remembered. Agamemnon returns. Neoptolemus. Philoctetes. But very few others reached their home. On the Trojan side, none were so lucky. Paris might've killed Achilles with an arrow to the heel, but he dies by the hand of Philoctetes in the later Greek assault, and the rest of Troy is sacked to dust.

Yet their names we know forever. Helen. Priam. Hector. Paris. And on the side of the Greeks, Achilles and Patroclus, forever remembered because in war they fell, and heroes they became.

My face hits the mat like a rock. Rarely have I hit it, but it's hardly soft. No wonder people avoid falling. I can hear the gasp of the crowd, the silence of the audience as they realize this is tragedy, not comedy, and death must befall the great. In my fall, Hector doesn't know what to do. It was the last thing he expected, and only after the count of the first second does he dive on top of me, his body weight holding me down, even though he doesn't need to. I'm not getting up. It makes me feel so uncomfortable, the weight of another man on my back. I only want Jesús, not Hector or any other of these people. I know this will be the last match I ever fight in. This is the death of Achilles. And then the whistle blows, making it final.

With the roar of the end of a bloody war ringing in my ear, I see in the last glimpses of light as Charon and Hermes head up the stairs of the bleachers, making for an early exit. But I smile on the warm and stinking mat. The slate is finished, the demons are slayed. I saw Hermes scratch a line through *alastor*, and then they left.

Chapter 19
Hades the Prom King

"Get in, losers," Carla calls out, hanging through the limousine's sunroof as it pulls up to our driveway.

"Bye, Mom," I say, grabbing my suit jacket with the flask of ouzo, the favorite alcohol of the Greeks, wrapped inside, desperate to get out of here before anyone sees Carla necking a bottle of sparkling wine in full view of the street.

"Bye, Mrs. McKenna," Jesús adds, for want of anyone else to say bye to.

"Wait, boys," Mom says, rushing out of her bedroom while trying to attach a hoop earring. "We'll follow you in the car."

"Fuck," I whisper to Jesús, "let's go."

We dive out of the house and straight into the limo door that Adam holds open, telling us to hurry up like this is the last helicopter out of Saigon. As we jump inside, he yanks Carla down from the sunroof and she plops down onto the leather seats.

"Drive!" Adam yells, banging on the roof. The unseen chauffeur knocks it into gear and we zoom along the street, burning rubber in our wake. Around the limo there's more booze than the four of us can drink, even after I've added my contribution.

"You know the school is only about fifteen-minute drive away," I say, cracking open yet another wine bottle, taking a swig before passing it to Jesús who is sitting beside Adam. "There's no way we can drink all this."

Adam's face falls. I've spoiled his good time as he realizes I'm right. I remember how forcefully Carla told me he's not dumb. Unprompted.

"Fuck, brah. Carla, babes, how we gonna drink all this?"

"Pedro," she clambers over to the divider and calls out in harsh Spanish, "condúcenos alrededor de la manzana nuevamente, por favor. There," she says, sitting down next to me and offering me a swig from her open bottle, "he'll take us around again."

"Carla," Adam says, looking offended. "You can't call every driver Pedro."

"He's my fucking cousin, you dumb shit."

The drinks loosen what could have easily been an awkward foursome as Jesús explains in luscious detail everything that had happened during the day's competition, even parts I hadn't been aware of.

"All of the gay internet is talking about it," Jesús says, showing Adam and Carla the gif of Jesús' running leap into my arms and our kiss captured by Channel Two.

"Aww, Achilles," Carla says, her arms and then entire upper body falling over me, "you guys are so cute together!"

I smile. At Jesús, at life in general. He's busy showing Adam the Twitter timeline. I sit back, watching him, loving him from across the limousine. After so much trauma, things start to seem...right.

"Oh fuck," I say, grabbing my bottle and Carla's and looking for a place to stuff them. "Oh fuck oh fuck."

"What?" she asks, swaying on her seat. The limo is slowing down, and pulling up right in front of our house, just like Carla had asked. Through the tinted window Mom and Mrs. McKenna are getting into the car. But Mrs. McKenna holds herself back from getting in the car fully and glares at all of us.

"She'll know what we're doing! Quick, hide all the booze."

"Hide the wha—" Carla asks through hiccups. Adam is laughing, so is Jesús. Only I see the crushing fear of the principal marching toward the limousine, sure as shit she can see through the tinted windows.

"Drive, Pedro. Drive!"

He hits the engine, and we leave a furious Mrs. McKenna standing in our wake. I dive in between Jesús and Adam to stare out the back window.

"She's getting back in the car…they're driving…fast. They're following us."

"Pedro!" Carla shrieks. "We got an old-fashioned prom chase on our hands."

Limousines are not built for quick getaways. And Pedro is not about to break the speed limit with a car full of drunk kids. So the getaway is somewhat muted, and more than once Mom's station wagon pulls up at the lights beside us, and we respond by hitting the floor and shushing each other to stop laughing so loud.

But, eventually, they have to drive to the school, and

we celebrate our victory by default by opening the ouzo I brought. The good stuff, fifty proof.

"Who cares about fucking prom, man," Adam says slumped in the seat, "This is so much better. I'm with the coolest guys in school. Aki, man. You're a fucking legend." He tries to raise his bottle, and almost succeeds.

"Here here," Jesús adds, raising his own bottle fine.

"Here-*hic*-here," Carla adds, not even trying to raise hers.

"Hey, Carla," Pedro asks, "you want to go to your prom now or drive around some more?"

"Keep driving until there's no more drinks!" Adam shouts.

"Okay, boss."

"Oh, and we need some food. Pedro, my good man." He lunges forward then falls straight into the divider as Pedro stops gently at the lights. "Take us to that McDonald's Jesús works at."

After all the drinks have been drunk and a hundred dollars of junk food later, we're ready for the prom.

"Now listen," I say, as all four of us stumble out of the limo, "We have to act very, very, very..." I forget the last word, but it was something like...undrunk.

It doesn't matter. The prom is in full swing. And, thankfully, in the dark lighting we can hide from Mrs. McKenna among the dancing crowd. But I'm not one who can easily hide. It's my first return to an official school event in almost two and a half years. I can hear the eyes, see the whispers. I'm the special guest, while most people are wondering how I was even invited. It's like stumbling through the disco square in the Underworld, but instead of hands, tongues lick out through the dark to spear me with their words.

"I can't believe he's gay."

"What's he doing out of jail anyway?"

"Fuck, he looks hot."

"Who'd he come with?"

"Who was he kissing on TV today?"

The downside to being a hero. The dance floor has swallowed me up, and all the lights and balloons and shimmering decorations make it impossible to get a sense of where I am, let alone the others. People move to the beat, crashing around me like waves on a lighthouse. I look for Jesús, high and low. I want to grab his face and kiss him right in front of every kid in this school that I don't give a shit about.

"Jesús!" I call out. I've spotted him in the far corner, by the wall near the stage. He's hugging the geeks…I mean his friends, and they're passing a hip flask between them. "Jesús!" But I'm so far away, stuck in a beat, trapped in a dance. I'm drunk enough I can go with the flow, move between these people that I once knew who are crying out for a dance with me, too.

"Uh, is this thing on?" a high-pitched male voice shrieks through the microphone. The DJ spins the music down low as this uninvited guest takes the stage. I'm still dancing with two girls I once had biology class with, my back to the stage. The voice sounds vaguely familiar. I assume it's a teacher ready to lecture us about "prom night choices."

"Achilles? Are you out there?" I stop dancing, and slowly turn around. The man on the stage is not a teacher, far from it. It's Yosemite Sam himself, and Mrs. Sam, standing smiling by his side and entrapping the vast majority of the male, and some female gaze with her obvious decision to forego a bra for this trip to earth.

Hades has at least put an overall on over his one-piece undergarment, tucked into his boots, and he's added a straw hat to complete the look. Even though he called me out, people are still staring at him, this cartoon-character Texan who's taken the stage.

"I just want y'all to know how proud I am of Achilles," he says in his coleslaw drawl. The audience burst out into applause with some whoops and cheering. But my heart drops straight down to The Styx. I don't think the crowd and Hades are on the same page.

"A terrible injustice was perpetrated against him," Hades continues to a rapt, if puzzled audience. Persephone stands next to him, like she's ready to present the Oscar as soon as the aged director finally finishes his speech.

"Achilles' father Christos betrayed him terribly. He told the authorities it was Achilles who done shot the meth dealer, when it was Christos. Achilles ain't had nothing at all to do with the crime."

A murmur of agreement, as opposed to a gasp of shock like in some courtroom drama sweeps through the audience. How long the school kept talking about my case I had no idea. How long was I on their collective consciousness?

After people hear about an injustice that's been done, how long do they keep thinking about it? Another week? A month? Maybe longer if they knew the person. But at some point they have to let go of the mistreatment of others. We cannot carry it around with us all day, every day. But from the reaction of the crowd I can tell the miscarriage of justice which happened against me has not been long forgotten.

"Achilles could have taken his revenge many times. He could've fought his case, got his own lawyer, testified against his father and appealed till justice got done. But he knew exposing the lies his father had told would tear his family apart, and put his father away forever, or even to the chair. This is the great state of Texas, after all."

A few people whoop at that, either the mention of Texas or the death penalty, but they are quickly shut down.

"But Achilles did none of those things. He served his unjust sentence, and spent every single day of it protecting the lives of others inside." Hades then fumbles in the front pockets of his overalls and pulls out a crumpled piece of paper which he unfurls and it falls down to his knees like a CVS receipt. "As King of the Dead, I can tell you the lives Achilles has saved—"

Persephone gives a throaty shriek and snatches the list.

"Oh, uh, right. Thank you dear," Hades continues to an audience now baffled at this performance of absurd truth. Persephone makes a wrap up motion with her hands. "Well, anyway, by taking his own injustice and using it to fight for others, by unanimous acclamation of the Olympians, Achilles has fulfilled the requirements to be a hero. Congratulations, Boy. And, as promised, I have released

Marcus from—" Hades quickly glances at Persephone who slices a finger across her throat. "I have released Marcus!"

The audience gives another perplexed smattering of applause. But, like most people, they choose to ignore the things they don't understand and focus on the bits they do.

"Well done, Achilles."

"Good job, man."

"We all had your back, dude."

People swarm around me, clapping my back, shaking my hand, hugging me. But it's all a strange haze like a Houston storm. My eyes are trained on the stage. When Hades steps back from the microphone, Persephone is smoothing down the white suit jacket of a man who's back is turned. As he turns, my heart stops as if I'm back in the Underworld. No breath. No beat. No tears. Just a smile, as wide as the earth itself. Marcus is staring right back at me from the stage, smiling in the way he always used to do.

I don't notice the DJ start up a slow song. I don't notice Persephone grinning like a stage-mom or even Hades wiping a tear from his beady eye. The crowd parts like a sea, peering at this strange, tall, impeccably dressed Black man in a diamond-white suit. The kind only Marcus could pull off.

Grinning, but anxiously out of place, Persephone encourages him forward and he takes the steps down from the stage and walks through the parted crowd which closes around us, stopping an invisible six feet away. Real. Life. Marcus. Standing in front of me in flesh and blood and an Armani suit.

"I…I can't believe it's you," I try to say, but every syllable sticks in my throat.

"I can't believe it's me, either."

The DJ starts to play a song I've heard before: *Secret Love Song*. Marcus places one hand on my hip, and the other on my shoulder. But I take his hand from my shoulder and wrap his fingers through mine.

"Dance with me?" he asks. But we already are. The crowd melts in awe as they expand to give us the entirety of the dance floor to strut around. Marcus pushes me to twirl under his arching arms, then pulls me back into a hug as our feet carry us with perfect agility. All those long mornings of watching reruns of *Dancing with the Stars*, then secretly practicing the dances in our cell long after lights out have made all the difference. Through beaming tears we keep on dancing, keep on dancing.

But there's one off note. One thing which I remember too late. Jesús. As we spin I search the corner where I last saw him, but he's gone. I look across the heads of the crowd as we spin around and again, but he's nowhere to be seen. But then the music screeches to a halt.

"Who the hell are you?" Mrs. McKenna shrieks from the stage at Hades and Persephone who are watching us dance.

"I am Hades, King of the—" But Persephone smacks a bejeweled hand over his mouth.

"We were just leaving. Goodbye, everyone." She waves to the crowd who, stunned, waves back, then she blows Marcus and I a kiss before they rush off stage.

"And who the hell are you, son?" Mrs. McKenna yells

at Marcus, starting down the steps of the stage, her face a storm of anger.

"Quick," he whispers to me, "Hermes is waiting out front." He grabs my hand and pulls me through the crowd who send us out with thunderous applause, but I have to look back. I have to find Jesús. The faces are a blur, and the one-woman stampede of Mrs. McKenna ready to restore order to her prom means I have to run.

We burst out of the doors into the night, and, true enough, Hermes is leaning against a stunning silver Audi with custom wheels and its soft top pulled down. The car looks like it cost almost as much as his gold sneakers.

"Let's go, boys," Hermes says, slipping his phone into his top pocket and jumping straight into the driver's seat without opening the car door. Marcus opens the back one for me as I go in first, then him after. The crowd has rushed out to see and gawk at the car Hermes is revving up. I scan the faces, all the ones I barely recognize, looking for the only one I care about. But I can't find him. My heart pounds faster than the spinning engine ready to shoot off into the night. But then it's too late. We're off, zooming into the glittering evening as Marcus turns my face away from what we left behind, toward his. I realize he's still holding my hand, still smiling at me.

As Hermes swerves out the school parking lot and onto the road, spinning our wheels in the direction of Houston, Marcus holds my chin between his thumb and finger. I can't believe his touch is real. But it is. The wind flaps through us both, but swerves around his short-cut hair, his perfect skin, his perfect teeth. Hades has not just returned Marcus to his body, he's given him the best version imaginable.

"Hey," Marcus says.

"Hey."

And then we kiss.

Chapter 20
A Heroic Attempt

"I was in this field," Marcus explains, as Hermes roars down the freeway toward Houston. "I don't really know how to explain, but it was like I was there, and I wasn't. Like I was there in spirit, but not in body."

"Was it bad?"

"No, not at all. That's the weirdest thing. It was peaceful. Like living inside a painting at a museum. And the field seemed to stretch onward to eternity, but there were rivers to swim in, and streams to drink from, and you could pull fruit from the tree, and it tasted like whatever in the world it was you wanted."

"It was heaven?"

"I don't think so." Marcus shakes his head. "Although it was like paradise, there was this sense we were all waiting for something. We all kind of kept our distance from each other though, and it was hard to see other souls even though we knew we were altogether, but it was like…I don't know. When you're in the movie theater and this extra-long promo comes on, and you're like, is this the movie? But you know it's not. You know it's just a preview.

"And I could hear whispers of conversations. One soul would be telling another they had been judged, and had to walk into the forest at the edge of the field. Then they would be gone."

"Is that what happened to you?"

"Sort of. Although I don't know how anyone knew they'd been judged, but all of a sudden I had this urge to walk toward this hill at the far end of the field. I went there and there was this bunny rabbit."

"You're kidding."

"No way." Marcus grins wide. "This real-as-shit bunny rabbit, and it hops right into my lap and says to me: 'Marcus, do you want another chance at your life, or do you want to be in eternal peace?' The only thing that went through my mind was you, Aki. That's why…that's why I did it."

Marcus' face turns to tears and I move closer to him while Hermes swerves between cars at a hundred miles an hour.

"Hey…it's okay. You don't have to justify, you don't have to…" but I'm crying as well.

"I'm so sorry, Aki. I was just so afraid. I knew by the time I got out you'd have forgotten all about me. You'd be gone, and I'd be alone again in the world…I just couldn't handle that pain."

"Shh…" I pull his head onto my chest and wipe up his tears. "You're safe now. You have life." I say it, but I don't know how to promise it. Marcus should, according to the state, be in prison serving his sentence. I can't imagine the state expunging his record just because he died and came back to life. But, for now, holding him is enough.

"All right, boys, here we are," Hermes says, pulling up

in front of the Hilton in downtown Houston, where I was just earlier that day. The Toyota Center is hosting a concert, so the streets are busy with lights and people. "There's a Lana gig here tonight," Hermes adds, rapidly tapping on his phone. "I'm gonna get *so* much emotionally-damaged tail. Hey, Marcus, you got everything Hades gave you?"

"Yeah." He pats the inside pocket of his suit.

"Well then, good luck. Now, fuck off, you're cramping my style."

A little shell-shocked, I follow Marcus out of the car and into the lobby of the Hilton. We're two well-dressed young people. Marcus in his silky white suit and me in my prom blazer, smart shirt, and tie. We don't draw any heads as I follow him to reception.

"Hi," Marcus says to the woman, "I think there's a room booked under my name? Marcus Palin…genesia." He struggles to pronounce the name as if he's just heard it for the first time that day. The word means rebirth. More than that, recreation, like the recreation of the universe.

The receptionist looks a little unsure about us both.

"Of course, sir. May I see some identification?"

My heart jumps into my mouth. How the hell will Marcus have any ID on him? But he reaches into the breast pocket of his jacket and pulls out a Greek passport, of all things. I stare open-mouthed as he hands it over, open at the photo page which I can see is very much Marcus.

"All right, sir, thank you very much. Your room is all paid for and any meals or drinks you'd like to order will be charged straight to your company. Your car will be here at ten AM tomorrow morning to take you to the airport." She hands back his passport and a folded card with two keys inside. "Enjoy your stay," she adds with a professional smile.

Fearful to say anything out loud in case someone from the hotel overhears, I wait until we are out of the busy elevator and into the multi-room suite overlooking downtown Houston.

Marcus pours us both a glass of whiskey from the bottle that's on the marble kitchen top and hands me a glass as I walk around in awe at the room.

"It's a shame I only have this for about twelve hours."

"Yeah," I say, drinking deeply to try and ground myself. It fails to succeed. "What the hell is going on?"

Marcus slides off his jacket and unbuttons most of his white linen shirt. He takes a seat on the sofa in the hotel room's lounge, and I sit across from him on the armchair, bringing the bottle of whiskey to the table and pouring myself another drink.

"I'm going to Greece," Marcus says, pulling his newly-minted Greek passport, plane ticket, platinum-tinged credit card from a Greek bank, and a pure black card with only a microchip out of the jacket pocket folded beside him and slapping them on the glass table.

"I guess staying wasn't an option." It's not a question, but a realization. Marcus nods his head in agreement.

"It's not like I have any family to miss," he says, holding the passport like he's amazed as well it is real. "And I can't stay in the US, of course. I'm not a citizen anymore. Not since I'm legally dead."

"Yeah, I guess there's no social security form to fill in when you come back to life."

"And if there was, I don't think they'd be too happy with me being out here living it up as a Black guy with a platinum credit card."

"Is this for real?" I ask, investigating the card which has the exact same name as is on his passport, both in Greek and English.

"One million euros a year for life," Marcus says with a grin, "I don't really know how much that is, but I assume it's a lot."

"What's this?" I ask, picking up the black card with the microchip.

"An apartment in Athens. I wish I could tell you where. Hermes just said there will be a car to take me there after I land in Greece."

"First class, of course." I can see from the plane ticket. "Man, it's nice being dead and coming back to life."

We look at each other across the glass table. Marcus smiling, me smiling. Us drinking. Somehow knowing Marcus is going to be taken care of for the rest of life is all I need to know. I can rest. The alcohol soars through me, lifting me up like on the wings of an eagle. Yet there's a face I cannot forget. There's a soul who went through Hades for me, for Marcus. The feeling of another man's weight on top of me, like when Hector pinned me on the mat hours earlier creeps up my neck. I don't want that anymore.

I drain my glass and stand up, a little uneasy on my feet, but I'll make it.

"Wait," Marcus says, reaching out and grabbing my hand, "where are you going?"

"Marcus…"

"Don't you want to come with me to Athens?" he says, finding the platinum card among the others. "It doesn't have to be tomorrow. Next week, next month, whenever you want." He says it, but I don't feel it. Maybe this is what it feels like to be on the opposite side of unrequited love, I don't know. It's bold of me to think someone like Marcus, tall, handsome, and with every resource the gods can provide at his disposal will want me. My silence is all the answer he needs. He puts down the credit card, but stands up, towering over me but pulling me into a kiss nonetheless.

His hands take mine, and run my palms all the way down his strong chest as his lips try to smooth my fears away. He turns my hands downward, and Marcus certainly doesn't have the same problem I had when I got out.

"No," I say, pulling back from the kiss and from him.

"Let me do this for you." He grabs me again, bringing me into his body, his front against my back, wrapping me in arms I thought I would never feel again. The scent of Marcus, the smell of his skin which used to drift through my dreams is here, holding me, offering me everything I ever wanted. He leans down and kisses my neck, and slowly undoes the buttons on my shirt, one by one by one.

"Stop," I whisper like a ghost. Against my own good sense, against my own self-interest.

"I want to say thank you."

"No…" His tongue licks up to my ear while his hand sails down my stomach. It makes it all the harder to say what I'm about to say. But I pull away, and I have to say it. "Being thankful is not a reason to do this. Do it because you love someone, do it because you like them, and they like you. Do it because you both want to make each other happy. But don't do it because you feel you should, Marcus. Don't do it because you think you owe me. You owe me nothing."

"But, Achilles, you saved my life. Literally, Hermes told me. You went into the land of the dead to bring me back."

"And I wish you all the best, Marcus," I say through streaming tears. "I swear. I only want you to be happy. You deserve the world, you deserve whatever future you choose. I am so happy for you, but we both know your future is not me. I am not your path, Marcus."

His eyes drop to the carpet, looking around at the clothes that were almost scattered on the floor, the touches which almost happened, the memories we almost made.

"*Efharistó*," he says, surprising us both with the Greek word for thank you.

"You speak Greek?"

"Eh…I guess?"

"The gods certainly keep their promises," I say, with a smile.

"I guess they do."

"I should go."

"I know."

We don't kiss. We don't cry. We don't hug. He doesn't watch me walk away, and I don't look back over my shoulder. I've already grieved for Marcus. I can't grieve again.

The elevator sinks down so many floors I fear it's going to take me straight to Hades for another round with the King and Queen of the Dead. For that, I don't have time. I walk across the gilded floor of the hotel lobby, blending into the background of a busy Saturday night, but as soon as I'm on the street, the TNT in my chest starts to tick down. I scan up and down the honking horns of the busy street as taxi cabs and Ubers swerve and fight against traffic, and the swarm of humanity that's exiting the Lana concert. Hermes and his silver Audi are not here.

It's not like I can hail a taxi or order an Uber. I'm here in downtown Houston with no phone or money, while every minute I am away from Jesús he's imagining the worst.

Then, like an electric blue bolt from above, I catch sight of the bar on the corner. Three six-foot-plus drag queens in even higher heels are standing outside smoking, so I push through the crowd of girls and gays leaving the Toyota Center and dance across crowded street of honking horns.

"'Scuse me," I pant, startling the three queens, "is Disco Styx performing tonight?"

"Well, hi there, honey," one queen wrapped in a crinkled pink body hugger says, blowing out smoke and measuring me up. "She should've just gone on."

"That's why we came out here," the other says, and the three burst out laughing.

"Thanks," I spit out, smashing through the door and hurling down a flight of stairs into the darkness of the busy bar. It's crowded. The tables in front of the stage are tightly-packed and full, and everywhere else is standing room only, everyone pushed close together to see the performer. I draw a few looks given my half-open shirt and smart suit, but not enough to distract from what's happening on the stage.

Disco Styx is there indeed. They've changed into a

gown that looks sewn from rainbows. Their wig though is styled to be Medusa's hair. A hundred snakes with eyes and tongues slithering around her head—which I swear are real, even if the audience doesn't realize—while she belts out *Fuego*, the song Cyprus nearly won the Eurovision Song Contest with, and Mom made me burn onto a CD for her the day after I got out of jail. Disco Styx dances, sings, and takes up the whole stage as the crowd cheers and begs for more. They flip one verse into Greek as they build up to the chorus.

"Disco!" I shout, trying to push through the crowd. But I've said the wrong thing at the wrong time, because then the beat drops and the crowd rises to their feet. With all the moving, I manage to spin toward the stage.

"Charon!" I yell over the thumping music. But they don't hear, although the snakes have spotted me, as a dozen of them snap their fanged teeth in my direction, threatening to strike if I come any closer to the stage. I didn't think I'd have to fight Medusa too.

"Charon," I say again, exhaustedly climbing onto the stage as the crowd starts to boo this interruption. Charon stops and helps me up, but the snakes hiss. "Charon—"

"Shh! Disco Styx...ah ha ha ha ha," they say to the confused crowd, "my godson seems to have lost his way." They lean into my ear as dozens of snake tongues tickle my face. "What do you want now?"

"I need Hermes. Where is he?"

"Oh, probably in the bathroom."

"Bathroom?"

"Yes! Check the cubicles."

"Thanks, Charon, I mean, Disco—"

"Don't ever cut me off in the middle of a song again." They pull back and smile and wave and the crowd which returns a huge cheer. They applaud and whoop even louder as Charon unceremoniously boots me off the stage.

"Now then, boys, girls, and genderqueers, who's ready for a little Greek Eurovision winner circa 2005? This is Helena Paparizou's *My Number One!*"

Charon has the crowd, but I don't need them. I can see the sign for the bathroom and I shove my way straight to it. Inside is even more tightly-packed than near the stage. Men push against each other in the dim light, swinging in and out of cubicles like it's a revolving door. Clearly I'm breaking some sort of code by pushing and shoving straight through the bodies and forcing the first cubicle door open. Nope, none of those three guys are Hermes.

"Sorry," I say, quickly slamming the door shut. I'm about to kick open the second of three, but then I see the top of his cap over by the urinals. He was on his knees, but gets up and sees me watching him.

"Achilles?"

"Hermes!" I shout across the pressing tin of sweaty bodies. I push toward him and he comes closer to me, and we meet by the sink. The guy he was previously attached to follows. He looks young enough to be at prom as well. Poor guy seems to believe he has some sort of claim on Hermes and wants to know what I want with his new man.

"Hermes, can you take me to Carla's house?"

"Who?"

"Oh, don't pretend you don't know."

"Ha, I know. I'm just kidding."

"Please, there's no time."

"Why, what happened?"

"I need to find Jesús."

"That cute little Latino twink from the wrestling tournament?"

"Yes, him. I need to tell him I love him."

"Aww," Hermes' companion says, clasping his hands together. But Hermes looks entirely unconvinced. "I'm not a damn Uber driver you know."

"I know, I know. But, please, please, can you do this for me? Jesús thinks I'm with Marcus and…"

"Marcus turned you down?" Hermes says with a careless shrug. "You guys *were* a bit of a mismatch."

"What? No…oh, fine, then yes. But I need to get to Jesús right now. He's at Carla's graduation party."

"A high school party? Sure, I can dig it." Hermes turns to the guy he was with. "Sorry bud, got a better offer." The guy doesn't seem offended, though.

"Good luck!" he calls to me as Hermes grabs me by the wrist and we snake out of the bathroom. The music is pounding, Charon is screeching, the crowd is thumping, and thankfully we are up the stairs and out into the busy street.

"Hold on," Hermes says, clipping his backpack around his front and lifting his cap to sweep more hair under it.

"Hold on? To what?"

But Hermes doesn't give me much choice. He grabs my hand and spins me toward his back like he's about to win a wrestling match. I'm barely able to wrap one arm around his neck before we soar into the air, like Hermes is a rocket launching from Cape Canaveral, and all I can do is scream.

"Jesús!" I cry, squeezing through bodies in the low, thumping light of Carla's after-party. Her mansion spreads out forever like a labyrinth, stairs and passageways crowded with teenagers, drinkers more interested in gawking at me than helping.

"Have you seen Jesús?"

"Who?"

"Have you seen Jesús?"

"Hey, aren't you Achilles?

"Who were you dancing with?"

"Are you really gay?"

"Does anyone actually know how to play beer pong?"

That's all the help I got. Hermes had made straight for the pool when he spotted the men's water polo team had stripped off to their underwear for an impromptu game.

"Jesús!" I keep yelling, running up one floor where kids are bouncing to the thumping music and no doubt wrecking Carla's mansion in the process. Guess her Mom is likely more than happy to foot the bill as long as her daughter remains the most popular, or at least most talked about, girl in school.

"I think I saw him in the kitchen," one girl I don't recognize says to me.

"Thank you!" I double back and run down the stairs two at a time, pushing people out of my way, although most clear anyway when they see a full-blown wrestler on the warpath. I make it into the kitchen, the busiest room in the party. Bottles crowd every available counter space, and the island in the middle is crammed with red cups and open bags of chips. The music thrums and a hundred conversations are going on all at once. The kitchen seems to be the main artery from the living room to the back garden, and the shouts and splashes from the pool out back echo around us. A small crowd has gathered behind me, clearly thinking drama follows wherever I go.

"Jesús…" He's at the farthest corner, by the back door, by the trash cans, talking quietly with a girl. His face is stained, his eyes are red and full of sadness. It looks like he's been here for a while. And it seems this day has aged him by years. He stares at me, not answering, just watching. It's so strange for him not to speak to me. Every moment we've been together he's never not talked to me. To tell me a story, to point something out, to kiss me when I felt sad or sorry or overwhelmed. And now I feel truly impotent; Achilles without his shield, without his spear. Without his Patroclus.

"Jesús…"

"Don't you have somewhere better to be?" Jesús turns back to his friend. I feel more and more people gathering behind, so much I'm pushed forward towards Jesús.

"Wasn't Achilles dancing with that Black guy at prom?" a voice says behind me.

"Yeah, so what does he want with the chimp?"

"God, he's a bigger slut than Carla."

But I ignore them all, and come closer. Jesús' friend suddenly looks nervous, like I'm about to wrestle her, and she quietly withdraws from the line of fire.

"Go back to Marcus, Aki. You got what you wanted. You used me perfectly well. But I think I've completed my subjugation to you."

"Jesús, stop,"

"I'm serious, Aki. Marcus is the one you always wanted, so go to him. I'm sure he's waiting. He can hold your sweaty towel at Nationals or the Olympics or whatever. Go."

Suddenly I smile, but it doesn't make Jesús feel any better.

"I'm not going to the Olympics."

"Fine, I'm sure you'll qualify at the next competition when you aren't distracted waiting on Marcus."

"No, I mean I'm not going, ever. I'm not wrestling again." I can see Jesús listening, and also glance back to see the rest of the school listening as well, but I'm not one to be bashful. "I threw the match. I let Hector win."

"What? Why?"

"Because of the job."

"What job?" Jesús looks genuinely confused. It hits me that I never got the chance to tell him. We were interrupted by that damn TV camera.

"The head coach at UCLA. He offered me a coaching job there after I told him I was moving to LA."

"But why throw the match? And let Hector win?"

"I can't coach full time if I'm training for the Olympics. I don't even think I'd be allowed to work at UCLA. And this guy was offering me a chance at a life…for us. A chance to make it in LA, to live like two normal people and just… be. That's all I want, Jesús. That's all I ever wanted. And I'm sorry about Marcus, really. It all happened so fast. He came down from the stage and then Hermes rushed us off to the hotel—"

"A hotel?"

"But I left. He's flying to Greece tomorrow, forever. And the only thing in my mind was getting back to you. To tell you…I love you. I truly do. I want a life for us. Together. Only us."

Jesús looks away, out toward the back garden, where shrieks and splashes are still going on full strong. Someone has just dived into the pool. I move further forward and seize his wrist, to make him look at me. I'm not letting go.

"Is that why Hermes is out there running a game of strip water-polo?"

"He flew me here himself."

The smile comes first, then the hug, then the "aww" of our watching audience. The public adulation Jesús never got at prom. The speakers crackle into life again, like someone is changing the AUX cable. *Secret Love Song* plays again, just for us, and I invite Jesús to dance with me around the kitchen. The second chance at a first dance. And we dance, all through the party, all through the playlist, all night long.

"Mom! There's no more room in the back of the car," I yell from the driveway through the open front door. It's not my bags that are the problem. Jesús has brought everything he owns as his aunt sold the house and bought him…us…an apartment in Pasadena.

"So put some in the back seat," she yells, bringing out

yet another cardboard box stuffed with foil trays of fresh dolmades.

"Someone's got to sit there," I say, as she heaves the box onto the one spare seat in the back of the station wagon since the other two have been folded down to make room for all the suitcases and boxes of house stuff. But Mom doesn't answer.

"Just one more box and a freezer bag of goat to go."

"Mom! There's food in LA you know."

"I know, I know, I just want to make sure you boys won't go hungry. And eat the goat with wine, I sacrificed it to Athena so she can grant you wisdom for your interview."

"It's a part-time teaching assistant job in the Classics department. The main requirement was to have a passing familiarity with ancient Greek, and thanks to you I am fluent in Attic, Doric, and Homeric."

"Fine, fine," she says, lighting another cigarette, although I'm sure there's another one lit inside. "But the wrestling coach position is only twenty hours a week. I just want to give you all the help you can get. Although the gods seem to like you." She squeezes my cheek.

"Yeah, they seem to."

We stand on the front lawn under the early morning August sun, but a soft breeze is blowing as Mom sucks in the smoke to save from the anxiety of me leaving. Us, leaving. If Jesús ever gets back.

"I still don't know how you expect the three of us to fit in this car."

"You've both got your license."

"Yeah…but it's your car."

Just then, a horn honks from the street and a Prius pulls up on the curb. It rolled up silently, no wonder I didn't hear it. Jesús jumps out the passenger seat and runs to greet me with a hug and kiss. Zotos clambers out of the driver seat and smacks the top of the brand new car.

"Oh my God!" I yell, suddenly putting it altogether and rushing toward the shiny new car. "But we just finished packing up the station wagon…it'll take ages to put everything in here." And who drives fifteen hundred miles in a new car?

"It's not for you, dumb ass," Zotos says, slamming the door shut and locking it with a beep from the keychain. "It's your Mom's." He hands her the keys. "You two can have the station wagon."

"Thank you, Zotos," she says, with a broad smile giving her brother a hug and kiss on the cheek. I take one more look at the new car, a little dejected.

"Zotos, Saphie," Jesús says, high as a kite, "it's way too kind of you, thank you!" He fawns over the ancient station wagon, just as I retreat from the new car.

"Fine," I say, grabbing Jesús by the waist and giving him a kiss on the cheek. "I guess it'll do till the acting jobs kick in and I can sell this piece of junk."

"You'll do no such thing," Mom says, "you were conceived in this car, you'll treat it with respect."

"Mom! Jesus!"

"Enough with that word," she says, but softly. "It's pronounced *hey-zeus*."

The four of us wander back into the house, where, right enough, a cigarette is burning in on the ashtray on the dining table and Mrs. McKenna is sitting there in her silk-patterned dressing gown, drinking black coffee with a stack of papers. Like any other morning this summer. Mom stubs her outside cigarette out, kisses Mrs. McKenna on the cheek and picks up her still-burning one.

"Sign these," Mrs. McKenna says, hurling some of the papers at me. "Both of you."

"What is it?"

"Affidavit of motor vehicle gift transfer, and your auto insurance plan."

"Why do I need these? It's Mom's car,"

"It's for his sake," she snaps, staring Jesús down. "You want him to get stopped by the police in LA driving a car registered to a Greek woman in Texas?"

"Okay," I say, bending over to sign the forms and then passing them to Jesús. "I guess you're right, *Dolores*."

But I say her name a little too loud, or with a little too much attitude because suddenly a strawberry—a large one—comes flying out of the kitchen like a discus and smacks me in the side of the face. Mom is nothing if not a good shot.

"You treat Dolores with respect!" she yells through pursed lips holding onto her cigarette.

"He was, Saphie."

"Oh, ha ha!" Mom shrieks, a ball of nerves today. "Just checking."

"When are you boys hitting the road?" Zotos asks to change the subject.

"Soon, I guess," I say, trying to find the map app on my new phone. Jesús quickly helps me out and I balk at the total driving time; twenty-two hours. "I booked a room in El Paso for tonight and we probably want to get there before it's too dark."

"Nonsense," Mom calls from the kitchen, as she pulls trays I didn't even notice out of the oven. "What do you think they've got streetlights for? So you'll get there half an hour later." She sweeps out of the kitchen and slams down an entire tray of pre-made pancakes onto the dining room table, a bowl of sugared strawberries under her arm and then pulls two cans of whipped cream from her apron pocket. "Sit down and eat something for the gods' sake! Zeus help us all."

The End

Author's note

There are an estimated one million[1] children behind bars around the world according to UNICEF, although a criminal lack of record-keeping and the variety of names child detention facilities use to dress themselves up means the real figure is likely to be much higher.

Many children were convicted of crimes committed when they were barely even in their teens, while others are imprisoned for acts which should not be crimes at all, from skipping school to fleeing abuse, having sex or seeking an abortion. Or sometimes just for drinking with their friends. Even more children are inexplicably tried in court as adults and sent to institutions to serve long, sometimes unlimited sentences alongside adults. Children held in adult prisons are nine times more likely to die by suicide. On any given day in the US, 4,500 children are held in adult prisons[2] where they are like lambs to the slaughter. Children in adult prisons often must commit more crimes in prison just to survive, adding to their sentence and creating an inescapable reality, like Sisyphus pushing a rock up a mountain.

In some countries like England, which has the highest juvenile detention rate in Western Europe, children can be

---

[1] Roth, K., *Children Behind Bars: The Global Overuse of Detention of Children,* Human Rights Watch, 2016
https://www.hrw.org/world-report/2016/country-chapters/africa-americas-asia-europe/central-asia-middle-east/north#:~:text=The%20lack%20of%20record-keeping,behind%20bars%20around%20the%20world

[2] Equal Justice Initiative, *Children in Adult Prisons,* Equal Justice Initiative, 2020
https://eji.org/issues/children-in-prison/

locked up from the age of just ten years old. And of all child prisoners in England, at least 85% admit to using drugs—harmful drugs—to cope with their incarceration.[3] How they access drugs in these supposedly secure units is anyone's guess (hint: it's abusive and corrupt prison officers).

In the United States, where at least 60,000 children are behind bars in juvenile detention, not to mention those held in adult facilities, a child can still be sentenced to spend their entire life in prison without parole. Only a few years ago could a person be executed for a crime committed when they were a child and only in 2005 did the US stop executing children.

In the Philippines, a child as young as five years old[4] can be convicted of a crime, and in many countries the so-called age of criminal responsibility is the age the criminal justice system will start to abuse children. More often than not in these cases, or to be more blunt, almost always, children are made the scapegoats for adult crime.

In the US, as in many other countries, some children's prisons are over a hundred years old[5], and still feature the torturous relics of the past from leg irons, solitary

---

[3] Johnson, M., *Children in prison aren't coping - but nobody seems to care,* The Guardian, 2018
https://amp.theguardian.com/society/2018/nov/07/children-prison-not-coping-nobody-care-young-people
[4] Fr. Cullen, S., *Viewpoint: On children in prison worldwide,* Independent Catholic News, 2018
https://www.indcatholicnews.com/news/38075
[5] No Kids in Prison, *The Facts Report,* Youth First, 2019
https://www.nokidsinprison.org/the-facts

confinement, chemical restraints, razor wires and hogties—all lawfully used against children.

Of the children who are sent to prison, a UK study found 30% have special education needs or are disabled, double the national average.[6] Two-thirds of incarcerated children have experienced some kind of life-altering trauma in their young lives and among adult male prisoners, 84% have experienced at least one major trauma in childhood such as physical abuse or sexual assault[7]. And of course, Black and Hispanic children are far more likely to be jailed.[8]

Doubtless some children commit crimes. Although according to data from the US, barely a quarter committed an offense involving any kind of violence and only 2% committed criminal homicide. Most are there for crimes against property, drug possession, public order offenses, or crimes which are not illegal for adults like running away from home or being truant from school.[9]

Not all children get the privilege of a trial before being

---

[6] Bulman, M., *Children in prison twice as likely to have special needs, figures show,* The Independent, 2019
https://www.independent.co.uk/news/uk/home-news/children-prison-special-educational-needs-jail-uk-a9034846.html

[7] Bangor University, *More than eight in 10 men in prison suffered childhood adversity - new report,* Phys.org, 2019
https://phys.org/news/2019-04-men-prison-childhood-adversity.html

[8] Child Trends, *Key facts about juvenile incarceration,* Child Trends 2016
https://www.childtrends.org/indicators/juvenile-detention

[9] *Key facts about juvenile incarceration,* Ibid

locked up. It is estimated that 15,000[10] children are held by US federal immigration authorities. Although records are not readily kept, and ICE has "lost" thousands of children held in their camps. The kids have just "disappeared" and continue to do so.

No child should be behind bars. There are infinitely more effective community and family-based rehabilitation programs for children who may require them. But if we normalize children being in prison, even after a trial, it also normalizes far greater abuses, such as children being held in adult prisons, children being executed or being sentenced to die behind bars, children being held indefinitely without having a trial, or even without having committed a crime.

No child should be in prison. Whether in a juvenile "jail" or in an ICE concentration camp, the incarceration of children is truly a Greek tragedy with no place in the modern world.

---

[10] Chalabi, M., *How many migrant children are detained in US custody?* The Guardian, 2018

https://www.theguardian.com/news/datablog/2018/dec/22/migrant-children-us-custody

About the Author

Harry F. Rey is a Pushcart-nominated author and lover of gay themed stories with a powerful punch.

Alongside *Of Gods and Boys*, Harry is also the author of the adult gay romance series *The Line of Succession* series and the gay rom-com *All The Lovers*, also available from Deep Desires Press. His other works include the queer sci-fi series *The Galactic Captains*, the WWII-era gay historical novel *Why in Paris?* And *Six Days in Jerusalem*. His work has also been featured in anthologies including *Not Meant for Each Other* from Lost Boys Press and *Queer Life, Queer Love* from Muswell Press.

Website: https://harryfredrey.wixsite.com/harryfrey

Also from Deep Hearts YA

Hunting Rabbits in the Dark
S.W. Ballenger

Hawk has the perfect life with the perfect girlfriend that he's loved since seventh grade. He's built his whole world around her, and he knows that once they graduate and enter the adult world, he's going to marry her and they're going to start a family.

This rock-solid life is shaken after a chance encounter with his former childhood best friend, Gabe. He's now the quarterback of the rival school's football team, tall, rugged, handsome...all of which awakens feelings Hawk thought he'd buried long ago.

When tragedy destroys Hawk's perfect world, he turns to the only one that can help him through—Gabe. With his best friend's help, will Hawk be able to rebuild his world and regain his footing? Or will he sink so deep into depression that he'll never escape?

Available now in ebook and paperback